D0393121

TROUBLE IN MIND: THE SHORT STORY AND CONFLICT

EDITED BY
KRISTINE SOMERVILLE
AND
SPEER MORGAN

Trouble in Mind: the Short Story and Conflict

Missouri Review Books

Edited by Kristine Somerville and Speer Morgan

Missouri Review Books

Published by Missouri Review Books
357 McReynolds Hall, University of Missouri
Columbia, Missouri, 65211

Missouri Review Books is published by the *Missouri Review* through the College of Arts & Science of the University of Missouri, with private contributions.

Trouble in Mind: the Short Story and Conflict

ISBN: 978-1-945829-18-5 (print)
ISBN: 978-1-945829-19-2 (digital)

Library of Congress Control Number: 2018960364

www.missourireview.com

Cover Image: "After the Duel," Antonio Mancini, 1872, De Agostino Picture Library, Gonella, Bridgeman Images

Cover design by Jane Raese of Raese Design, Boulder, Colorado. Interior design by Scott McCullough.

Special thanks to Associate Editor Evelyn Somers who edited the stories when they first appeared in *The Missouri Review*.

For Jeffrey Smith and Jeffery Viles, the two sailors who have stuck with us through storm and calm.

Table of Contents

Foreword

No single author invented the short story. However, certain American writers were among the most important early creators of the form as we know it today. In the early nineteenth century, Washington Irving, an expatriate living in England, published two picturesque tales, "The Legend of Sleepy Hollow" and "Rip Van Winkle," that were genuine short stories. Both are presented as stories and nothing else, not journalism or essays with fictional elements but narratives with characters that go through a complete narrative trajectory.

The "lateness" of short stories and novels in mass culture was partly due to the fact that fiction was considered suspect, just as movies, television, or gaming are sometimes suspect today. Moralists deemed the very medium of fiction corrupting, fearing that it taught bad values and behavior. Being by definition "not true," fiction was deceitful and dangerous and could instill bad habits such as laziness or lewdness. To counter this, early fiction writers often made extravagant claims—on title pages and in prefaces and advertising—that their purpose was to afford moral examples.

During the four hundred years following the invention of typesetting, slow-moving advances in publishing and distribution delayed the spread of fiction. Yet between 1825 and 1850, publishing made up for lost time with the number of magazines increasing in this country sixfold. Within a quarter of a century, more than five thousand new magazines sprang up. The growth was fueled by new technologies in printing, a network of railroads for distribution, the rise of literacy and public education, and improvements in and availability of eyeglasses. Reading had suddenly become a common pastime, and periodicals needed to fill pages. Rather than continuing to steal material from England and Europe, publishers wanted homegrown content—by Americans, for Americans.

As an ambitious writer, Edgar Allan Poe had the good fortune to come of age during the dawn of American periodicals. New York had not yet become the epicenter of book and periodical publishing, making it possible for aspiring editors and writers to find opportunity across the country. After attending the University of Virginia and West Point, Poe saw magazine work as a viable calling and quickly found a position. Richmond printer Thomas Willis White hired him to assist with the editorial duties of the *Southern Literary Messenger*, which highlighted the literary talents of the South. In his first magazine job, Poe learned all aspects of the business, from subscription sales, layout, and proofreading to writing anonymous filler on a hodgepodge of topics ranging from gymnastic equipment and housekeeping advice to women's purses and Chinese romance writers.

The *Messenger* was competing with hundreds of periodicals, and Poe worked hard to attract a readership. While his taste tended toward the genteel, he believed that readers wanted pieces on sensational subjects, written in a charged style. He also felt that they sought a range of techniques, from short, elegant prose pieces and rhymed narrative poems to epic voyage narratives. He had the talent for writing in any genre, though he preferred what he called the "tale of sensation," a narrative in which the central action, typically an improbable event, is heightened with sensory details and a dire mood. Influenced by the German romantic writers, he wrote stories of violence, mental aberration, and diseased lovers.

While his journalistic and creative work brought him little money, he took the vocation seriously and was committed to America's gaining artistic and intellectual independence from England. As a critic, he became a tastemaker and arbiter of American literary standards. He refused to lavish praise on mediocre writers and called for "constructive accuracy." He scorned casual writing and demanded conciseness and grace. His publishers often cringed at what they labeled his "tomahawking style."

The popularity of the short story coincides with what Poe saw as the "illimitable power" of the magazine. Magazines and short stories suited the mid-century's condensed style of thinking and its pace—"the rush of the age"—and the artistic possibilities in subject matter and style. Irving's sketches, Nathaniel Hawthorne's *Twice-Told Tales*, a two-volume collection of stories, narrative sketches, and allegories of his native New England, and Poe's *Tales of the Grotesque and Arabesque*, published two years later, are among the first powerfully imagined and technically adroit story collections by American authors.

Poe popularized the short story and in his essays and lectures argued that it was a discrete art form. He defined the short story as a prose narrative meant to be read in a single session, absorbing the reader so that "external or extrinsic influences" would not disturb its single effect. He connected intensity to economy of form. Regardless of how serious its subject, the function of the short story was to entertain, amuse, and delight.

While the short story would develop gradually from Poe's time, between 1880 and 1910 it expanded internationally, with major practitioners whose works became classics. These included Guy de Maupassant and the transplanted James Joyce in

Trieste and Paris, Anton Chekhov in Russia, and Joseph Conrad and the American Henry James in London. This variety of authorship continued during the decades between the two World Wars. While today America again seems to dominate the form, impressive short stories can be found all over the world. American literary magazines now receive submissions from authors worldwide.

The *Missouri Review* plays a role in maintaining the popularity of the short story. The stories of this collection are Jeffrey E. Smith Editors' Prize winners or runners-up from the last twenty years. In the tradition of Poe, *TMR* subscribes to the belief that the short story matters.

In Fiona McFarlane's "Exotic Animal Medicine," veterinarian Sarah, distracted by the thoughts of her very new marriage (earlier in that same day), fails to avoid a car that turns directly in front her on the rural road near Cambridge. The collision leaves Sarah and her new husband in dire need of help to save the life of the injured driver. In a mere few hours, a day of joy turns into one of tragedy. Jason Brown's "Instructions to the Living from the Condition of the Dead" tells the story of John, a geriatric World War II vet ambushed by his extended family on the day before Thanksgiving. All he wants to do is get away from their infantilizing treatment and spend time with his equally venerable girlfriend, reading Emily Dickinson and celebrating her birthday. He makes his escape to her house on a scooter, only to discover through a powerful confession he finds himself making that his beloved isn't the woman he imagined she was.

In Alice Fulton's historical fiction "Happy Dust," set in 1908 rural New England, Mamie must deal with "the married woman disease" on her own. She delivers her baby while the men dawdle with their errands and her sister-in-law and brood of children run around excited and terrified. Roy Kesey's "Double Fish" is set in Beijing many years after Mao's Great Leap Forward, though the lingering effects of the chairman's reign of terror are still felt by those who lived through it. When an unlikely visitor shows up and insists on being acknowledged, Zhao, an old man who runs an amusement concession, discovers that no matter how solitary or orderly he has made his life, he cannot escape his own past betrayals during Mao's three-year murderous campaign for ideological "purity."

The conflict in Jennifer duBois's "The City of the Dead" focuses on Jo, a high-functioning alcoholic who provides care for the sick and elderly when they become too much for their families. Jo's own family, a troubled daughter and her two children, provide as much grief as her client, Dr. Hill, a brilliant man now quickly sliding into dementia. After his death, Jo must contend with the grieving widow and Dr. Hill's daughter from another marriage who feels shut out. Jo discovers how many unceasing demands we make on the dead and the living. Ben Gibson, the diabetic amputee in Tamara Titus's "Exit Seekers," creates his own chaos. Consigned to life in a nursing home and a certain early death from his own bad living, Ben finds a way to maintain his renegade spirit and gallows humor. While he rages against the controlling caregivers who dole out small favors, he finds ways to assert, through secretive, subversive acts, his limited power.

This collection reveals characters in struggle with love, work, family, or community. External and internal battles show them to be resilient and tenacious but also leave them changed. Many of these stories are dramatic at their cores, with powerful event and mood radiating revelations that readers may sense even before fully comprehending them. Details may be as knotty and difficult as life, but beneath it all is the pitch toward meaning.

KS & SM

Consider this Case

Melissa Yancy

This is the one day each year they come to him, enshrouded in blankets and footed rompers, matching sets of pink plaids and blue stars or T-shirts proudly declaring personal interests in trucks or ladybugs. Nowhere else do so many twins and triplets, all under the age of five, congregate en masse. Julian, stationed with a chair and a photographer, looks something like a wasting Santa Claus. He scoops them up—one in each arm if they are small enough—to smile for the camera. The babies rarely cry. They touch his thick eyebrows, his prominent nose. They have to be coaxed to look at the photographer.

The reunion is one of Julian's favorite days each year. It is the only day he works in the sunlight, one of the few times he allows himself to relax. He spends half his life in the operating room. The lawn between the hospital and the parking garage has been set up with rental tables and a tent, and a food truck stationed in the entry drive serves burgers to the families. Older children, now four and five, race around the perimeter with blades of grass stuck to their sweaty faces, waving their sticky Popsicle fingers—exhibiting their dominion over this place, their right to be.

He first encountered these children as fetuses. The same jokes get told. From him: "I knew you when!" From the parents of the triplet toddlers: "Did you have to save *all* of them?"

After lunch, the photographer sets up for the annual group photo, positioning Julian in the center of the crowd. She perches high on an A-frame ladder, directing the dozens of children. More tables have to be cleared to fit everyone.

They are nearly in position, ready for the group wave, when the telephone in his pocket vibrates. It is his sister, Liv, calling from London; she never calls just to talk to him. Everyone in his family has this uncanny ability to call at the worst possible moment, usually to deliver bad news.

"It's Father," Liv whispers through the phone, as though their father hovers nearby. "It's time. He can't be in-de-pen-dent anymore."

"Why are you whis-per-ing?" Julian mimics. "I can barely hear you." All around him hips bob, pacifiers are offered. A few toddlers are chased down at the fringe.

"I can feel his anger from across the Atlantic," she says.

The photographer gesticulates like a conductor. It is time to wave, time to smile.

He misses half of what his sister says, but he knows what she's asking of him. He tells her to hold, smiles for the camera. Then he excuses himself and squeezes through to the edge of the lawn.

"He only has a couple of months," his sister says. "It's not like a permanent situation."

"Life is not a permanent situation," Julian says.

Liv is an actress, currently on the West End. Their mother is long dead. Their brother, Jay, is also dead, from an overdose that may or may not have been accidental. Their father is still at home in Virginia, which makes Julian, all the way in Los Angeles, his nearest relative. Julian offers to pay for residential care, but this is not what his sister has in mind.

"He needs to be in hospice," Julian says.

"You could get a nurse to come to the house every day. And you have the space."

"He'll try to redecorate," he says.

"So what?" she says. "The place could use a woman's touch."

At the airport, Julian parks the car and goes to wait inside, in the cordoned-off area where they allow it. He can't remember the last time he has gone to the trouble to do this.

"They don't let you come to the gate?" is the first thing his father says. "So much for welcomes."

He is wearing a seersucker blazer and tan slacks and a tie with a print of tiny sailboats. His loafers look brand-new. His father looks around at the abundance of flesh, flip-flops and bedazzled sweat suits.

"It's like the apocalypse," his father says. "Like everyone was looting, and this was all they could find to wear."

"It's the West Coast, Dad."

"It's something, all right."

He has brought only two bags—a matching leather set—and tells Julian that he has sent his other belongings through "the United Parcel Service." He has a lifelong aversion to acronyms and abbreviations.

Perhaps his father will be impressed by the location of his house, if nothing else, Julian thinks. Some people are taken with Malibu. But the weather hasn't entirely cooperated. When they arrive at the beach, it is dull and brown outside. Julian's house, like most of the homes in his neighborhood, is unimpressive from the street, just a simple clapboard square wedged between the highway and the ocean. But when you step through the front door, the highway seems to recede, and the water extends in front, giving the sensation, as the enthusiastic Realtor had called it, of "having stepped off the continent."

But the ocean view from Julian's living room might as well be of a cinder-block wall for all the impact it makes on his father. It's cold like a Rothko out there.

His father eyes the floating staircase in the modern house. Julian has almost forgotten that his father is truly ill. His hair is white but still thick, with the soft sheen of old age. His posture is erect, too, but the footsteps are smaller, nearly a shuffle. Julian has rearranged things so the space he uses as a downstairs office can serve as his father's room. He goes to help him unpack, but his father pushes his hand away hard.

At dinner, Julian tries to remember ever having sat alone like this across from his father at a meal. When his siblings were in college, there were times his mother went out to play bridge with her friends. But had they sat together, or retreated into their rooms? Julian only remembers how hollow the house had felt in his mother's absence. Even though his father selected and arranged most of the décor, he never seemed to inhabit the house in the way Julian's mother did. Without her, none of them knew how to behave as family members. She'd had to keep reminding them, like children, to share, to set a good example for their siblings, to call on each other's birthdays.

"I didn't know you could cook," his father says. Julian has made penne with sausage and greens and French bread. He remembers his father's weakness for the tang of fresh bread.

"Mom taught me in high school," he says. "So I could fend for myself in college."

They talk of Washington. His father chronicles the current first lady's fashion in great detail. A glimmer comes into his eye. Her style is classic, he tells Julian, but fresh and bold. He is particularly pleased with a recent mint shell paired with a coral pencil skirt. There have been missteps, too, he reports. He did not care for an ombré evening dress. "It looked like she had been wading in mud," he says.

He stares at his son, as though he, too, will feel sufficiently worked up about ombré. Julian does not know what ombré is.

"You know," his father says, pushing himself back from the table and eyeing the open floor plan, "modernity is all about poverty. Cheap reproduction and delivery to the masses. Like that case-study house the Eameses lived in. That house looked like a rabbits' warren."

It is not so much Julian's taste that bothers his father as his disinterest in taste, his failure to take a position. Julian has delegated the furnishing of the house to his friends who care about that sort of thing. He knows his father associates this disinterest with his career, with a predilection for science, when in fact it was cultivated in childhood, a path of least resistance to his father.

"A warren has mounds and tunnels," Julian says. "It hardly looks like a box."

"I was speaking metaphorically of the specks of junk everywhere. And the terrible use of textile."

Julian wants to laugh. But his father is deeply serious about the "terrible use of textile," whatever that could possibly mean.

"How are you feeling?" Julian asks. He begins to think his sister has tricked him, that his father has years more to live.

"Quite well. Physically, I mean. Aesthetically, I am suffering at the moment."

Despite his father's protests, Julian takes him to see one of his friends in oncology at the hospital. Walking in through the sliding front doors with his father beside him—when he usually enters from the staff entrance at the rear—he no longer feels ownership over the place. He feels almost out-of-body, as though he's never worked there at all.

His friend confirms that the lung cancer is stage IV, the kind that, to his father's great pleasure, will kill him quickly. His father is the sort of man who will gladly choose death over loss of dignity. He is known, in fact, for pronouncing death as a preference to many things: American cheese, West Texas and prime-time television, to name a few.

The oncologist prescribes pain medication and says they can get an oxygen tank for the evenings if Julian's father gets short of breath. The oncologist keeps telling Julian how lucky he is. The cancer is killing his father softly. Julian thinks that's a strange way to put it. He pictures the cancer kissing his father all over his body, spreading until its lips cover his, until it snuffs out his breath.

To get out of the house, Julian agrees to attend a political fund-raiser at the home of a wealthy philanthropist. One of his nurses, Terri, has convinced him that a few eligible bachelors will attend. Julian's nurses, all women, are like a tribe, and he has given himself over to them completely. Most of them have known him since medical school, and even though he is only forty-three, they treat him like a helpless old man, picking out his car and his furniture and arranging his kitchen cabinets. For the fund-raiser, Terri has picked out his clothes; Julian spends his days in scrubs and is always at a loss when he approaches his closet.

He wears a tapered suit and a skinny tie that strikes him as too feminine. The house where the party is held is indiscriminately ostentatious—a style a Realtor might call Mediterranean—and with his cocktail in hand, Julian feels like an extra who has stumbled onto a bad set. He keeps catching glimpses of himself in the large gilded mirrors that fill the home's foyer. Some of the mirrors high on the wall are strung by wire and angled, giving a bird's-eye view of the guests. He sees that he is getting balder on top. He has hair everywhere except his head. Why hasn't he noticed this before?

Terri introduces him to an architect, a handsome man with the confidence of the newly, rather than perennially, single. Julian feels himself shrink beside him. On the subject of his work, the subject that should give him confidence, he falters. How he describes his profession is always calibrated to the listener: he calls himself a doctor, or an ob-gyn, or a fetal surgeon, depending on the kind of conversation he wants to discourage or engender.

He settles on doctor.

"Is it too cliché to ask you about health care reform?" the architect says. "Normally I wouldn't talk politics, but I suppose that's why we're here." He smiles. He is one of those men who age well, Julian thinks; he undoubtedly looks better than he did fifteen years ago. His teeth are so tidy and white. Sometimes Julian feels angry at those men.

"I'm for it," Julian says flatly, "if that's what you want to know. Although it doesn't impact my patients. Fetuses. They don't really have a status." His patients, in fact, are the mothers, but he spends his days in the womb.

He waits for a reaction. The word "fetus" carries a charge for anyone who is not a physician. And yet he throws it out there like smut.

He sees the architect formulating a question, wondering if he is a quack or an abortion doctor or just being funny.

"I imagine it's hard to bill and collect," the architect says. "Fetuses tend to have a weak credit history."

Julian actually smiles. Why has he been an asshole? "I'm getting another," Julian says. "Would you like me to bring you anything?"

But the architect shakes his head.

At the end of the night, Julian goes out back to get some air. One of the caterers is smoking a cigarette. He is scrawny and fey, and Julian feels more comfortable out there with him.

"What's this party about?" the boy asks.

"Politics," Julian says.

"I got that much. For what?"

Julian is a gay man who saves fetuses and performs medical research on sheep: he is always an abomination to someone. He is accustomed to strange political company.

Julian shrugs. "Our side," he says.

He has a new triplet case referred from one of the status hospitals in town. Most of the families seem impossibly young to Julian, but not this one. The mother is an executive in her forties, pregnant with triplets because of in vitro fertilization. "An embarrassment of riches," she says to Julian as they sit waiting for the father to arrive. He is a television producer, she explains, and it is difficult for him to get away during the day. When the father arrives and takes a seat, he keeps his cell phone balanced on his knee.

Terri sits beside the family while Julian tells them what is happening. He explains that even though the babies are in their own amniotic sacs, they share the placenta. Two of the babies aren't sharing the placenta equally because of a problem in the connected blood vessels. One baby is providing too much blood to the other. On the ultrasound, Julian points out the donor and the donee. The donor is dangerously small and can't urinate enough to make amniotic fluid. The baby could become shrink-wrapped in its own sac. The donee has too much blood and too much urine, and its tiny heart is working far too hard.

"You mean they pee in there?" the father says.

"Well," Julian says, "as the pregnancy progresses, more of the amniotic fluid is made up of urine."

The man looks over at his wife. "I guess that makes sense."

"What about the third one?" the mother says, running her hand over her stomach.

"He's an innocent bystander," Julian explains. "Off to the side doing his own thing."

If they do nothing, at least one and maybe both of the twins will die. The parents understand, so they agree to the surgery.

"Three," the father says. "We're going to need a bigger house."

Julian and Jay and Liv had been three, but they came in a trickle instead of a flood: Jay two years after Liv, Julian two years after Jay. His brother had been the reckless one, the one who gleamed—not on stage or in the darkness of an operating room or in Washington but in life, with real people, when intimacy was actually required. Jay's death had broken their hearts. When Julian thinks of his father as a father and a husband, his mind always goes to Jay's funeral, which stands like a wall between the father of his childhood and the one he now knows. His father refused at first to attend the service, but his mother wouldn't allow it; in her usual way, she forced them to behave as a family. But he wouldn't comfort their mother. He wouldn't lay a hand on her at all.

At the time, Julian had hated his father for his stoicism, what had felt like a rejection of each of them. It was his sister who had explained, "He's ashamed, Julian. You don't see that? His son died from addiction."

Liv spent her life inhabiting people—not invading the body, the way Julian did, but gaining entry in ways that led to different understandings. He was envious of that sometimes.

"Jay was sick," Julian said. "He can't treat this like an affront to his *manners*."

If their father acknowledged that shame, Liv told him, if he allowed himself to live in it, he would expose himself to deeper shame, shame he would not be able to manage. This was a fragile little carapace, she said.

Carapace, Julian thought. Like a crab, like cancer. He had never thought of it that way: emotion could explode that shell, letting what was soft and rotten inside metastasize throughout the body.

"But what's he got to be so ashamed of?" Julian said.

Liv only put her hand on his shoulder and shook her head.

The surgery does not go easily. Julian cannot insert the scope in the usual place because of the innocent bystander. He will have to work around the third baby.

The surgery begins as it normally does. His nurses stand off to the side of the operating room watching the monitors; they help him find the vascular equator and build the road map of large and small veins that he will ablate. But it is cloudy in the uterus, the turbid amniotic fluid like watery milk speckled with mucus. Just finding all the connections takes him twenty minutes. He can often finish a surgery in that amount of time.

He has to pump in Ranger's solution for visibility, then use the diagnostic scope to get a look at the spot he is going to laser. But when he pulls the scope out and slides the laser into the cannula, the landscape has already gone cloudy again. It feels like he is walking down a dark hall, brushing cobwebs out of his face all the way.

The babies won't stay where he wants them. When the solution rushes in, one of the babies raises his hand up to feel the water moving against his palm. He closes his fingers to grab onto the scope. Normally, Julian finds this cute. Sometimes he will even point this out to the mother if she is alert enough.

"I need you to scoot over, baby," he says.

He has to find a rhythm, and the rhythm is fast: he has to add the solution, put the diagnostic scope in, find the next connection, then whip out the scope and get the laser in while he can still see. But he keeps getting lost. He gets a large vein that should have been adjacent to two smaller ones, but the smaller ones are not there.

"How many are left?" he asks Terri.

"Three large, five small," she says.

"Scope," he barks. "Scope, scope, scope."

"How many are left?" He asks it a dozen times. He needs to hear Terri's voice telling him that he is almost there.

"We're winning," he finally says. "Did we get them all?"

"Last one," Terri says.

It doesn't feel like the last one. It still feels like new veins are proliferating, swelling with blood when his eyes are closed.

When he gets home, the house is empty. He goes to his father's room, where antique whale-oil lamps and Canton vases now cover the mid-century dresser. At the far end, closest to the bed, his father has set out a series of frames—photos of himself with American presidents and visiting shahs and kings. In the largest photo, he and Pat Nixon stand in the Green Room, one of dozens of rooms they had rescued, in his words, from Mrs. Kennedy's handiwork. His father spent almost thirty years redecorating the State Department's diplomatic reception rooms and then curating the White House, but it was only Pat who really let him have his way.

His eyes go to one photograph of his father alone. The photograph is more recent, yet in it he looks more youthful than he does in the older pictures: he wears a yellow-and-green floral blazer with creased cream pants and black-and-brown saddle shoes. He is leaning back against a wall of black-and-white Moroccan tile in what looks like an exotic locale. The photograph looks professional.

"Excuse me." His father has propped himself in the doorway behind him.

"Where have you been?" Julian says.

"For a walk."

"On the beach or the highway?"

"I found a little tributary," his father says, making his way slowly to the corner chair. "Who lives in a place where there's nowhere to take a walk? Private beaches. Hmmph."

"Where's the nurse?"

His father leans back and closes his eyes. "I let her go, I'm afraid. She wasn't amenable to my shopping trip. She was supposed to be a nurse, not a warden."

"But she was in *my* employ," Julian says.

"Please. It's a service. They'll send a new one tomorrow."

Julian stands there, waiting for his father to open his eyes.

He phones the nurse. "I'm so sorry, Doctor," she says before he has even begun. "He wanted to go shopping for antique furniture. He said he was going to have a mover come and take your furniture out of the room. He had a list of the furniture he needed to buy. I told him we couldn't go, not until we spoke to you."

Once, when Liv was eight and away at summer camp, their father had redecorated her room. She'd wanted a princess room—in the pedestrian pink sense of princess—but she'd returned to find a room that was practically Elizabethan. Julian hasn't thought of it in years—the big reveal, his sister squealing, dancing through the velvet drapes that hung from the four-poster bed, gesturing as though about to give a monologue. He always thinks of his father as a disinterested figure hovering at the edge of their childhoods. But perhaps it is Julian who wasn't interested in him.

"You did the right thing, of course," he says. "You're not fired. You should come back tomorrow."'

"They've already reassigned me. I think it's for the best," she says. "He requested a male nurse."

The architect calls. Julian has so excluded this possibility—they had not exchanged information, for one thing—that he sits there dumbly on the phone, wondering if his father has called an architect to redesign his house.

"It's Wesley," he says. "From the fund-raiser," he says. "Do you remember me?"

"Of course," he says. He didn't remember even learning the man's name. He has thought of him only as the architect. "I didn't expect to hear from you. How did you find my number?"

"Terri."

"Oh, yes. I must not sound too resourceful."

"She also told me you're more charming than you came across."

"Is that so?" Julian says. He should just admit to having been intimidated by the architect's good looks. But he can't manage it.

"I thought I'd give you the opportunity to redeem yourself," he says.

The architect wants to see Julian's house, so he invites him over for the date, with the reassurance that his father will keep himself entertained. The housekeeper has just come, but Julian patrols the house for anything to straighten.

His father comes out of the guest room. "I thought you were having company," he says.

"He should be here soon," he says.

"Then why do you look like a farmer?"

Julian has put on a thin denim button-down and tucked it into his khakis. He does not look anything like a farmer in these clothes, but he does not feel like himself, either.

"It's unstudied gay," he says to his father. His father hates it when he says the word "gay" aloud.

His father comes over and lifts his reading glasses up.

"This look is neither happy nor what I would deem homosexual," he says. "So it fails both senses of the word. Why don't you put on a nice striped shirt?"

So Julian does. He looks like a junior professor, but he feels more comfortable. When he comes back, his father has poured himself a drink.

"Let me give you a word of advice, son." He pauses for effect. "You may live in California now, but nothing about you will ever be unstudied. This house, your clothes, your gait. It is not in your blood."

The architect arrives, wearing a light blue V-neck sweater, linen shorts and loafers, his salt-and-pepper hair effortlessly combed back with natural wave. Apparently the look is in *his* blood. Julian feels an unexpected charge, seeing the man on his doorstep like that. Perhaps it's because he brings so few men home that it makes him feel familiar, as though their relationship has already progressed past awkward beginnings.

When Julian brings him into the kitchen, his father has thankfully disappeared. Julian opens one of his best bottles of white wine—he knows nothing about wine, but one of his tribe has stocked the cooler with the cheap ones on top, ones for entertaining on the bottom—and pours them both a glass.

The architect has wandered off and is showing himself around the living room. "Occupational hazard," he says when Julian brings him the wine. "I tend to help myself around other people's homes."

"You probably think you can tell a lot about a person by their house and what's in it," Julian says. "But not me. I haven't picked any of this."

"What could be more telling than that?" he says.

They sit on the couch that faces the ocean. It is dark already, and Julian has left just one lamp on in the living room. He apologizes for his behavior at the party. "I can't imagine what would have made you call. Was it my incredible charm, my sense of style? It must have been my body."

The architect just smiles. Julian can smell ginger and amber on his skin. It makes him want to lean in.

His father comes out—for a glass of water, he claims—and the architect gets up to greet him. A consequence of being well-bred.

His father picks up the bottle of wine. "And what are we having, Wesley?"

Wesley falls for it all. He offers to pour. He insists that Julian's father join them for a drink, and suddenly Wesley and Julian are not knee-to-knee on the couch but outside on the deck chairs because his father thinks they need some ocean air. Julian goes to fetch blankets for them, and when he returns, his father and Wesley are laughing like old friends. He stands in the living room for a moment, watching. His father leans in, the way he does when he approves, when he wants to know more.

"Your father was just telling me about his career," Wesley says. "About a certain naughty first lady who kept gilding the silver fixtures."

"I thought an architect could appreciate my stories," his father says.

"I think most people would," Wesley says. "Everyone is fascinated by first families."

"And did you share your thoughts on architecture?" Julian asks his father. "The modernism-poverty-communism speech?"

The architect frowns: Julian is being mean again. So Julian wraps his father in the cashmere blanket and prepares himself to endure.

He knows the stories. His father's favorite is how he swindled collectors by asking to borrow their favorite pieces of art and furniture to have them reproduced, only to place the originals in the White House and slyly suggest that this was the more fitting home. Some of them—either too stunned to protest or flattered to see their belongings take residence in the White House—had agreed to give the originals up.

Wesley looks charmed. He asks about the first ladies, the marriages, the changes in what constituted formal entertaining. His father could have rivaled Emily Post in the area of social graces; it was the intimacy of domestic life behind closed doors that seemed to paralyze him.

"This is fascinating," Wesley says.

"You really think so?" his father says. "That's nice of you to say. I didn't suppose we would be discussing all this this evening."

"Nor did I," Julian says.

"Could you top me off?" his father asks Wesley.

"I'll get it," Julian says, but Wesley is already up, leaning over his father.

"Wherever did you meet my son?" he asks now. "Do you run in the same circles?" He says this as though that couldn't possibly be the case.

"It was at a political event. Although he didn't seem interested in the politics. Or in me."

"Oh, never mind that," Julian's father says. "See his face right now? That's interested. That's what a surgeon looks like skydiving."

The wind is coming through Julian's blanket and reaching his toes. He has been hiding them not just for warmth but out of vanity, too. He almost has more hair on his toes than on his head.

"Dad, aren't you cold?" Julian says.

"Who cares? I'm dying. I should enjoy it. Maybe I'll never feel wind like this again."

"How about we not accelerate death?" Julian says. "The wind will still be here tomorrow."

It is a long good-bye. His father shakes Wesley's hand in both of his, grasping onto him like a railing. Wesley kisses his father's cheek.

It is a chore to get his father back into his room. He wants water from the kitchen, then a magazine from upstairs. With his father in bed, they move back into the house, onto the long gray sectional again. But Julian can't completely relax. This is what it must be like to have small children. Even once they are in bed, the parent is still spring-loaded, ready to go into action.

"Is he very ill?" Wesley asks. "He looks so healthy."

"Either that or my sister lied to me," Julian says.

"It must be interesting to have a father who's gay," Wesley says. "I've always kind of wondered what that would be like. How it might have made me different."

"He is not gay," Julian says.

"Oh. But—" Wesley sits back against the couch with a strange smile on his face.

"What?"

"I misunderstood. I completely misunderstood."

"He's Southern," Julian says. "He's deeply Southern."

His father has no complaints about his new nurse, although Julian comes home every day in fear of a home remodel. But his father no longer has the energy to coordinate an attack. His health is diminishing in a quiet, almost invisible way not noticeable day-to-day; yet it's markedly worse than when he arrived.

The nurse gives Julian thorough reports, even sharing news from Liv, who calls a few afternoons a week, just after her evening show is over. Julian supposes the time zone is to blame, but she never calls when Julian is home.

Julian tries to sit with his father, but he rarely looks up from his biographies. "What does he do all day when I'm gone?" Julian asks the nurse.

"Reads. And asks me to talk to him. He seems to think my life is a telenovela. He wants to know all about the romance."

At work, Julian has a breakthrough. For a year, he and his collaborators in engineering and cardiology have been trying to implant a fetal pacemaker onto the tiny heart of a sheep fetus, spending long afternoons at the research barrack at the edge of the medical center. They've been working with a small intramural grant from the hospital's research institute, an award that covers the cost of the sheep and the anesthesiologist's time, and not much else. The team uses sheep because of the ewe's paper-thin uterus, the way it lights up like a zeppelin, all the ramuscules and arcades easy to trace. Today, for the first time, the prototype of the pacemaker has stayed put. It is the kind of career news a person wants to share, however difficult it is to explain. He drives home thinking of telling his father, how he could relay its significance, if he wanted to.

But when he arrives, the architect, the nurse and his father are all having drinks in his living room.

"Join us," his father says. "We were just getting started."

Wesley turns to Julian apologetically. "I was down the street visiting a client. I thought I would stop in."

"Stop looking so scandalized," his father says. "We were just swapping stories of Rio."

"You've never been to Rio," Julian says.

The nurse gets up and comes to him, wrapping an arm around Julian's shoulder and pulling him into the kitchen. Julian flinches at his touch.

"It's happening," the nurse says.

"He's never been to Rio," Julian repeats.

"Listen to me," the nurse says. "It'll be fast now."

"Should he be drinking?"

"The drink is weak. A little is fine. It'll help the pain."

"He's in pain?"

"Why don't you join them?" the nurse says.

But when the nurse heads home, Wesley gets up, too. It is only later that Julian realizes this is because his father wants a moment with him. He wants to show him the outfit he'd like to be buried in. "I already showed it to them. Both approved."

"Dad."

"It's happening soon enough. And you think I'm going to let you pick it out?" he says. "You'll dress me like it's my first dance."

He follows his father to the bedroom, where he rolls open the left-hand side of the closet. On a wooden hanger is a cream-colored evening suit. His father lifts the hanger off the rod and pulls it out, gently running his hands along the back of the suit to show it to Julian. Next, he holds up a light teal dress shirt with French cuffs.

"When have you ever worn that?" Julian asks.

"If you can't be yourself when you're dead, when can you be?"

His father maneuvers past the bed to the dresser. From the top drawer, he pulls out a pocket square, then sits down on the bed.

"This is the most important piece," he says, fingering the cloth. "Come look at this."

Julian sits down on the bed beside him. His father holds a small printed square of teal, cream and coral. He is staring at it as though looking at a photograph.

"This is a medallion print," he says. "That's a man's word for flower. They didn't used to use the word flower for anything for men."

The medallions are lined up in neat military rows, rimmed by a teal border. He holds it up to Julian. "See this? These are hand-rolled edges, not machine finished. See how plump they make it? This is what you're looking for."

He lays the square out across his knee, and Julian sees how slim his father's leg has become. "I haven't taught you these things," he says. He folds the square neatly. Julian rises and opens the top drawer for him. "Perhaps the architect can attend to these things when I'm gone," his father says.

Julian is washing up from supper when he hears his father cry out. He almost doesn't recognize the sound at first—it is high and muffled, like a cat's scream. He runs to the bedroom and, finding it empty, realizes his father must be in the bathroom. The door is locked.

"Can you unlock the door?" he asks.

His father moans. "Leave me be," he says. His voice is coming from a low point; it sounds as though he's on the floor.

"Did you fall? Can you reach the lock?"

"I must have eaten something that disagreed with me," he says. Despite his father's best efforts, Julian can hear the high pitch of pain. "Call the nurse," his father says.

"He's gone home. I'm here now."

"He'll come back if you ask."

"I'm a physician, Dad." Julian presses his ear to the door.

"I don't have a uterus," his father says.

"Jesus Christ, Dad." Julian bangs on the door with the side of his fist. "Can you reach the lock? Let me in." He listens through the door but hears nothing. "I'm a doctor," he says.

The hole on the outside of the doorknob is very small, so Julian gets an ice pick from the kitchen, comes back and drops to his knees to get a better view of the outside of the privacy lock. He threads the ice pick in and feels around for the groove, but the pick won't catch. He tries a few different angles with no luck. He could get a paper clip, but it would be no better. He is a surgeon, and he cannot unlock a privacy door. He jams the ice pick in lazily, like a child without a strategy. He needs a tiny screwdriver, the kind used for eyeglasses. His father might have one in the dresser. He is about to go searching for it when the lock clicks.

Julian opens the door and stands there with the ice pick still in hand. His father is wet, prone on the floor between the shower and the toilet; there is a smear of feces across the floor in front of him, and Julian cannot quite piece together the order of events. Without his clothes on, his father looks more than naked—he is a sea creature yanked from its shell.

The intensity of residency is meant for moments like this; it leaves a muscle memory that is more like a scar. Although the son wants to scoop his father up, the doctor knows better. He assesses him first, and only when he finds nothing broken, no signs of internal injury, does he carefully lift him up and set him down in the shower chair, where he can wipe off the feces with a warm rag. The son doesn't really see his father—only the doctor does. It is not until later, after he has dried his father and put him in his proper pajama set and gone to sleep out on the couch so that he can come to him in the night, that he closes his eyes and finally sees his drooping breasts, the last tuft of hair sprouting proudly on his concave chest, his skin so transparent it's a roadmap, a surgeon's dream.

He cancels all his work except for surgeries. Those cannot wait. The next closest fetal surgeon is in San Francisco, and, like Julian, he is always at capacity.

At home, his father sleeps most of the days. He calls Liv, and she arranges to come to Los Angeles for a three-day trip in two weeks. Julian wanders and waits. He edits a journal article he has been putting off. He cleans his home office. He works in a hospital, yet he knows nothing about illness, not really.

One morning, his father wants to take his tea in the living room and watch the morning light on the water. There is no fog, and the ocean looks lit from within. Julian sits with him. They are both wearing robes and slippers as if it is Christmas morning. His parents always wore matching robes, which, as a child, Julian interpreted as a symbol of deep love. It is hard to clearly remember his parents on a holiday morning; the memory of his own anticipation is stronger. He remembers running downstairs without using the bathroom, trying hard not to pee on the floor by the Christmas tree. He can see the extravagance of the house, perfectly decorated with old-fashioned ornaments his father liked: lace snowflakes, golden orbs, wooden Santas carrying trees. He can see his father leaning forward in his high-backed chair that he positioned near the tree, while his mother sat with her legs tucked up beneath her on the end of the couch.

"I can't complain about this view," his father says. "Although it could get lonely looking out at this."

"It does," Julian admits.

"Trees make me feel insulated," his father says. "You and your sister always had a higher tolerance for loneliness. In different ways. She's surrounded by people, of course. But there's no lonelier life. Jay was always more like me. Looking for something to fill it."

His father never speaks of Jay and certainly not in relation to himself. "I hadn't thought of it that way," Julian says carefully. "As you two being alike."

"Unfortunately for Jay, I'm afraid so," he says. "But you—the work you do. I don't know what kind of person one has to be to do that. It frightens me. I thought it was crazy enough when you decided to study gynecology."

Julian tells his father about the pacemaker, about the federal funding he could get. He does not fill in the gaps or explain that he researches on sheep. He tells him instead what it could mean for the babies.

"The lengths a person will go to to bring a child into this world," his father says. "It's the only thing that still astonishes me. People are so predictable in other matters. But not this." He is looking out at the water, the rim of the cup grazing his lips. Julian feels he has stepped into a private moment that perhaps he shouldn't be witnessing.

"Look at me, for example," his father says. "Consider this case."

"Yes?" Julian asks.

His father turns to face him. "Look at me," he says.

Julian is looking. His father is a shrunken man, skin now barely hiding what lies beneath. And yet somehow he still looks royal.

Julian has always believed he and his siblings were a nuisance or a social obligation to be fulfilled. He has been telling himself a particular story for so long—has had, in physician terms, a cognitive disposition to respond, the kind of bias that leads to errors in diagnosis. As a boy, he could identify the symptom: a coldness that swept over their home. But the only cause he could attach to it was his father's preoccupation with his work. He had understood the work to be the cause, but what if it had been the compensation instead?

"It's been worth it," his father says. "You and your sister and Jay. I know that you're more than a doctor. I've understood that all along. But that's exactly what I'm afraid of. When all I want for you is a great love. That's all I want for your sister, too. That's what I wanted for all of you. And yet I suspect I did the thing that has made that impossible for you."

In medical school, Julian thinks, they would call his blindness "anchoring": the tendency to lock on to salient features in a patient's initial presentation and fail to adjust in the light of later, contradictory information. Julian reenvisions his father's life now—a life, as he's always understood it, of sacrifice—but with different bargains than Julian has previously understood.

He says to his father what he says with great intention to every patient he encounters: "It is not your fault."

Terri briefs him when he arrives. They have done an ultrasound, and they are missing one heartbeat. This mother is at the follow-up visit alone; the father was unable to get away from the studio that day.

Sometimes the nurses are wrong. Sometimes a shift of position changes the scene. But not this time.

"We are missing a heartbeat," he tells the mother.

She does not need to ask him what that means. He takes her hand and watches her face. She blinks slowly, her eyes rimmed with laugh lines he doesn't see in most of his patients.

"We have to run some tests," he said, "but it appears the ablation was successful. But the donor's bladder is still very small. It would indicate that the kidney failure was already too advanced."

"Will I have to deliver now?" she says.

"No, the vessels are severed, so the donee is safe," he says. This is, technically speaking, good news. But he has always found this the hardest news to share. "Eight more weeks," he says. He squeezes her hand. "You can do this."

He is lucky. Days with bad news are fewer and farther between. He is not entitled to ask why this woman must now live for two months with a dead baby inside her. If things happen for a reason, he has not figured that reason out yet.

What makes him saddest about his work is not those he disappoints but the shame his patients feel. Some of them are young and superstitious; others have gone to great lengths to get pregnant, but no matter the level of education or circumstances, they feel a deep responsibility. This is why he has learned to absolve them out loud. They need to hear it said explicitly, more than once, and by him. It is not the same when they hear it from someone else.

He thinks of his patient in the months ahead, of the baby shower, of strangers touching her belly in the supermarket, of the innocent questions people ask. Of how some people can bear hidden knowledge inside them, buried under skin and muscle, half-formed, something they will never betray.

The nurse warns Julian that there may be a little burst of energy near the end. The light doesn't just dim; the switch has to be turned off—and that takes a final push of spirit. Julian remembers this phenomenon mentioned briefly in medical school, but he is skeptical, as there is no real switch, no physiological need for this burst. But there may be evolutionary reasons, he thinks: the energy to pass on one final piece of survival knowledge: *Watch out for bears near the far ridge of the mountain!*—that comes straight from the cavemen days.

So when he finds his father making breakfast one Saturday morning, he has forgotten. He is so surprised to see him there that he just smiles. Only the night before, his father seemed half-conscious. He wasn't eating or drinking and wouldn't tell Julian the last time he had had a bowel movement. Julian sat at his bedside like a doctor on a house call, taking his temperature, listening to his heartbeat. The beat was irregular, his father's eyes glazed.

Now his father is in the kitchen making chocolate pancakes and scrambled eggs. The house is filled with the sharp sourness of real buttermilk. "I can't stop thinking of chocolate." His father smiles. "I had to have some."

Before the pancakes are ready, Julian is called in to work. There's an urgent case from Arizona. It is his father's nurse's day off. He would call Terri, but she is at work, of course, waiting patiently for him with the couple.

He calls the only person he can think of: the architect. He considers for a moment what favors of this kind usually mean, how advanced a relationship must be to call one in. But Wesley doesn't hesitate. Julian wonders if it is his father's illness or his father himself or something about Wesley that has allowed them to bypass so many preliminaries and what, if anything, this portends for their relationship.

When Wesley arrives, he is a weekend-morning beauty, hair tousled, tan feet in flip-flops. His father delights at the sight of him, smooths his own hair back with a quick gesture.

"I hope you haven't eaten breakfast," Julian's father says. He pulls another mug out of the cabinet and places it next to the coffee maker.

"I can't thank you enough for coming," Julian whispers to Wesley. He wants to hug him but settles for squeezing his elbow instead. "This is a real gift."

Wesley goes to the kitchen, helps carry the plates and the mugs to the dining room. He goes back for the syrup and the juice, then pulls out a chair for Julian's father, who sits at the head of the table. His father's hands just graze the beam of morning light that slices across the dining table. It will only take a couple of hours. Julian quietly backs out of the room, leaving the two to their breakfast, smiling over their mugs like old mates.

Instructions to the Living from the Condition of the Dead

Jason Brown

The door hinges creaked, and the thudding footfalls of his family shook the beams. What were they doing here today, the day before Thanksgiving? Voices, the crackling of grocery bags, firewood clunking in front of the hearth (because they thought he was too old now to carry it from the barn himself). They swarmed into every corner of the parlor and the kitchen with no thought to the most important question, the same this year as every year: Who had brought the goddamned cheddar? Indeed. Two years ago he'd put his foot down and said he would no longer provide! So this year would be the same as last year: crackers and hummus from California.

"Dad? Where are you?" called Melissa, his mealymouthed, psalm-singing sycophant of a granddaughter-in-law, a lawyer from California who always talked about the importance in old age of regular bowel movements. A sharp slap on the staircase, then another and another. Nowhere to retreat to except into his bedroom. Not safe! The first place Melissa would look. The bathroom, and once there, into the cast-iron tub? Forced to evacuate because these people had shown up on Isabel's birthday. His family didn't even know about Isabel and wouldn't approve if they did. Their beloved Grandma Sarah departed, and here he was sneaking over to Isabel's house. Tut, tut, the old Heathcliff. No cheddar for him!

The slapping grew louder as he decided to stand his ground in the bathroom (they had just once, he and Isabel, lain side by side in her great bed, with their clothes on, and he had leaned over to kiss her). "Your wife was very pretty," Isabel said. "She is," he replied, and this would've been a good chance to explain (though he decided it was not wise) the overwhelming feeling that his wife was not dead but everywhere around him at all times.

He heard no sound for almost a minute, so he opened the door to the bathroom. Five small fingers rested on the top step. The scruffy blond hair. The blue eyes and tanned face of his great-grandson, William Palfry Howland (Will), resident of Ojai, California, a place, he gathered, where people lolled around in the sun like overfed housecats. Having summited the top step, his great-grandson sighed.

"Daddy wants to talk to you," he said and cocked his head.

"The grand one or the regular one?" John asked.

He heard his wife, Sarah, clucking in the air around him. She didn't need to tell him to leave the boy be.

His great-grandson frowned and pursed his lips. The smallness of his mouth reminded John of Melissa, the boy's mother, who measured her words like a butcher adding slices of roast beef on the scale. The more she spoke, the more he would have to pay. She'd actually been born in Maine, not California, but she was a Yankee in name only. Her branch of the John Gorham Palfrys suffered from dry rot, but none of that was the boy's fault.

"Ah, I don't know what dayyy wants," Will said and shrugged. Cocking his hip and raising his hand in the air, Will flashed that sly smile, head tilted. Were all the children from California born to sell insurance?

"Do you want to play a game?" John asked.

"No—." Will shook his head.

"Well, you're in luck because I have a secret stash of cookies. . . ."

"Why?"

"Why? So no one else will eat them."

This seemed to cause horrible confusion. Will put his palm up to the side of his head.

"I don't like cookies," Will said.

"Everyone likes cookies," John countered.

"Do they have sugar in them?"

"Do they have sugar? Of course. They're cookies."

Will shook his head sadly. As always, John had lost the battle before it even started.

"What the heck do you like to eat, then?"

"Mangoes. I like mangoes."

"Would you like to do something for me?" He was out of tricks.

"Yes, I would!" Will's eyes flashed blue.

"Go downstairs and tell your dad and your granddad—tell anyone you see—that you spotted me down by the river in back of the house."

"But you're not down by the river."

John knelt in front of Will's face.

"That's the point of the game, Will. If I were down by the river, it wouldn't be a game at all! Don't you see?"

"No." He shook his head. "I don't see."

"Well, you will someday. Now hurry up before it's too goddamned late."

"You swore," Will pointed out, but he didn't seem upset about it. He descended the steps carefully and, with a good deal less urgency than John would've liked, turned the corner to tell everyone that he had spotted his senile great-grandfather headed for the shore. John heard the side door slam. Everyone spilled out into the field behind the house and started calling his name.

Even on days when he managed a decent bowel movement, the narrow staircase was an iffy proposition (not recommended by Doctor Pingree or Janine, the attractive acupuncture woman, without whom he would never have a bowel movement). He grabbed his volume of Emily Dickinson, creaked down the stairs, stutter-stepped to the landing like a teenager, plucked his Irish tweed hat off the hook, and headed out the front door to his electric tricycle parked at the head of the drive. Didn't need the motor going downhill. He slipped past the cars at the end of the drive, banged a left, and coasted toward Boynton's Market. Couldn't show up without a cupcake. She was only eighty-five—a younger woman! Flowers, too much. She always had flowers, anyway. How did she manage that in the winter? They hadn't even taken away her license yet, so maybe she drove to Portland for them. A girl with a license. They'd taken his away, even though he could see an osprey pluck a mole out of the grass at a hundred yards. He pedaled along the flat on Water Street and rode up onto the curb in front of Boynton's Market.

Charlie Boynton manned the counter today.

"John," he said in his usual flat voice. Anchored there for twenty-five years.

"Got a house full of people," John said.

"Happens this time of year."

"Half of them seem to be from goddamn California."

"Sure. Heard of it."

"Ever been there?"

Charlie just looked at him with raised eyebrows. Course he hadn't.

"They weren't supposed to come 'til tomorrow. Charlie, I need a cupcake. A large cupcake if you have one. Two. Do you even have cupcakes?"

"We have cupcakes."

Thank god, and tremendous cupcakes they were. He bought one carrot with thick cream frosting and one double chocolate. Charlie fit them up with a box, no great shakes, tied with string, just right for Isabel. A no-nonsense Radcliffe girl, weren't many of them around, and two books of poems to her name. Isabel Vaughn Bowditch, though everyone called her Bella Vaughn, because she was a Vaughn first, especially as far as the town was concerned. The last Vaughn still living in Vaughn. Trim and strong in her yellow slicker and Wellies, drove the old Volvo to the post office for mail at exactly 10:45 every single morning. Her grandfather would've been Henry Vaughn, the one who ran the mill into the ground. Not his fault. Her brother the one who turned it into a retirement center. Her husband, Walter Bowditch, bald as a harbor seal, dead five years now, a "fancy mechanic," wanted to be a specialist in Portland, people said, but Bella said no, so he stayed in Vaughn and dispensed pills and cough syrup.

His own wife, Sarah, had grown weak around the ankles in her last years. John had to do the shopping and cooking and cleaning. Then one morning he woke with the light as usual, swung his legs out of bed as he shivered in the cold bite of the bedroom air, and said, as he always did, "Going to take the dog out." Instead of saying, "Okay," in her perfectly clear voice (she always woke before him and lay in bed waiting for the sun to come up), she said nothing. Made no sound. She lay on her back, mouth open, eyes closed.

Unsure that the half-charged tricycle battery would power him up the hill, he pedaled as far as he could before hitting the power switch and letting the motor take over. If he could make the next rise, he could coast the rest of the way past the Smalls' and Nasons' to reach Isabel's driveway. She'd told him when he last visited . . . ten days ago? Said he shouldn't worry about her birthday. "No big ship," she said, using a phrase he'd heard on a trip to Nova Scotia in 1952 to deliver a schooner from Canso to Newburyport for a man named Rogers.

The motor on his trike started to whine a hundred yards from the crest of the hill. He pressed down hard on the pedals and, in the final stretch, stood up as sweat pooled on his brow. Over the top, he ran before the wind down the other side.

"For me, all that business with the body is over now," Sarah's voice entered his ear. "Go to her if that's what you want." Sometimes she spoke from above, high in the clouds, or from across the room.

He did want to smell Isabel's hair and rest his lips on the nape of her neck. He wanted to pull her to him.

"What if I lose track of you?" he said to his wife.

"You won't," she said.

He glided past the Boynton house, the Wells house (someone from Massachusetts lived there now), the Coffin house with the windows shamefully fallen out of the cupola. The same was true of the Dill house, where Betsy had lived alone since her husband, Henry Dill, owner for forty years of Foot Wise Shoes in Augusta and active member of the Volunteer Fire Department, had stepped in front of the snowplow, either on purpose or not, according to what you believed. Having only recently sold the store, he had talked to John about buying an electric tricycle for himself (one, he thought, with a stronger battery). No person who wanted to own an electric tricycle could possibly want to throw themselves in front of a plow, but, as Sarah had pointed out more than once, why was the man out on Water Street at twelve midnight on a Thursday during a snowstorm? No one would ever know the answer to that question.

Second Street swept down to level ground. The sky began to clear, and the air, tinged with wood smoke, turned sharp in his sinuses and hard as a fist in his chest. The body mechanic Pingree had said he had emphysema years ago, yet he felt it was only yesterday when he first stepped up to Sarah's parents' house and asked to see their daughter. "No, you may not!" It was a Sunday, the father reminded this young man. No piece of information had ever seemed as trivial and funny as the day of the week. He told her father he'd come back the next day, the eighth day of the week. "There is no eighth day," the father said, clearly baffled. "There is now," John told him.

And there was, and there is, still.

He slipped right into Isabel's driveway. The ground grew too rough and the ruts too deep, and he stepped off the trike. Eager to reach the black front door, he forgot the box of cupcakes and had to turn back.

"You should've brought flowers," Sarah said.

"She has flowers already," he said.

"But that's not the point."

He knew she was right, and he stood in front of the door wondering if he should turn back to Boynton's. For the past two months he'd called Isabel before sleep each night, and they read Emily Dickinson to each other as they both gazed out their bedroom windows at the moon hanging over the twisting current of the river.

I had been hungry all the years;
My noon had come, to dine;
I, trembling, drew the table near,
And touched the curious wine. . . .

After more than sixty years of marriage and almost a century on earth, he could now feel himself pushing against the front of his pants like a schoolboy. He wanted to touch Isabel today, before the sun went down, before his family realized he'd abdicated his post the day before Thanksgiving (who would cut the turkey, light the plum pudding, start them off singing *We gather together to ask the lord's blessing . . .*)

He pounded the brass knocker and listened with his ear to the door. For a moment, when he heard nothing, he stopped breathing. Then the house creaked under her light step. Those old pine floors with loosened rosehead nails, the horsehair plaster itself as alive as the hide of an animal.

"You would have been better off with her, John," Sarah said, and he shook his head. His father had said more or less the same thing when he first brought Sarah home: "Are you sure, John?" But what had John done with his life? A schoolteacher, correcting the spelling of the town. No great shakes. Sarah had risen to rule the school board. He hadn't deserved *her*.

The knob turned, and the door swung open. There she stood, trim in her white blouse and gray bob, a cup of coffee poised in her right hand. Her eyes jumped away from him, slid off his shoulder, and came to rest on the granite step. He didn't understand; there was no reason for her to be embarrassed. They'd done nothing that they couldn't take back. He could explain; he just wanted to come in, to not be outside.

"John," she said, and his patience gave out.

"Please, can I come in?"

"Of course." She bowed slightly and stepped out of his way, and he entered the foyer and then the cool parlor. The threadbare oriental, the portrait of her grandfather, old Henry Vaughn, his chin like a rifle butt. He set the box on the sideboard and started to undo the string. She'd understand when he showed her the cupcakes. He struggled with the tape on the edge of the box and finally took out both cupcakes and placed them on the sideboard. The sight of them seemed to make her sad. He knew she liked chocolate.

"For your birthday," he said. How could anything be more simple than that?

"Today," she said slowly, "is not my birthday, John. It's next week."

Next week! He looked from the cupcakes to her. He'd spent so many afternoons looking right into her green eyes. She smiled out the window toward the brown straw of the field. At the end of the field the barn, and beyond the barn a scattered veil of pines partially obscuring the river.

"I was going to call today and invite you to supper next week," she said.

He took *The Collected Poems of Emily Dickinson* out of his pocket and rested it next to the cupcakes.

She smiled and moved the cupcakes to the kitchen table. She would be right back. When she returned from the pantry, she carried a bottle of wine, her last bottle of Bocksbeutel, she said, from a case she and her husband had brought back from a trip to France and Germany in the late 1980s. He hadn't seen one of the distinctively round bottles of the Franconian wines in fifty years. She pulled the cork and filled two glasses. He toasted her birthday, and they both drank.

He lifted the book he had brought and was about to open to the poem "Hunger," when she sighed and told him that her favorite town in the wine region had been Tegernsee, and he set the book down on the table.

"Tegernsee?" he said, and she nodded. He asked if the wine in front of him had come from this town. She nodded and lifted the bottle to pour him more.

"It was such a beautiful village, with those old hotels right on the lake and the mountains in the distance." She leaned forward, still smiling.

"We almost destroyed Tegernsee," he said.

"What do you mean?"

"It was the war," he said.

"Yes, of course," she said. "I didn't know there was a battle there. When we visited, the residents said none of the buildings had been destroyed. That there hadn't really been any fighting there."

She was right. His company commander, Bill Spears, had spared the village because of a man named Heinz Shaeffer, a wounded German tank commander who walked toward them across a field with a bandage around his head and his one good arm raised in the air.

John had never spoken to anyone about the end of the war, not even Sarah. Now as he talked, he began to search, like a man in a dark room, for an excuse to shut his mouth.

"We were chasing an SS unit down from Munich. They stopped in Tegernsee and started to shell us. So my commander told me to get on the phone and call for artillery. It was May 3."

"But then this man, a tank commander, walked out of the village?"

"He told us the village was full of 12,000 unarmed German soldiers who were not SS, and war refugees, and that the war would be over in days, and he was right—we knew that. The war ended five days later."

"So then it was a good thing you didn't destroy the village," she said, still smiling.

"But the armed SS unit was there, too, and they would get away down the back end of the valley into Austria. We didn't want to let them escape."

"But the war was almost over," she said and leaned forward to lay her hand on his forearm.

"We didn't care. We planned to execute every last one of them," he said.

"I don't understand. Why would you kill them if you knew the war was about to end?

"Not kill—execute. Two different things. Because of the goddamned mess we found at Gardelegen and Kaufering, that's why." She tilted her head and squinted at him, and he lowered his voice. "Because of what we found."

"Oh, I see," she said and leaned back in her chair, the afternoon light turning to liquid in the reflections of her eyes. The corners of her mouth tucked in like the wings of a bird folding against its body. "Come now," she said and quickly shook her head.

The words might have come from his own thoughts—he couldn't be sure—and he spoke to argue with himself.

"A thousand burned bodies inside one barn in Gardelegen," he said, "and that was nothing compared to Kaufering and Dachau . . . and all along the roadside to Tegernsee."

"Dachau?" Isabel shook her head with her eyes closed. "No, John," she said.

"I'm sorry," he said. "I shouldn't be telling you this." After they'd failed to attack Tegernsee, he and the others in his unit had never talked about what they'd seen.

"It's nonsense, John," she said, and she placed her hand back on his arm. He looked at her hand, at the Dickinson, at the cupcakes, then at the walls of the kitchen with pictures of her family: her late husband, her only child, Katherine, who lived in Boston, and other Vaughns, most of them gone now, the descendants of people who had, along with his own ancestors, started this town.

"But I was there," he said quietly, not to her, and now he was forced to picture the man who had wedged his head under the wall of the barn and died with his eyes open to the sky. Had he seen that? The others they found in smoldering piles by the doors. Following the trail of the destruction south, they found more charred bodies inside the barracks at Kaufering. Skeletons with blackened skin stretched as tight as the heads of snare drums. Between Dachau and Tegernsee, more bodies in the woods and along the side of the road. Then they reached Tegernsee, and the tank commander with the bandage over one eye and another around his chest begged them not to shell the town where the murderers hid among the innocent.

"The SS is still there," John had said to the CO, Bill Spears.

"And a hospital and 12,000 people without guns," said the tank commander in perfect English. Dried blood flaked off his dirty neck. John remembered the German tank commander's hazel eyes, the chip in his tooth, the feel of the air, the impossibly blue sky as John held the handle of the radio in one hand and the crank in the other. Bill Spears raised his palm and shook his head. Later, they walked into the town with the tank commander. The SS had left already, and thousands of people, many of them children, mothers, grandmothers, wounded soldiers, all the people they would have killed, came out to greet them. Many people were dying in these last days of the war, Germans and prisoners both. Hundreds of thousands in the camps died of typhus before and after they were rescued. Many German villagers not killed by the constant Allied firebombing committed suicide just before the Americans or Soviets arrived.

"I know," Isabel said, "we are all supposed to think . . . Walter and I, we just never believed any of that—at least not in the way we were told it happened."

He realized she meant Kaufering, Dachau, and similar places. She looked him in the eyes. They had grown up in the same town. He'd known her as a girl until she left for Dana Hall and college. When he saw her after she returned already married, she wore the same warm expression when she shopped at Boynton's store, chaired library committee meetings, and read her own poems in public. He was married, and she was married, of course.

"It's Thanksgiving tomorrow," he said, and when she nodded, he looked at the floor. The deep blues and reds of the worn Persian carpet. When he stood, he focused on the dark oil portraits of her ancestors down the hall. He needed to be out of here, and he pushed himself from the table and limped (his knee aching again) down the hall past the door to the study. All those leather-bound volumes, her father's and her grandfather's books from Harvard, which she'd read as a girl on summer afternoons when her mother propped open all the windows and the breeze from the river billowed the curtains and stirred the leaves of her father's newspaper resting on the arm of his wing chair. In the last year she'd painted him a picture of her whole life.

She touched his back. "I'm sorry, John," she said, and for a moment he thought she would take back what she'd said. "I am sure you saw many horrible things." Her hand on his seemed to weigh more than any man could lift.

He nodded and limped as quickly as he could out the door. Not the first time he'd run for his life. On the granite landing, his heart jumped but didn't stop. He jog-hopped with his bad knee toward his tricycle, but when he turned the trike around, he realized the battery was dead. He'd never be able to pedal—or walk, for that matter—up and over the hill to the house.

He hobbled around the edge of the woods. His breath seized every time a dry branch snapped under his boots. He had left the Dickinson in her kitchen, but he didn't think he would read any more Dickinson in the time he had left.

Isabel kept an old wooden rowboat down by the river for when her daughter and grandchildren visited. He spotted the upturned blue hull, made of plywood, half its paint gone. He flipped it over and found the gray oars rotting but still solid. Larry had pulled the dock for her already. With his back to the river, he tugged the boat a few feet at a time to the marshy shore. The tide would pinch any time now. He waded up to his knees and pulled the boat in after him. Sensing Isabel watching him, he tried to climb quickly into the boat, but he couldn't raise his feet. He dove headfirst over the side and used his arms to right himself. When he craned his neck, he spotted her halfway between the river and her house and moving fast on her springy legs.

"John," he heard Sarah say in his ear, "why did you never tell me what you saw?"

"I just wanted to forget it," he said.

"John . . ." Isabel, calling his name. Though he'd launched himself into ebb tide, he did have the wind in his favor. Before he could set the locks and oars in place, he'd already drifted out of Isabel's view and traveled fifty yards, maybe seventy-five. Rowing, he picked up speed and felt the satisfying whoosh of the oars and the bow cleaving the water. He had rowed this stretch as a boy many times, and now all he wanted to do was get home to Sarah.

The three-story shops lined the waterfront. Behind their sagging roofs, the square captains' houses and church spires of town stretched up the hill toward the top of the valley, where his Puritan ancestors had arrived hundreds of years before to claim this shore—the farthest upriver into the belly of the state a deepwater vessel could travel. What had he done with the life they had prepared for him? Running around a field with a whistle, parsing lines of poetry for children who could think of nothing but chasing each other around outdoors.

The men from the SS unit—five hundred, maybe—slipped into Austria, and from there he never knew what happened to them. Some might have been caught. Others must have escaped. John had been killing Germans since D-Day, and now his commanders told him to stop. Just like that.

The boat was leaking. Up to his ankles now. Nothing he could do but row harder. The rotten oar cracked, and his shoulder seized with pain. He sighted the field in front of his house and gave an extra hard tug. A small person stood at the shoreline, shielding his eyes. His great-grandson, Will, shouted, "Grand, grand," over the water. "What are you doing?"

John thought he would save his wind and attempt to answer the question later. The technique he'd used with his children and grandchildren, of putting them off until they forgot their questions, never worked with Will, who remembered everything and had a backlog of unanswered—and frequently unanswerable—questions that he brought to bear with a tax assessor's persistence. Will's mother, the lawyer, had placed a stick in the ground to mark the spot past which her son should not venture closer to the water. Will leaned against the stick like a ballplayer leaning on his bat.

The boat nudged into the grass. The water had come to within six inches of the gunnel.

"There's a problem with your boat," Will observed from the safety of his position on the bank.

John stood in the shallows of the river and looked up at Will's blue eyes and unruly California hairdo.

"I wish I could ride in the boat with you," Will said sadly. He pursed his lips. Despite his California origins, possibly Will had inherited a tendency to look at all boats, even this boat, with longing. "My mother thinks I'm going to the bathroom." Will turned his miniature hand palm up. "I *was* going to the bathroom, but then I looked out the window and saw *you* in the river. In that boat," Will said.

When John tried to trudge through the mud, his boots stuck and wouldn't move. He undid the laces and pulled. The socks stayed with the boots as he freed his feet and fought the reeds to solid ground. The bank remained, and his right knee and now his hip had stopped working altogether. His back, his neck, his ribs—his whole body ached and burned and resisted taking one more step. He stumbled, turned his ankle and scraped his forehead on a root.

"You didn't make it!" Will said, more thrilled than troubled, it seemed to John.

John grabbed the branches of a bush and pulled and crawled his way up the slope. At the top, he collapsed, wheezing, in front of Will, who looked from his face to his wet trousers and bare, sliced feet.

"You have blood on your head!" Will said. He leaned close to John's face and frowned. In California—and especially in Will's little genius private school where they taught astrophysics to eight-year-olds—people didn't get knocked around. They didn't make emergency landings on hostile shores. John touched his forehead, and his fingers came away bloody.

"Here they come," Will said, pointing to the side of the house. The family had spotted him and started across the field. They would surround him.

"Stay here," Will said. "Take a time out. I will go tell them you're sleeping."

The black soles of Will's shoes snapped as he sprinted through the pale grass.

"Sarah?" John said and looked for her in the apple trees his father had planted along the shore, in the windows of the house at the head of the field, in the rowboat, submerged to the gunnels and turning in the current, and in the faces of his family waving to him from halfway across the field. They would want to know where he'd been. "Sarah," he said, no longer recognizing the sound of his own voice, "what do I tell them?" He closed his eyes to listen for her answer and heard only silence.

Exotic Animal Medicine

Fiona McFarlane

The wife was driving on the night they hit Mr. Ronald.

"My first drive since getting married," she said.

"First this, first that," said her husband. He looked at her, sitting high in the seat: her hair looked flimsy and blond in the late sun. It was ten-thirty and still light. These were the days for marrying—the long days, and the summer. It hadn't rained.

"You've got to be thankful for the weather," the registrar had said to the husband. The husband was thankful for the weather and for everything else. He wore a narrow suit and his wife wore a blue dress. They came out of the registry office into the pale summer, and St. Mary's rang the hour.

"Listen!" said the wife. "Just like we've been married in a church."

It was midday, and because they were in Cambridge, the college bells rang.

Their witnesses—two friends—took photographs. The four of them went to a pub on the river to celebrate among the tourists and the students who'd just finished exams. The tourists pressed around them, clumsy at the bar; the students slipped in among them and were served first. The bride and groom were rocked from side to side in the crush of people. They cooperated with the crowd, and liquid spilled over their glasses.

They began to drink.

Their friend Peter swayed benevolently above their table. He motioned over their heads with his arms.

"I suppose I'm best man," he said. "By default. So, a toast: to David and Sarah. To Sarah and David. I'll make a statement about love. I'll say a few words."

"You've already said more than enough," said the other witness, Clare.

"Not nearly enough," said Peter, and sat down. By now it was four in the afternoon, and the June town was keeping quiet. The scent of the roses in the college gardens increased, and the black East Anglian bees responded, hanging lazily above the scent. The lawns maintained their perfect green. The river was laid out straight like a track for trains. David and Sarah and Clare and Peter walked along it to find another pub.

The swans idled on the brown river, the ducks chased punts for food, the geese slid against the wet banks. Tinfoil barbecues were lit on Jesus Green, one by one, and the smoke hung in morose columns above each group, never thick enough to form a cloud. The husband and wife and their friends picked their way among the barbecues. They encountered dogs, friendly and wayward.

"Stay well today, canines," said David. "Stay happy and healthy."

Sarah was on call that night.

"I'm not worried about them," said Sarah. "It's the Queen of Sheba I'm worried about. But he'll be good."

(At the surgery, the Queen of Sheba lifted his haunches and lowered his head to stretch his grey back. He walked figure eights in his cage the way a tiger would. The nurse poked her fingers through the grill as she passed Sheba's cage and Sheba, blinking, ignored them.)

"He'd better be good," said David.

"That bloody cat," said Sarah, happily.

The crowd at the pub parted before the bridal party, and they found an outdoor table, newly abandoned. Their happiness was good luck. Sarah said, "Just one more drink. I might have to work."

"You might," said Peter. "And you might not."

"Remember, this is your wedding reception," said Clare, and she placed her arm around Sarah, coaxing.

Sarah looked up at David.

"Just one more, then," she said.

"We'll make it vodkas," said Peter.

"My first vodka as a married woman," said Sarah. She sat against David and felt the day carry them toward each other. The hours passed at the pub, and they didn't think of going home, although this was what they looked forward to: the privacy of their bed against smudged windows, its view of small gardens and the beat of trapped bees against glass that shook as the buses moved by. Their bed was a long way from the colleges and the river, but the bells would still come over the roads and houses, and they would be alone, and married. The day moved them both toward the moment in which they would face each other in their bed, utterly familiar, and see that despite their marriage there was no change, and that this was just what they wanted.

Sarah's phone rang. She knew it would be work. David creased his face at her, disbelieving, but he wasn't disappointed. This way he would have her to himself. They would drive in the car, and she would tell him her impressions of the day: the mannerism she had disliked in the registrar—a tendency to blink too often and too hard. He would rest his hand on her warm leg and lean his head back on the seat and watch the way her driving forced her to keep her usually animated hands still. This animation would pass instead into her face, where her eyebrows would knit and rise across her forehead. She would lean a long way forward to look left and right at intersections, as if she needed to see vast distances. Sarah drove as if she were landing an enormous plane full of porcelain children on a mountaintop.

"What a surprise," said Sarah. She placed her phone on the table. "The Queen of Sheba needs a catheter."

Clare said, "There must be someone else."

"No one else," said Sarah, standing now, slightly unsteady on her feet but graceful. "Sheba's all mine. He's a friend's cat."

"And does this friend know you got married today?" asked Clare. Sarah laughed. No one knew they had been married today.

"Your wedding night, and you have to go stick something up a cat's dick," said Peter.

(Sheba rolled in his cage, snapping at the nurse's fingers. The pain felt familiar to him but newly terrible, a hot pressure. He flicked his paws to shake it off, shake it off. He couldn't.)

Sarah led David from the pub. He leaned against her the way he did when he was on the way to being very drunk. In fact, he was just perfectly, amiably, generously drunk, inclined to pause in order to kiss his new wife. He looked proudly at her. He felt grateful. He felt an expansion in his brain that he enjoyed—a sense that finally he had found his life or was finding it, was on the verge of finding it, although he was still a graduate student and suspected he always would be. He said to himself, "This is my youth, at this moment, right now," and because he was drunk, he also said it to Sarah.

The walk home wasn't far, but they took their time. Sarah had a sense of urgency about Sheba but couldn't translate that urgency into hurry, like those anxious dreams when she was due somewhere important but was unable to find the items she needed to bring with her. They spent whole minutes stopped on the side of the road to watch a woman move around her lit basement kitchen, ironing. As they approached their apartment, David said, "You know I'm coming with you," and she didn't argue. They changed their clothes and it felt to Sarah, briefly, as if it had been David's suit and her dress that had married each other earlier in the day. David followed her to the car. Before lowering herself into the driver's seat, she shook her head from side to side, just a little, as if she might clear it. She didn't feel drunk.

It was an old car, friendly but unreliable, that flew with dog hair when the windows were down. It required patience, particularly in the winter; even now, in June, it demonstrated a good-natured reluctance to start. Sarah turned the key; the engine kicked in and then out. David played with the radio to find a good song, and when there were no good songs, he turned it low. As if encouraged by this decrescendo, the car cooperated. Cambridge was lit with orange lights. They passed through the city and were in the country very suddenly, with dark fields pressing round them and the lights of airplanes far overhead. England became a long, dark road, then, with bright windows visible across wet fields, and trees against the sky.

"What's wrong with this cat?" said David.

"Urinary tract."

"I know that. But what's *wrong* with it?"

Sarah grew defensive on behalf of Sheba. "He can't help it."

"Why call a tomcat Sheba?"

"They let their kid name it," said Sarah. "It's the name of a brand of cat food. It uses real cuts of meat rather than by-products."

"Crazy."

"Don't," said Sarah.

"It's crazy. It's like your mum naming your brother Leslie and your dad doing nothing to stop it."

"Leslie's a family name. It's a boy's name! And I don't want to think about my mother. Right now I'm pretending she doesn't exist. I left my phone at home," said Sarah. "If she calls, I don't want to tell her we're married, and I don't want not to have told her."

"So just don't answer."

"I'd have to answer. I couldn't not answer. And then—you know." She spread her hands to indicate her predicament and then quickly placed them back on the steering wheel.

David lifted in his seat to feel at his back pocket and then said, "Shit. My phone's still in my suit."

"What do you need a phone for, darling? Call all your girlfriends?"

"I've given them the night off."

She hit at him with her left hand.

"Watch the road!" he said, laughing. She watched the road.

"My first drive since getting married," she said.

"First this, first that," he said. At this moment, a car pulled quickly out of a dark side road and turned directly in front of them. Sarah's veer to the left met the back corner of the other car. Trees moved in front of the window-screen; tires made a long noise against the road; the car jolted over the grass and stones of the verge; they hit a low, wooden fence and felt the engine splutter and stall. And as this took place they were aware of something more urgent occurring behind them: the spin of Mr. Ronald's car, its dive into a roadside tree. Sarah and David remained still for a moment and then realized they were both hunched over, preparing for an impact that hadn't come.

"Fuck," said Sarah, looking back down the dim road. The muted lights of tiny Cambridge hung orange at the bottom of the sky behind them. The car radio continued to play.

"You're all right?" asked David, but that was obvious. He opened his door and stepped out onto the road. Mr. Ronald's car made him think of him of a cartoon dog, excessively punched, whose nose had folded into his face for a brief and hilarious moment. Soon it would relax out again, intact. He watched Sarah run toward it and then ran after her. The driver's door had opened in the crash, and Mr. Ronald sat, his legs pinioned inextricably, but his right arm rested against the door frame as if he were about to casually lean out and make a comment on the weather. He wasn't moving.

"He's alive," said Sarah.

She knelt beside the car and held Mr. Ronald's wrist, and when she released it she wiped her fingers against her skirt. David leaned against the tree and passed his hand across his face. He felt the air press in around him, and he wanted somehow to press it back. Sarah had found Mr. Ronald's wallet on the front passenger seat.

"His whole name is just three first names," she said, inspecting his license. "Ralph Walter Ronald. He's seventy-six."

Sarah looked at Mr. Ronald reverently, considering his age and misfortune. His awkward name had lifted him out of a past time in which she played no part and deposited him here, in his crushed car.

"Which way to the nearest house?" asked David.

"I don't know."

"Forward or back?"

"I don't know."

"This is your drive to work. You drive this way almost every day."

"It's dark. I haven't been paying attention."

"All right, all right. Should I try the car? Otherwise I'll have to walk for help. It seems like ages since we saw a house."

"Nothing in England is ever very far apart."

"Maybe I should cross the fields. Do you see lights to the left?"

"I don't see anything."

It began to rain, very lightly. The rain seemed to rise out of the ground and lift up into their faces, a cheerful mist.

"All right, try the car, quickly," said Sarah. "I'll sit with him. His car won't blow up, will it? Is that just in movies?"

"It would have blown up by now. Right?"

They stood helpless in their combined ignorance, considering Mr. Ronald's car and Mr. Ronald trapped within it. The passenger's seat was intact, although the accordion-fold of the front of the car left almost no leg room. Sarah brushed glass from the seat and slid in beside Mr. Ronald, tucking her legs beneath her.

David pulled himself away from the tree with great effort and crossed to the car with caution. It wouldn't start. It would never start when he was late for a seminar or a critical train; it required tender solicitations after particularly steep hills. Of course it wouldn't start now, when his need was desperate. Perhaps it was finally beyond repair. David tried again. It wouldn't start and wouldn't start. He ran back to Sarah.

"No good," he said. "Fuck it. I'll run. I'm sure I'll find someone. Another car."

"Go forward, not back," said Sarah. "Keep following the road forward. I think there's a service station. God, I have no idea of distances on foot."

"Baby," David said, leaning farther into the car, "it wasn't your fault."

"I know," she said. "It was his fucking fault. But darling, I'm a little drunk."

She watched him comprehend this. He was drunker than she was. His eyes filled briefly. There was a scar above his right eye, half hidden in the eyebrow, left over from childhood chicken pox. He often walked through their apartment on his toes, adding to his height, bending down over her as she lay on the couch. He would lay his head on her stomach and look up at her face, and when he did this he reminded her of an ostrich. This was how he looked at her now.

"I'll be back soon," he said. "It's going to be all right. I love you. Don't be scared."

He bent down to kiss her, bent his long, beautiful bird neck, and then began to run. Sarah was amazed at how quickly he vanished into the vanishing light. She looked at Mr. Ronald. He wore corduroy trousers and a neat shirt, a woolen vest and bulky glasses over thick eyebrows. He lay with his head thrown back and to the side, facing Sarah, and his facial expression was bemused and acquiescing. She felt again at his wrist. His legs were caught up with the buckled car, and it was impossible to tell what damage had been done. She sat on her side, looking into his face, and felt the faint breath that hung around his mouth. It smelled like a doctor's waiting room: just-extinguished cigarettes and a human smell rising up through disinfectant. She heard David try the car again, and she heard the car fail. Then his footsteps on the road, and then nothing. Sarah felt loneliness fall over her quickly, and fear.

"The Queen of Sheba," she said.

(Sheba paused in his tiger-walk, his head lifted toward the surgery door, waiting. No one came through the door, and he dropped his head again, letting out a low, small sound that startled the macaws opposite into frantic cries.)

Sarah was married, and no one knew but herself and David, Peter and Clare. Her mother didn't know. She wondered now about the secrecy—how childish it seemed. They only wanted privacy. They wanted a visa for Sarah, to match David's student visa, and they didn't want to bother about the fuss that went with weddings. The last of the vodka wound itself up against the side of Sarah's head that tilted against the seat; it hung there in a vapor. Mr. Ronald's burnt breath came in little gusts up against her face. Was he breathing more, or less? Sarah pulled the door as far as it would go behind her in order to feel safe and to guard against the slight chill in the wind. This was summer, she thought. You waited for it all year, shoulders pushed up against the cold and the dark, and this was your gift: the sun and the bells, the smoke over Jesus Green, geese on the river. A midday wedding. A cat's catheter and Mr. Ronald by the side of the road.

Mr. Ronald's eyes opened, and Sarah pulled back from his face quickly. They studied each other. His eyes were yellow at the edges; they were clever and lucid. They looked at Sarah with calm acceptance, and at the windscreen, shattered but half in place, and at the close proximity of the tree.

"I've had an accident," he said.

"Yes, you have. How do you feel? Stay still," said Sarah. She felt composed. Everything she did felt smooth and immediate.

"I'm all here," said Mr. Ronald. "Everything's attached, at least." He gave a small laugh. "It happened so fast, as they say. I see I've hit the tree." He said "the tree" as if there were only one tree in the whole country; as if he had always known he would hit it.

"Good of you to stop," he said.

"Of course!" cried Sarah.

"Plenty wouldn't. Decent of you. I don't suppose he even thought for a minute about stopping."

"Who?" asked Sarah. She looked into the back of the car in panic, as if there might be someone else crushed inside.

"The lout who swiped me."

Sarah remained quiet. Then she said, "My husband's gone to find help."

She had been waiting to use this phrase: "My husband." Her first time.

"Ah," said Mr. Ronald. "I don't suppose you happen to be a doctor. That would be convenient."

"Not a human doctor," said Sarah. "An animal doctor, though."

"My leg, you see," he said. "I think it should hurt, but at this moment it doesn't."

"You're probably in shock," she said.

"You're not British, are you? Antipodean."

"Australian."

"I thought so but didn't venture it. For the first few sentences you might just as well be a New Zealander."

He pronounced it "New Zellander." Sarah found this charming.

"No, no!" she protested. "We sound completely different." She demonstrated the difference: "Fish and chips," she said. "That's us." And then, "This is a Kiwi: fush and chups."

"Nonsense," said Mr. Ronald. "No one speaks that way at all."

Sarah felt chastised. She didn't resent it—there was something so pleasantly authoritarian about Mr. Ronald, who seemed to her like a school principal driving home from church, or the father of a boyfriend, to whom she must be polite at all costs.

"A veterinarian," said Mr. Ronald. "Dogs and cats."

"Actually, I specialize," said Sarah. "Exotic animal medicine. But dogs and cats too, sometimes. Mostly for friends."

"What counts as exotic these days?" asked Mr. Ronald. She could see that he was keeping himself occupied as he moved his right hand slowly over his chest and toward his legs, testing for pain and damage.

"Chinchillas," said Sarah. "Ferrets. Hermit crabs. Monkeys."

"Monkeys?" said Mr. Ronald. "Good god. Does anyone in England actually own a monkey?"

"You'd be surprised."

"And is it legal?"

"I'm afraid it is."

"And people will bother to spend thousands of pounds curing a hermit crab?"

"People become very attached to their pets," said Sarah. She had defended her clients on this subject before, at parties and college dinners, and whenever she did she saw them all in the surgery waiting room, bundled against cold and worry, holding cages and carriers and shoeboxes with holes punched in them.

"Yes, you're right," said Mr. Ronald, and he mused on this for a moment. "Dogs I understand, and cats too, in their own way. I grew up with a bullmastiff. He could knock me down until I was eleven, and then I could knock him. Once ate the leg off a rabbit."

The bullmastiff walked through Sarah's mind, eyeing her with care. Hip dysplasia, thought Sarah. Hypothyroidism. A heavy dog. Need help lifting it.

"And you've treated a monkey yourself? You seem very young."

"A capuchin once, yes, with a broken leg."

This mention of a broken leg reminded Mr. Ronald of his situation. His face altered, suddenly, in pain.

"Do you feel it now?" asked Sarah. The skin whitened around his mouth, and he let out a sound that reminded her of a tiger she had seen on television once, whose roar sounded like a long and drawn-out "ow."

"It won't be long," she said. "My husband will be back soon."

She looked out the window. The road was dark in both directions and overshadowed with trees. There were dark shapes in the trees that looked like small monkeys, escaped from backyard sheds all over England, swarming with their rotten teeth and cataracts.

Mr. Ronald had recovered from the attack of pain and now lay back against the seat and breathed quietly. His head was larger than most people's. This gave it a resilient look, although it reminded Sarah of a puppet. There was a band of sweat across his forehead. Without thinking, she placed her fingers on his wrist in order to measure out his heartbeat. It was steady now, and slow. She kept her hand where it was, despite feeling suddenly revolted by the dampness of his old skin. They sat together listening for cars. Someone will come in this minute, thought Sarah; but the minute passed.

"A capuchin, you say," said Mr. Ronald. "A kind of monk, isn't it?"

"Well a monk, yes, I think. But also a kind of monkey."

"I once saw an orangutan in the Berlin Zoo painting on the wall with a dish brush. Looked just like my wife cleaning the shower. But here Douglas is against primate testing. I can't go in for that. Douglas calls me speciesist." Sarah decided not to ask who Douglas was. "If they cure Parkinson's, then it's worth those gorillas, I think. Not a popular stance, I'm told. I myself can't stand vegetarians."

"I'm a vegetarian," said Sarah.

"Well, in the abstract. It makes sense for someone like you. A veterinarian. Why heal them and then eat them? But I always say vegetarians ought to eat meat when it's served to them. Imagine being a guest in someone's home and turning down food that's offered."

This reminded Sarah of her own grandfather: perplexed and indignant in the midst of his self-imposed wartime privations, carried on secretly and with pride. Food might run out—eat what you're given. Life might be lost—don't mind the monkeys.

Sarah liked to argue on this topic, calmly maintaining her position, but in this case she would not.

"Oh, but I'm sure you're a charming guest," said Mr. Ronald, "And here you are, helping an old man in distress."

He chuckled, and the pain came again, stronger this time. It lifted him from the seat a little, and this lifting caused more pain. He shut his eyes against it. Sarah waited for this to pass, as it had the last time, and when he was quiet she asked, "What can I do? Anything? Is it your legs?"

He laughed again, sucking in his cigarette breath, and moved his wrist away from her hand. The rain grew heavier, and the trees on the road began to move their monkey arms, high above the fields. The fields grew damp and gave up their deeper smells of night mice and manure. No cars passed by. Sarah worried about David in the rain. He couldn't have been gone for longer than ten minutes, she reasoned; perhaps fifteen. She wondered briefly if the woman was still ironing in her house.

She asked again: "How are your legs?"

"Funny," said Mr. Ronald, and his breath was shorter now. It left his throat unwillingly. "Funny, but one of them's not even a leg. Left leg, below the knee. Plastic."

Sarah imagined him at other times, rapping his fingers against the plastic of his leg, knocking it through his neat trousers while chatting on a bus. The war, she thought, he must have lost it in the war; she saw him and other men moving quickly over a French field. Poppies blew in the grass, and he was a young man, strong of limb, and the sea was behind them all as they ran.

"Diabetes," said Mr. Ronald. "Didn't know, did you, that it could take your leg off?"

Sarah shook her head, but she did know. She'd seen diabetic dogs; cats too. She'd cut off their legs. The French field fell into the sea, and the rain still fell against the roof of the car.

"Started as a blister, then an ulcer," said Mr. Ronald. "Just a mishap. A blister from new shoes. No one tells the young: be careful of your feet. Feet should last a lifetime. What can be prevented? Everything, they say. No, they don't. They say not everything."

He laughed harder now, in a thin straight line, and his cheeks drew in over the laugh, so that Sarah could see the shape of his skull and the crowded teeth, nicotine-stained, that swarmed in his mouth. Perhaps this wasn't laughing, but breathing. The steady rain and wind moved the car slightly, back and forth, and it felt as if they were floating together gently at sea. The branches of the tree against which the car was pressed were black shapes at the corner of Sarah's eye, like Sheba at night, stalking rats with his stomach full of jellymeat.

(Sheba himself lay panting in the corner of his cage, overwhelmed entirely by a calm fury and a pain on which he concentrated with a careful doling out of attention. He kept himself steady, but his small side rose and fell, rose and fell, higher and then deeper than it should. His eyes moved toward the door and his mouth sat open, showing pink.)

The laugh was a clatter behind Mr. Ronald's teeth, a rough edge over which his breath moved hectically. Sarah huddled close to him as he moved against the back of his seat, placed her arm around his shoulders and touched his damp forehead. She felt her hair lift away from her skin, all along her arms and the back of her neck. The summer passed through the car, windy and wet.

"Hold on," said Sarah. "Just hold on." Her mouth was against his ear. David would come soon. You could swear at a cat that rocked this way, crowded close in pain and confusion; you could talk softly, not to the cat but to the idea of the cat, to the faces of the family you must explain to about the cat. You could sing to the cat, and if you had forgotten its name you could call it Kitty—you could say, "Hold on, Kitty," while your hands moved quickly and your neck craned forward and the parts of you that understood the machinery of a cat, its secret and moving parts, worked quickly beneath the cat's terror. You could set the leg of a monkey and watch it, later, as it limped back and forward across the surgery floor, scowling and shaking its funny fist at you.

Noises came from Mr. Ronald's throat now, and these sounds seemed accidental, the by-product of something else. They continued past the point Sarah was certain he had died; they rattled on in the can of his throat. Sometime after they had subsided she became aware of the sound of a radio playing. In her own car, or this one? Who could Douglas be? A son? A grandson?

Sarah was unsure of how long she had been sitting beside Mr. Ronald, and how long it had been since he had stopped making any sound at all. Gently she laid his head back against the seat. His wife cleaned the walls of their shower, and he had been to see orangutans in Berlin. He was too young to have been in that war.

Without warning, David filled up the space in the passenger door of Mr. Ronald's car. She had been so certain she would hear his footsteps on the road, but he was here in the door, as if she'd summoned him out of the field.

"I'm sorry, I'm sorry, I didn't find anyone." He was wet and his breath came quickly. "I ran and finally found a house, but there was no one home. I thought about breaking in. Kept going for a bit but no sign of life. No cars on the road, even. So I headed back to try the car again."

He looked at the stillness of the man in the driver's seat. He saw the blood on Mr. Ronald's trousers and the way that it crept toward his belt and shirt, and searched for blood on Sarah.

Sarah concentrated carefully on David's face, which swam in the noise of the rain and the radio and the end of the vodka. My husband. Then she placed the wallet in Mr. Ronald's lap.

Sarah moved to step out of the car, and David made space for her.

"How is he? Has he woken up?"

When a cat died during an operation, when it was necessary for a macaw to die, then Sarah must tell its owners. That was difficult to do, and so along with the truth she added other, less true things: that the tumor caused no pain, that the animal hadn't been frightened to go under anesthetic. Still, it was difficult. It made no difference to Sarah that words were inadequate to her enormous task. Of course they were. There might be a time when she would have to tell her friends, Sheba's owners, that he wouldn't survive his infection. Their grief would be altered by a slight embarrassment that they felt it about a cat. Each loss of which she had been the herald seemed now to lead to this new immensity, her own: Mr. Ronald, dead in a car. But they didn't know Mr. Ronald. David had never even spoken to him. They had been married that midday, with no rain. There were no witnesses.

"He's dead," said Sarah.

She stood and shut the door behind her. David fought the desire to lower his head and look through the window. It was necessary to make sure, but more necessary to trust Sarah. He held his hands out to her, and she took them.

"My god," he said. She shook her head. When she shook her head in this way, it meant: I'm not angry with you, but I won't talk.

"What now?" he asked. "Should we take him somewhere?"

It seemed to David that Sarah owned the wreck, owned the tree and piece of road on which Mr. Ronald had died, and that he need only wait for her instructions, having failed to find help. He thought of her sitting alone with the unconscious body of an old man, and he thought of the moment at which she must have realized that he was no longer unconscious: that he was dead. David saw with certainty that Sarah was another person, completely separate from him, although he had married her today. His wife.

"We'll try the car again," said Sarah. "We just have to get to the surgery."

"And use the phone there," said David.

Sarah crossed the road, and he followed her. She didn't look back at the wreck. Waiting on the grassy rise slightly above the road, their car had a look of faithful service, of eagerness to assist. It started on the third try with a compliant hum. Sarah had always been better at coaxing it; even before trying the ignition she'd been sure it would work. She didn't know if this resurrection was good or bad luck or if, beyond luck now, it was simply inevitable. Now that she could see the rain in the headlights, she realized how soft it was, how English. She missed home, suddenly:

the hard, bright days and the storms at the end of them, with rain that filled your shoes.

It grew dark in Mr. Ronald's car as Sarah's headlights passed over and then left him, and it remained dark as she left that piece of road and that tree. David watched Sarah drive. They didn't speak. As the distance between their car and Mr. Ronald's grew, it seemed that the roads were all empty—that all of England was empty. It lay in its empty fields while the mice moved and the airplanes flew overhead to other places, nearby and faraway.

They reached lit buildings and then the surgery so quickly it seemed impossible to David that he couldn't have found help within minutes. Sarah walked calmly into the building, and she spoke calmly with the nurse. She didn't look at the telephone. There was no blood on her clothes. David watched his wife as she made her way toward the Queen of Sheba, who rubbed his head against the bars of his cage. He was waiting for the pain to stop. And then he would be let out, healed, to hunt mice in the wet grass.

Double Fish

Roy Kesey

The wife is moaning, her time now come. The husband puts his arm around her, guides her out the door; her parents follow, ecstatic—a grandchild at last—and together the four of them make their slow way down the street, but at the hospital there are no doctors, just nurses, the doctors all long since executed or imprisoned or sent off for reeducation, and the nurses are very young Red Guards—too young, practically children themselves —but now they and their comrades are in charge, here and everywhere. They lead the wife into the delivery room, shoo the parents out. They assure the husband that they know everything that needs to be known; there is no reason to worry.

As the grandmother-to-be sits down on a chair in the hallway, Zhao An pauses the film. He hurries to his kitchen for another bowl of *jiaozi*, returns to the bedroom, dips one in the dish of vinegar, soy sauce and chili oil, puts it in his mouth and is about to start the film again. Then he sits straight up.

Something was wrong today. He missed it when it happened, but now, yes, there was definitely something. He thinks through his day: dawn, bus, work, lunch, work, bus, home. Nothing comes to him. He rubs his face, takes another bite, chews slowly. As he'd walked up the alley toward his front door, there was a truck stacked with furniture blocking the far end, someone moving in or out, but then someone was always moving in or out. The driver, leaning against the door of the truck, had thrown a cigarette butt to the ground as Zhao squeezed past. Of course, none of this means anything. Perhaps he is mistaken, and there was nothing. He has not been sleeping well.

Zhao wishes he could skip the rest of the scene—the hemorrhaging as the baby is born, the nurses panicking, the doctor brought from prison to assist but too weak from hunger to even stand. Watching only the easy parts of these films is not an option, however; playing the scene only in his head is insufficient. He starts the film again, settles back into the old time, and it is just as he remembers: everyone so well-intentioned, but yes, this is how it was, and how we were.

The following day, half an hour until closing time, and five children lean over the edges of Zhao's small inflatable pool with their scoop-nets in their hands and their buckets half submerged. Three of them are Chinese, one is half Chinese and half something European, and one is black. The half-and-half smells odd, not the stink of a full diaper but slightly sour; the smell comes and goes, at times disappearing beneath the constant Happytime odors of feet and child-sweat and rubberized plastic.

Zhao is quite sure that no one here knows how much money his little stand brings in. The habit of watching without being watched is something the janitors and snack vendors and activities staff are all too young to have learned properly. They see the children around his pool but make no note of how often they come and go, paying again each time they return: ten yuan for a net and a bucket.

He pays rent, of course, on the forty square feet he uses, but he covers that expense in the first few days of each month. The Happytime bathrooms provide the water, and in seven years no one has yet bothered to charge him for the electricity needed to run the bubbler and the pump that keeps the pool inflated. Even the fish he gets for free: there are two pet stores near his house and three more in the area around Happytime, and he visits each one once a week to take whatever the owners are willing to spare—the sluggish, the sick, the malformed. The owners think they are donating the fish to local orphanages and brag to their friends about the worthy cause.

He kneads his hands, tries to work the stiffness from his fingers. Twelve minutes now, and only two children left. Each has an adult sitting alongside, parent or nanny, aiding in the scooping and dumping out, and why would anyone bring a child to Happytime on one of Beijing's few clear summer afternoons? There are small parks throughout the city, temple grounds and play areas, but instead the parents pay to come here. Five years ago it was mainly foreigners, the wives of diplomats and businessmen, but now the majority are wealthy Chinese who should know better.

He's been thinking on and off about which film to watch tonight. If he still hasn't decided by the time he gets home, he'll turn once again to the shelves closest to hand. The staff begin chiding the parents who have not yet gathered their belongings and dragged their kids from the Olympic-sized ball pool or the video games or the four-storey jungle gym. His remaining customers wander off, but then up comes a woman who has been bringing her daughter here regularly for the past two years. From the mother's accent it is clear that she is from the southeast. She is in her late twenties, is thin and sad and beautiful, and he likes to think of her as the Woman from Hong Kong.

As she sorts through her purse, she chats into her cell phone about her recent divorce, talking mostly in Mandarin with bits of English scattered in. She pauses to let whoever is on the other end of the line commiserate and pays Zhao without looking up. The little girl is already at work netting two at a time—he keeps the pool well stocked so that no one will notice when one of the fish floats wrong-side-up to the surface. But now the whistles are blowing, far louder than is necessary, as always. The woman folds her phone closed with a click, says something to her daughter in Cantonese. The girl complains, and the mother touches her shoulder. The girl nods and empties her bucket back into the pool.

Zhao brings out a plastic bag, scoops it full of water, tells the girl to catch one last fish and dump it in, says that she can keep it, free of charge, and this can be their secret. The girl laughs and reaches out, nets a white one with small black and orange spots. Zhao ties the bag closed, holds it up, and already the fish is swimming not quite erect. It will be dead by morning, but no one will blame him. He hands it to the girl and smiles at the mother, who thanks him and seems almost to smile back, then leads her daughter away. This is the longest chat the three of them have ever had.

It takes him half an hour to clean up: ferrying the remaining fish to the holding tank in the storeroom, emptying the pool two buckets at a time, deflating and folding and carrying it to its place beneath the tank, mopping the floor, rinsing out the mop. He wonders what the Woman from Hong Kong would think of his apartment. Her daughter is exactly the sort of child he once hoped for, quiet and neat, polite and obedient but also clever, trapping the fish easily along the edge instead of flailing the net around out in the center. It's been twenty-five years now since a doctor said there weren't any children in Zhao's future. Then his wife's anger, her insults, her leaving—

Zhao stops short in this reverie: his supervisor is standing in front of him, and he wonders how long she's been there. He leans the mop in a corner and nods to her. She is perhaps ten years younger than he is, a thick, sallow, officious but not unpleasant woman from Tianjin. She asks how his day went. He smiles and shrugs.

—Perhaps tomorrow will be better, she says.

He thanks her and says good-bye. Back in the storeroom, he picks up the canvas bag in which he brings his lunch each day and sees a small piece of paper taped to the outside. He pulls the note off and opens it. The characters are smudged but still clear enough to read:

It took me years to catch up with you.

He glances around. There is no one else in the storeroom. He steps to the door. Everyone is gone but the janitors. He watches them for a moment, but none of them look up.

Zhao pushes his way onto the first bus that comes, observes everyone around him, waits for the bus to start moving and then shouts to the driver that this isn't his bus, that there is an emergency and he has to get off immediately. The brakes screech, and the other passengers glare and mutter. Zhao ignores them, hurries down the steps, stands on the sidewalk and waits to see if anyone follows him off. No one does. The bus pulls away. Zhao heads back to the bus stop.

The next bus he boards loops up to Dongzhimen, then cuts west across the Second Ring, the road thinning and strung with lanterns, the terraces of the small restaurants to either side now full. Finally it reaches his neighborhood bookstore, where he steps down. He moves quickly up the street to the hospital, turning to glance behind him every few steps. Around to the back of his building, and he looks up, checks each window, sees nothing unusual—bird cages, plants, clotheslines hung with laundry. Up the alley to the entryway, wincing at the sound of a table being slid across a floor. Up the stairs.

It is not that just now he is too nervous to notice the cobwebs and dust, the dirt pooled in the corners of the landings, and it is not that he doesn't see the stacks of broken clay flowerpots, the empty plastic bottles and scraps of plywood—it is that he has never seen the staircase otherwise and stopped caring long ago. He climbs to the sixth floor. Perhaps his neighbors wonder about the number of locks he has installed. He does not care about this either. He pulls out his ring of keys; the first lock is sticky as always, the next three easier. He is breathing hard as he steps inside.

A year ago he did not need so many locks. Then he spent his entire savings on the plasma-screen television that takes up most of one wall in his bedroom. He has since started building his bank account back up, but everything he can spare goes into his collection: thousands of DVDs filling the shelves that cover the other three walls of his bedroom and the walls of the short, wide hall he calls his sitting room. All of them are pirated, and some do not work so well—they are missing scenes, have audio from other movies entirely or are marred by the shadows of cinemagoers who stood up in front of the illicit camera. He has a copy of every film he has ever seen except two, and nearly a hundred he has not yet had time to see.

Zhao sets down his keys, runs his hands through his hair. The note could mean so many things, and all of them are bad. It has not been pleasant, this business of making lists in his head. Nearly all of his acquaintances have reasons—and that is only to speak of the present.

The pet store employees stand in formation on the sidewalk, shouting in unison about how hard they will work today—a common enough scene on the early-morning streets, but still it gives Zhao a small shiver. When they have finished shouting and have been sent to their posts, Zhao greets the owner quietly.

—Not many for you today, says Li.

—That's all right. I'm in good shape this week. And I'd like to buy a healthy one as well.

—Since when do orphans need perfect fish?

Zhao nods, rubs his face, watches the man's eyes.

—This one will be a gift for a friend.

—Yes? And what's her name?

Zhao smiles, mumbles the first name that occurs to him, follows Li into the store and down the dark center aisle, pretends not to hear the man's questions about how old his friend is and what she does for a living. They stop at a series of small tanks, and Li points out the fish Zhao can have. He nets them into his large plastic bucket and points to another, small and white with black and orange spots.

—A special friend like Yunhua deserves something a little more interesting, says Li. How about a crown pearl scale or one of these orandas? And how long have the two of you been together?

—She's only a friend, and this little one will be fine.

—Are you sure? I've got the most beautiful panda butterfly—

—I'm sure. But let's make it a pair.

The two identical goldfish go into a small bag of their own. Zhao pays, fits the lid onto the bucket and heads for work. The traffic is loud, and the air is fat with smog. His arms are strong, but the bucket is heavy, and his hands begin to ache.

Finally he arrives. The purples and greens and oranges of the jungle gym have always been overly bright, but today, compared to the sick gray sky outside, they seem almost to throb beneath the fluorescent lights. He puts the healthy fish aside; with luck they will still be alive the next time he sees the Woman from Hong Kong. Already he feels ridiculous for having bought them. He wonders if she thinks of him as the old man who scoops dead goldfish out of an inflatable pool or as the middle-aged man who provides toddlers and preschoolers with joy. Then he wonders if it matters at all.

Instead of heading to the storeroom, he tucks his lunch bag beneath his stool, keeps an eye on it each time he stands to help retrieve a dropped net. All morning he watches his coworkers, the way he was once taught to watch. None of them act any differently than usual.

He waits for a moment when there are no children at the pool, turns on the bubbler and lays a piece of cardboard over the top. He fetches his shoes and steps out into the muggy day, walks around the corner of Happytime and down the side to the back. Here at least he can eat in relative peace: generators and air extractors grind and sigh, but no one will come to bother him. He has shade, a brick to sit on, a tin can in which to extinguish his cigarettes. It is all he needs.

As he sits down, he thinks again of the two films still missing from his collection. He was only a child when he saw them and does not remember the titles, the directors or actors; he is not even sure of the stories. The only things he remembers for sure are sounds, one from each film: a reed flute echoing in a cave; a bamboo fan waved sharply through the air, bringing coals to life at some woman's roadside stand. These are not things he has dreamed; he is sure of it. But none of the video store owners has any idea what he is talking about.

He takes out two plastic dishes, one filled with steamed buns, the other with stir-fried tomatoes and cauliflower. He removes the lids, then opens his thermos, recently refilled—the leaves have lost most of their flavor, but at least the tea is warm.

He eats slowly, observes traffic through the chain-link fence, wonders which film he will watch tonight. Not long ago he found a DVD that was actually called *A Woman from Hong Kong*. It wasn't a proper movie, just a few episodes from some old Japanese television series, but it might still be worth a try, once he has earned it.

When he has finished his cigarette, he puts the dishes in the bag, heads back to work. There is a scrap of paper resting on the cardboard that covers the pool. He picks it up and unfolds it. There is a single word: *Yes.* Zhao glances around. No one is paying him any attention at all.

Closing time, the last children borne away, the scrap of paper warm in his shirt pocket. Zhao stores his things, mops hurriedly, doesn't hear the supervisor come up behind him; he nods to her as she chatters, and goes for his shoes. Again the bus, but this time out one stop early, across the avenue to the mouth of an alley. At the corner he steps into a hardware store and buys a fifth lock for his door—a useless gesture, but the only one he can think to make. Then he heads up the alley to his favorite DVD shop.

The entrance is locked. There is no sign, no note. He looks in through the window. The shelves are empty. He walks back down the alley to another DVD shop. This one specializes in recent releases and foreign television series, but he drops by from time to time just in case. The owner remembers him, nods, asks what he's looking for.

—Has Shen moved his store?

The man looks around at the few customers who are browsing, takes Zhao by the elbow, leads him outside.

—They took him.

—Who?

—The police.

—For selling pirated copies? But every store around, all of them, even you . . .

—Exactly. So it was something else.

—What?

—I have no idea.

The man stares at him. Zhao looks away, shakes his head. Perhaps Shen was selling more than DVDs. Perhaps it was a random warning shot fired at counterfeiters. Or perhaps it was the man's particular stock, the films that Zhao himself often comes to buy. Many of them are illegal to sell or own, of course, but it seems awfully late in history for people to be arrested over that sort of thing. Still, the police would not have taken him without first watching for a time. They would know who came regularly and what was bought. They would know everything.

He walks toward his house, pausing at each corner to pretend to tie his shoes, listening for footsteps behind him. Up the street and the alley, around the corner, and he is nearly run down by a woman on a bicycle; she shouts at him to watch where he's going but does not stop. The window of the first-floor apartment is cleaner than it's ever been. Up the stairs, in through his door. He goes to his bedroom and stands staring at the loaded shelves. Then he hurries to the kitchen for plastic bags, comes back and starts shoving DVDs into them as fast as he can.

Ten minutes of this, and then he stops. There are too many films, and he has nowhere else to store them. He pulls them back out of the bags, restocks his shelves. When he is done he returns to the kitchen, puts away the bags, looks through the refrigerator and realizes he is not hungry.

He sits on his bed, wondering what else is to be done. He can't think of anything. He roots through the stacks looking for something he hasn't seen yet. Nothing feels quite right. At last he puts *The Blue Kite* on to watch for the twentieth time. He stops it when the landlady is questioned, isn't sure he can watch anymore, and starts it again. He stops it when Shalong is sent to the labor camp, and starts it again, and the tree falls, of course, it always falls; and again as Tietou tells of denouncing his teacher and cutting off her hair, and again, the stepfather denounced and dying of heart disease, and a stretcher is brought, carried not by hospital orderlies but by the screaming mob.

Zhao's supervisor meets him at the door as he comes in from lunch. As she begins to speak, he interrupts.

—You have beautiful handwriting, he says.

—What?

—Your handwriting. It's very graceful.

She stares at him, her mouth slightly open.

—There is nothing special about the way I write. Do you need to go home for the day?

This is a trick or it is not. He considers telling her how much he truly makes, how much he would owe in taxes if forced to declare his full income. But surely she wouldn't do it this way if she knew for sure. She would instead bring in the NICMB, would point him out to the gray-uniformed officers and stand back.

—I am fine, he says.

—You look very tired.

—I will be fine. What were you going to say?

—Why were you late this morning?

—I was late?

—Eighteen minutes.

—I'm sorry.

—Many parents were angry to see your stand closed. If it happens again you will be fined.

So she has no idea. Zhao smiles, promises that he will be more careful from now on and tells her that what he said before about her handwriting was the honest truth: her instructions on the blackboard in the storeroom are always beautifully printed.

His back aches, and his knees; perhaps it is time to see a doctor, but the one he has been visiting for years retired a month ago and he does not have the energy to find someone new. He heats water for tea and lights a cigarette, goes to his bedroom, and as he sits down his elbow brushes the nearest stack. The films scatter. He stares at them, gathers them up, takes the top four and sets them beside the DVD player. Together they will last until morning.

He falls asleep halfway through *Devils on the Doorstep*, snaps awake, relaxes, gets up for a glass of water. Then he hears something—a small animal, it sounds like, out on his landing. A cat most likely. He glances at his door, and a slip of paper comes under it. For half a second his mind hangs on the idea of the cat, and the piece of paper makes no sense. Then he knows and is striding, works the inside locks and slings the door open, sees someone hurrying down the dark stairs. He follows as quickly as his body will allow. The figure below is not getting any farther away, is in fact descending more slowly than he is. From the second-floor landing he sees that it is a woman, old from the way she moves—as old as he is or older. He grabs the back of her shirt as she reaches the bottom floor.

He drags her to the wall, but there is not enough light, and he holds her there, tries to catch his breath, but it lunges and barbs inside him. She too is straining to breathe, does not try to pull away, stands and gasps and coughs. Finally he gets out one sentence:

—Who are you?

The woman doesn't answer, though now she is breathing more easily. Zhao holds on to her with one hand, feels around for the light switch, finds it, but the bulb has burned out. He takes her by the shoulders, brings her face up close, shakes her.

—Who are you and what do you want?

—Let go of me, she says.

It is a voice he has not heard in thirty-five years.

He releases her, steps back. She unlocks the nearest door, opens it, turns on the light and yes: it is Jiang Chen, his childhood neighbor from the *hutong* north of Tiyuguan. She is a few years older than he is, must be sixty by now but looks closer to seventy; she is heavier than he would have guessed, gray at the temples, and there's a scar on her chin that he doesn't remember.

She walks into her apartment, turns on another light. Zhao stays at the threshold. The unease from a few days ago is back, surges stronger, and then he knows: the wooden chair that his mother gave her, its scrolled back, one armrest broken and repaired; he'd seen but not noticed it in the back of the moving truck, and here it is, at a writing desk below the window.

—The note you just left upstairs—what does it say?

—It says, *I hope you have not forgotten.*

—I have forgotten nothing. I have forgotten everything. I live among the million nothings I forget every night.

—So you're a poet.

—And you're still insane.

She turns, and her arm arcs back. He ducks as she throws. A small plate shatters against the wall a few feet away. He straightens. Her face is perfectly calm.

—If you come near me again, he says, or leave me any more notes . . .

—You'll do what? Call the police?

—I mean it. Leave me alone.

—But I have come here to be near you.

He leaves her then. He walks up the staircase, loses track of the number of landings he has passed, knocks his shoulder against the wall as he makes a turn, nearly falls. He is so very tired. Of all the things the notes could have meant, an unbalanced woman from the old time come to live in his building cannot possibly be the worst, though, yes, a problem—hopefully not large. He picks up the note, and it is as she said. He tapes it beside the other two, then pulls down all three and throws them away. The film is still running. He finds the remote, turns off the television, climbs into bed.

For two weeks there are no more notes. To his surprise, she never opens her door as he enters or exits the building, never comes to bother him at Happytime. He sometimes sees her face in the window as he arrives in the evening, but that is all, and even then her eyes do not appear to be following him. She has tracked him down and moved into the same building. So what? She obviously has her reasons, and sooner or later she'll tell him what they are, and they will be nonsensical. For now he will simply have to put up with her, or at least with the knowledge that she is near.

In the empty hours at work he thinks about her, about that time. He'd been very young when her parents were killed. The fire—but no, that came later. Her parents died when something collapsed. Not their house, but . . . the roof of a factory? Something like that. And then she had no one—her older brother was already dead, killed by the Americans in Korea—and Zhao's parents took it upon themselves to provide for her. They protected her even after the fire that destroyed half the houses around their courtyard, claiming that she hadn't started it, though everyone knew it couldn't have been anyone else.

Not that Jiang was particularly stable even before the accident. He remembers screaming that went on for hours and silences that lasted days. And he certainly remembers his own resentment later on—the toys his parents wouldn't buy for him, the money going instead to someone who talked gibberish to cats, to parked bicycles, to the swept dirt of the courtyard. His mother had lectured him on generosity and solidarity, and so had his sister. For several years they had simply lived their lives, and then came the other time, when it wasn't just Jiang, when they were all insane, everyone, the entire country. She had disappeared at some point, and that was the last he'd heard of her.

He should be sleeping better now, but instead it's gotten worse—the pain in his hands, in his back. Shen's store has not reopened, and no signs have appeared, but there are rumors that he has been seen, that he is simply resting at home, that he will open the store again soon. The Woman from Hong Kong has not returned to Happytime. Zhao asked his colleagues about her, and no one had any idea whom he was talking about. The two fish are still healthy and live now in a small bowl on his windowsill.

Zhao comes slowly up the stairs carrying a bag of colored gravel and a plastic plant. As he opens the door, a scrap of paper lifts off the ground. He picks it up. There is nothing written on either side. He strides down to the first floor and bangs on Jiang's door until she opens it.

—I told you. No more notes.

—That isn't a note. It's just a piece of paper.

He looks at it, wonders if in fact it's something that fell from his desk— but no, it is the same size and shape and texture as the notes she sent him.

—What do you want?

—I want you to invite me to your apartment.

—Why?

—For a visit. For tea or water or beer, whatever you drink.

The thought of having her in his home makes him nervous, but he's been expecting this request since the night he caught her on the staircase. There is no other way to end this, and now is as good a time as any, or at least no worse than most.

He nods, and she steps past him, closes and locks her door. They climb the stairs, remove their shoes as they enter his apartment. There is an odd, anxious deliberateness to her motions. He waves her to the one chair in the sitting room, but she does not sit down. Instead she stares at the shelves full of DVDs, steps closer, reads the titles. He starts the water boiling, can hear her walking through his apartment, knows that now she is in his bedroom staring at the massive television, at the films on the nearest shelves.

When the tea is ready he calls to her, and she comes.

—So that is how, she says as she sits down.

—How what?

She smiles.

Zhao serves her and then himself. He lifts the lid on the teacup, blows across the surface.

—And how are your parents? she asks.

—My father passed away two years ago, my mother a few months later.

—I'm sorry. Are they interred here in Beijing?

—No. We . . .

—Harbin, yes, I know. And how is your sister?

He stares at her. She nods, sets her cup down on the armrest, speaks again:

—So each year the day comes, and you have no tombs to sweep.

He gets up, sits back down. He looks at the floor, the walls, at her again, and she shakes her head.

—Not anymore, she says. I take pills. They give them to me for free, and believe it or not, most days are all right. The nights are hard, of course, but not as hard as yours.

He takes a sip, replaces the lid.

—I drive a taxi, she says. Doesn't that seem like a good job for me?

—It's a good job for anyone.

—Yes, but for me in particular, at least for another year or two. I now have one of the new ones, orange and blue. It's so nice not to have that metal grate surrounding me anymore. Though sometimes I miss it. And have you seen the price of gasoline recently? Terrifying.

He frowns and nods. She stares past him, stands, thanks him for the tea, puts on her shoes and departs.

—Sir? Sir?

Zhao looks up, sees the Woman from Hong Kong staring at him.

—Would you mind? she says.

He looks where she is pointing. A fish is floating in the center of the pool, and now she points to a second, and a third. He apologizes and nets the dead fish out. He smiles at the woman, says that it's been so long since they've visited.

—We need to be going, says the woman.

—Of course, but I've . . .

Already she has taken her daughter's hand, and the two of them hurry away. It doesn't matter. The fish on his windowsill aren't any trouble at all. He nods to his supervisor as she passes by. So Jiang is no longer insane, or at least not like she once was. The question is whether this makes things better or worse. He has taken the trouble to scout around their building, and sure enough, a new taxi is parked each night near the mouth of the alley, her picture on the license taped to the dashboard.

Four days since her visit to his apartment, and he has not seen her, not even through the window. He wonders if the tension in her movements is the result of some struggle between medicine and sickness. He has no idea how she knows so much about what happened with his parents and his sister. And it makes no difference.

Except that it does.

Late in the afternoon, a young boy asks if the fish are all right. Zhao looks down, and they are all swimming at the surface, gulping air. He turns on the bubbler, hopes for the best. Last night he stopped by Shen's store, and it was open again, but he no longer carried the films that interest Zhao. Zhao asked what had happened, and Shen said nothing. Zhao lowered his voice, asked if he should be worried, and Shen said of course not—there had been a problem, but now it was resolved.

The day ends. Zhao stores his things, catches his bus, walks up the alley through the sticky heat. He stands outside her door for a time. There is music coming from her apartment, and he remembers the song, remembers every word.

Finally he knocks. She comes quickly, opens the door, smiles and invites him in.

—Four days, she says as he sits down. More than I would have thought.

—"Returning After Target Practice."

—Yes.

—Of all songs, why that one?

—You choose your movies carefully too.

—Yes.

—Do you find it strange that no one else wants to remember?

—I find it stranger that anyone does.

It has been so long since he was in any apartment but his own. He kneads his hands, stands and paces back and forth, sees a row of CDs along a shelf. They are all from the old time.

—How did you find me?

Even as he asks, he realizes that he doesn't care. She must sense this, and tells him the shortest possible version: three years now back in Beijing, keeping her eyes open, hoping, and one morning a woman and a young girl flagged her down, asked to be taken to Happytime, and there he was walking in.

—Did the woman sound like she was from Hong Kong?

—No, they were locals. What does it matter?

—It doesn't. Would you like to come up for tea?

—I would love to.

When they are settled and he has served her—not his usual *zhejiang mao feng* but green pearls from a new shop around the corner, expensive, in a beautiful bronze-colored tin—he starts a question, reconsiders, finally speaks:

—You've told me how. Now tell me why.

—So that we can remember together.

—I haven't forgotten anything, and neither have you.

—I'm glad to see that. But there's another reason. I remember things you don't even know but need to, if all is to be fair.

—There's nothing I need to know. And I do not believe anything is fair.

—Denouncing your parents, for example.

—I had no choice, says Zhao.

—We all had choices. Even if none of them was good. Your parents were also my parents by then, even if for some reason your father wouldn't speak to me.

—They were still collecting rents! If I hadn't done it, someone else would have.

—They were saving that money for you.

—And for you.

—Yes, says Jiang. All right. But your sister never hurt anyone.

—She was preparing to denounce me.

—No, she wasn't.

—You have no idea.

—The notes you found? Two pages, typewritten?

The teacup slips from his hand. The stain spreads across the carpet. Jiang kneels to pick up the cup, but Zhao catches her by the arm, pulls her up, and she sits back down.

—Your sister didn't write those notes. I did. She came over to visit, saw them on my table, took them and ran. I should never have been so careless, but it was hard then, so hard to concentrate at times, Jiang says.

—You were going to denounce me?

—You deserved everything you would have gotten.

—That can't be right. My sister would have told me.

Jiang looks at him.

—Why didn't she tell me?

—I don't think she knew what to do. She was angry at you, of course. But I doubt she would have spoken against you. She might have denounced me instead, but you didn't give her time.

—Even so, she could have told them.

—It wouldn't have mattered. They had her. You remember how it was.

She hands him her teacup and is gone.

A month now. Zhao has been to three different doctors, none of them able to help. He rarely sees Jiang—only when they happen to meet on the stoop, leaving for work or coming home. This happens once or twice a week, often enough that for a time he wondered if she was doing it on purpose, or if he himself was. But there is none of that.

He sits and stares at his stacks of films. So they were insufficient or unnecessary, as this was coming all along and now has come. It is nothing like what he thought it would be.

Then the phone rings, and of course it is Jiang. He tells her he is busy, and she says it is only one quick question, pure curiosity: Some of his comrades moved so far and so quickly ahead, politics and business, while he was left behind helping children to play with fish. How had that happened?

He says he has no idea what she is talking about and hangs up. He wonders how she got his number. Hers, of course, is now in the memory bank of his telephone. Finally he dials, and when she answers he does not say hello, simply starts speaking: yes, some of them advanced, are now rich or powerful or both, but far more are neither. Some of us sweep streets, he says, and some of us take care of fish—a question of bad luck or missed contacts.

She is silent at the end of the line.

—Or perhaps the others were simply more clever and more diligent than I was, he adds.

She says that she doesn't believe it. He says he doesn't care, and hangs up again.

There is a military parade on television, and Zhao watches. The camera pans from a distance: an army of millions. It draws closer, zooming finally to the faces of the soldiers. Even now they are not men but children. Why had his father been so cold to Jiang? Zhao had forgotten that part of the story. Perhaps his parents had simply disagreed, and his father had felt that they should take care of family first and worry about others later. It could have been something else, of course, anything at all, and now there is no one who can tell him.

Last night, in Jiang's apartment, Zhao asked her what had happened after she left the *hutong*. The stories were long and complicated—an aunt in Suzhou, a hospital for months and months, a man who loved her and then died, a small amount of money left in her name. Her first taxi. The waiting and watching.

He walks to his goldfish, takes out the bag of food, remembers that he's already fed them. The two fish swim just below the surface, their fins hardly moving. The Woman from Hong Kong hasn't returned to Happytime, and Zhao can't remember her face. He sets the fish food on the sill, grabs his keys, walks down the stairs. At the store he tells Shen that today he's not looking for films. He goes to the music rack, finds the latest releases and chooses a CD at random.

From there it is not far to the closest pet store. As he walks, he strips the cellophane from the CD. The owner is surprised that instead of fish he wants only another bowl and a tiny ceramic temple. At home he calls Jiang again, asks her to come up.

She arrives, and he hands her the music; he says someone at work was giving it away, and he thought she might like it. She looks at it, smiles, thanks him. He leads her to the pair of goldfish, and Jiang asks if he's suggesting what she thinks he is. It takes him a moment, but then he understands—the two fish floating nearly head to head, the exact tableau of a million paintings good and bad, the pattern embroidered on the sheets and pillowcases of every newlywed couple, an image of happiness and abundance, conjugal unity and connubial bliss, the very breath of fertility. He shakes his head sharply, then looks up and sees that she was only joking.

He brings out the second bowl and sets it on the table. She laughs, thanks him for the gesture and says that she doesn't actually like goldfish. He says that he doesn't either, and asks if she would please take one all the same. She shrugs, says that he shouldn't expect it to survive for very long, but yes, all right, she will take it.

And that is enough. He serves tea, and tells her about the two films still missing from his collection—the sound of the reed flute in the cave, the sound of the bamboo fan. She doesn't remember anything like that from the few movies she's seen but will ask her customers. It is only a question of patience, she says. Sooner or later she will meet someone who knows.

The City of the Dead

Jennifer duBois

The first time I went to visit Dr. Hill at Park View, I brought him a bouquet of flowers. It would be six weeks before the headstone would be in, and the grave was gutted-looking still, like new gardening. It all looked a little vulgar and exposed, and I didn't like to look at it straight—though it was true I'd seen Dr. Hill much more exposed than this. "Don't get used to this," I said, laying the flowers on his grave. Dr. Hill didn't respond, but then he'd never been talkative when I knew him in this life, either.

In the car, Stephen and Andy were listening to some awful radio, their little heads bobbing up and down like chickens pecking at the ground. After a while I went to sit with them, and we all bobbed together. Nothing happened. I changed the radio to the news, and the boys yelled. There were depressing numbers about Afghanistan. There was classical music.

"Grandma," said Stephen, "why are you making us sit in a cemetery?"

I changed the radio back. It's a nice cemetery, mostly because of the view. The cemetery sits on top of a hill and looks out on a dramatic wash of sea and sky. The cliffs crumble down into the Pacific like they might at the edge of the world—if the world had an edge. And if you're going to sit in a cemetery for most of the day, it's best to sit in one as old as this one. Most of the people here would be dead by now no matter what had happened to them, and that makes the whole project somewhat less depressing.

The boys were getting antsy and mildly violent. They started to kick at my seat, and I told them to quit it. The owlish groundskeeper came by with a rake, and we all waved. She waved back. She'd been apprised of the situation. A woman came with a Christmas wreath, but she wasn't the right woman. A man came and stood in front of a grave with a look of silent fury.

"What is he doing?" said Stephen. Stephen is six and towheaded and has a girlish lisp. Andy is four and floppy-eared and looks strikingly like a mouse. Neither of them will make attractive men, but as boys they are heartbreaking.

"Visiting his daddy, probably," I said.

"Where's his daddy?" said Stephen.

"It's weird here," said Andy.

"Do you boys want gum?" I said.

They did want gum. I wanted a drink. I never drink my first day on a job, and this felt like a new job, though in a lot of ways it wasn't. I wish I could say I never drank when the boys were with me, but that's not entirely true. I can say, though, that I was always meticulous about the drive. I'd stop drinking a full hour before I had to head down the switchbacks to the other side.

"Grandma," said Andy, "I'm cold." That boy was always cold. I turned on the engine, though there was no way I was wasting an afternoon's worth of gas on a child who refused to wear a sweater.

"All right," I said. "Five minutes."

The light grew thinner, and the wind kicked up. The boys played tic-tac-toe on the window panes. We watched and waited, but no one else came.

I do eldercare, which makes for problematic job security—each job has its own layoff built in. The details vary, but my time with each client follows the same general arc. At first I sit with them for half-days and set up their movies and drive them out to the same cheap buffet lunches and keep them away from the stove. They eat microwaved mashed potatoes, and I daub seltzer when they dribble. I read them items from the newspaper, usually local bits about rescued animals, or schoolchildren doing volunteer work. When I go to full days, I sit in the afternoons and do the crossword puzzle. They doze on the couch, gearing up for nightmarish evenings when they'll zombie-shuffle through the house, insensate as sleepwalkers, their fingers groping desperately at all the surfaces and doors. For me, this is the easy part. I watch TV. I use the Internet. I've joined Facebook now, though my daughter Penny seems to find this amusing, on days when she finds anything amusing. I play endless rounds of word games, and I've built up an entire fantasy farm, complete with pigs and an egret.

This is the part where the families start to wonder if they are overpaying me, especially when they find their crosswords always done. I let them wonder. I know how it will be, and I know what I'll mean to them then.

When it gets worse, I wrestle the elders into showers, and I duck when they spit and punch. They bend back my wrist, and I know how to lean into them. They swear and snarl. They escape, and I chase them. I wrangle them back inside. I live with claw marks on my arms, bracelets of bruising around my throat. The families stop wondering if they are overpaying me. When it gets worse again, I change their bedpans. I turn up the morphine when they holler, if it comes to that. I rotate them so bedsores don't bloom on their papery skin, like the first blushes of bubonic plague.

By then I'm like family, but better—family doesn't do this stuff for family, not if they can afford not to. I am the goddess of capitalism, of the specialization of labor. The families talk to me in solicitous voices, most of the time. They remember my birthday. They love me and hate me like you do the person who knows all the worst things about you. I am the patron saint of their lives.

The first time I went to meet Dr. Hill and his wife, Angela, we sat at their beautiful oak dining room table and talked about the plan for care. According to Angela, Dr. Hill had been a charming, brilliant man once. Not all families claim previous charm or brilliance for their demented, but everybody claims something. Everybody reminds me that their relative was not always so. They don't have to remind me. I flatter myself that I'm charming, too—but I don't flatter myself that I won't exit raving and drooling, like everyone else. And I only hope that when I do, I have compassionate and pragmatic care.

Angela had been taking care of Dr. Hill for six and a half years before she called me. She was a bit of a holdout; you could tell this was the first disaster of her life that no amount of research or effort had been able to mitigate. Angela wore a cashmere sweater and tasteful makeup, but she looked like shit anyway. She had inky pits under her eyes. Her arms were ropy, and her hands were ruffled with elevated veins—as though she were a professional weightlifter, or severely dehydrated. Some caregivers fill out, and some waste away, but none of them, in my experience, look wholly normal. Next to her sat Dr. Hill. His mouth hung open, and he was wearing a tie flecked with pumpkin-colored stains.

"He traveled to twenty-seven foreign countries," said Angela, handing me a cup of tea. "It's hard to believe it now."

I told her she had been doing a terrific job. I said I understood how exhausted she must be. I told her that dementia is like a black hole—it is insatiable, and it will consume every bit of light in its proximity. And I didn't mention it, of course, but Dr. Hill was taking a particularly long time to die.

"Have you had any help from relatives?" I said, though I supposed not. Responsibility, like luck, is never evenly distributed in families.

"No," she said quickly. She was glad I had asked. She had been waiting for someone to ask. "He has a daughter from a previous marriage. Long defunct. But she doesn't come."

"I understand," I said.

"They weren't close," she said. "He was away on research a lot. But even so, you'd think she'd come. Wouldn't you think she'd come?"

"Well," I said, "everyone reacts differently."

She stared for a moment. "Yes," she said. "I guess they do."

I looked at Dr. Hill. He was staring into space and meditatively probing his nose with two fingers.

"Do you have any children?" said Angela, pulling Dr. Hill's hand away.

"A daughter," I said. I didn't like to go into it any further than that with clients' families. Penny is clinically depressed. She can barely manage to feed her own children and brush her own teeth. I'm told some of this is my fault.

"Oh," said Angela. Now she was using her thumbnail to remove some of the dried squash from Dr. Hill's tie.

"And grandchildren," I offered, because everybody loves grandchildren. I produced pictures of Stephen and Andy from my wallet. Stephen's missing a front tooth in the photo, and he's tilting his head proudly so you can see the little spot of gore where the tooth had been.

"Adorable," said Angela, but she wasn't really looking. Dr. Hill was trying to pull his teabag out of his tea. "Fuck," he said. "Fuck." Angela held his hand, lightly, to keep him from scalding himself. "You cunt," he said to her.

She looked at me apologetically, though she didn't need to. "I don't know," she said. "He was a professor of anthropology. He was beloved. He had tenure."

She was wearing earrings, I noticed. She was going grocery shopping. I wondered how long she had been waiting to wear those earrings—how long she had been fantasizing about this simple, silly thing—to listen to the radio in the car, maybe. To buy herself a coffee. To walk through well-stocked neon aisles without fear of anybody in her care pooping in the frozen foods section.

"I understand," I said.

She took her hand away from his and wrapped her silver scarf around her neck. Then she asked me the question that everybody asks.

"You'll take good care of him, won't you?"

And for the most part, I did. When I started with Dr. Hill, I was drinking less than I would later—only in the evenings, usually, and often only a drink or two. Once he was really sick, I never would have dreamed of it. You need to be ready to get in a car and drive the patient to the hospital; you need to be ready to take their gloves off the stove. You need to be ready to duck if they punch. You need to be ready to go in if they aspirate. You need to be sharp.

But in those first few months, when Dr. Hill was mostly sleepy and dozing through every afternoon in his chair, I will admit it was a temptation. There were a few times I slipped up, and a few times I planned to slip up. Sometimes I brought a flask. It made me feel young.

I'd only drink on easy days, after he was fed and medicated, after the violent anguish of the shower was completed. It was so easy to let him sit on the sofa, emitting little honking snores, his eyeballs roiling underneath their lids. The dreams of the demented, I've often figured, are among the last things we have in common with them—even after seven years of atrophying cortex, their dreams probably make no less sense than ours. Once he was fully out, I'd take a sip or two—or more. And then I'd wander the house.

The house was notable in a lot of ways, and most notable perhaps for its vast collection of books. In particular, there were a lot of souvenir picture books documenting the different places Dr. Hill had gone, I suppose, when he was charming and brilliant. Angela had set the books out for Dr. Hill to look at—rich people in particular like to treat their demented like gifted children and ply them with crayons and clay and Mozart CDs. Dr. Hill had no interest in the books. But I liked to look at them sometimes while I was drinking and Dr. Hill was sleeping through another brittle afternoon. The one I liked best was about Egypt. It had a whole chapter on Cairo, and there was a two-page spread showing an enormous cemetery called the City of the Dead. It was four miles long, and people lived there among the graves of their ancestors. It was a slum, of course. Rich people bought themselves space away from the dead as soon as they could; it was probably one of the first things anyone did with money. I remember staring at that picture for a long time—at those long blocks, white as bleached bone, intersecting for miles. You couldn't tell which buildings were crypts and which were houses, and the book didn't specify. I'd stare and stare at that cemetery-town until it blurred into a monochromatic mass, wondering which structures contained grey morasses of lingering ash and which contained crying children and shouting wives. I'd stare until darkness fell and my buzz wore off and it was time to microwave Dr. Hill his dinner.

Dr. Hill took four more years to die. This was lucky for me because I needed the money. It was less lucky for Angela—and, by the end, for Dr. Hill.

After the funeral, of course, there was some ugliness in the family. The details vary, but trouble happens almost every time. People turn on each other for money or the competing claims on memories that the dead person can no longer arbitrate or the accretions of rage when one person cared for the dead in their derangement and another person did not. There's a chasm between those who turned away and those who looked. And so often, a family is like a vase that's been broken for years but that nobody's ever moved. Death is like the moving, and with it, things come apart in big, raggedy pieces, sometimes, or a shimmer of porcelain dust.

With the Hills, the trouble came from the absent daughter, Lorraine—which I suppose was predictable enough. I'd never met Lorraine. After Dr. Hill died, though, she made herself known. She disputed the will. She disputed the obituary. And then, two days before the funeral, she went to the funeral home to demand some of Dr. Hill's ashes. She wanted to put them in a necklace.

The funeral home director called Angela to ask about it. He said this was getting to be a fairly common request, and he seemed to regard the whole thing as a benign kind of fashion trend. But Angela was adamant that it would not happen. She said it was not what Dr. Hill would have wanted—that it was making a fetish of death, and it was vaguely incestuous, vaguely Oedipal. This is how she talked. She said it was ghoulish. She said it was a violation. She said, in one of her more emotive moments, that it was blasphemous. She'd never given any indication of being religious before, but religion has a way of coming upon people in these circumstances, swift and irrevocable as a terminal disease. This is another thing I've seen time and again.

The day before the funeral, there was a lot to be done. I'd already arranged the flowers and the music and the catering for the reception, and I was putting together a photo board of Dr. Hill's travels. Angela lay on the sofa with a cold compress over her head. She'd been eating a lot of Ativan, and Lorraine had called six times that morning. We'd been letting her calls go to voicemail.

The phone rang for the seventh time while I was tacking a picture of Dr. Hill at the Taj Mahal to the bulletin board. Angela lifted her head, which she hadn't done in a while.

"For Christ's sake," she said hoarsely. "Can you get it this time?"

I pushed the tack through Dr. Hill's head and into the cork. In the picture, Dr. Hill is charming and brilliant—you can just tell. Behind him, the ivory mausoleum is palatial and bright white. "Okay," I said.

"Tell her to fuck off," said Angela and giggled girlishly. Ever since the death, she'd been exhibiting a sort of giddy libertinism—she'd been laughing strangely at small things, and using language like a sailor, and drinking some. She'd tried to get me to split a bottle of wine with her, but I'd begged off, knowing what a disaster that would be.

I answered the phone. "Hello?"

I heard a scratchy sort of voice. "I need to speak with the lady of the house," it said.

I shifted the phone to the other ear and cast a sidelong glance at Angela. She was watching me with wide, helpless eyes. "I'm Jo," I said. "Who's this?" I'd never spoken to her before, but I knew who it was.

"Put Angela on, please," said Lorraine. She sounded somewhat unpleasant. Still, she didn't sound like the kind of person who would do what she was doing.

"It's her," I mouthed to Angela. Angela dropped her head back on the pillow. In the last few days, she'd gotten paler and even ropier than before. She looked all tendon, and her face was sharp as an Italian greyhound's.

"I'm sorry," I said to the phone. "She's not available."

"What's she doing, lying on the divan and fanning herself?"

I looked at Angela. She wasn't fanning herself.

"Can I take a message?" I said, even though the message was already pretty clear.

There was a pause.

"Tell her I want a piece of my father," she said finally. "I think it's about time."

I hung up. I took my time fiddling with the receiver.

"What did she say?" said Angela. The cloth was back on her head, obscuring the top of her face.

"She does seem pretty determined."

"I'm afraid she'll disturb the grave," said Angela. "I'm afraid she'll dig around up there and find a piece of ash for the necklace." She curled up her feet under her quilt so I could sit at the edge of the sofa.

I sat. "I don't know about that," I said. "It sounds a little farfetched."

"It is farfetched," she said. "But I wouldn't put it past her."

It seemed like a stretch to me, though I didn't know the woman, and I had heard of such things happening before. Back in '89, a client's entire newly buried urn was removed, and though the family had suspicions, no arrest was ever made. That Lorraine might try something similar seemed remote but not unthinkable.

"I'd like you to sit up there," Angela said. She still had the cloth over her eyes. Talking to her was like having a conversation with a disembodied mouth. "I'd like you to watch him."

"Watch the grave, you mean?" This struck even me as strange, and I'm no stranger to strange.

"Yes. Just for a little while. Just until all this blows over. Just until all this ends."

She started to uncurl her knees. She was ready to have the whole couch back.

"Oh," I said.

I didn't know if I believed it would end, and I had no idea how Angela would know when it did, but I didn't say anything. I didn't want to sound as though I was desperate for such a wretched thing to continue—though it's true I needed the work.

"I'll have to reduce your pay some, of course," she said. "Since it's easier than what you were doing before."

I swallowed. I try not to judge. If you were a judgmental person, you'd never last a minute in my line of work—you have to sustain too many tantrums, too many wounds from both the patient and the family. Also, I am a high-functioning alcoholic. So I know a bit about shame, myself.

"Of course, Angela," I said, patting her quilted feet and standing up. "That makes perfect sense."

The first time Lorraine showed up at the cemetery, the boys were with me. We'd been playing I Spy, though it's a hard game to play over and over in the same landscape. She'd materialized like weather, and I didn't notice her until she was already halfway to Dr. Hill's grave. I put my water bottle down quickly and popped a mint in my mouth.

"Who's that?" said Stephen.

"That's Dr. Hill's daughter," I said. "You remember Dr. Hill."

"Not really," said Andy.

She wore sunglasses, though the day was descending into a cloudy early twilight. Behind her, the cliffs looked menacing and biblical in the falling light. In the distance, Carmel was starting to twinkle with automatic porch lights. Lorraine had worn sunglasses at the funeral, too.

"I'm going to say hello to her," I said to Stephen and Andy. "You boys can play a round without me."

I made my way down the hill. In the office window I could see the avian face of the groundskeeper watching with concern and, I imagined, a kind of breathless interest. This whole drama was probably the most excitement she'd had at her job in a long while. Lorraine was kneeling at the newly placed headstone, and she didn't see me until I was practically standing on it. She'd taken off the sunglasses. I felt intrusive and awkward, all of a sudden—like it was me who was doing wrong, and not her.

"Hey," I said. I meant it like a greeting, but it came out like a threat.

"Who are you?" she said. She'd put down flowers—lurid yellow things that lay limply in the shadows—and I stared at them instead of at her.

"I'm Jo," I said. "We spoke on the phone. I took care of your dad."

"Oh. Right." She squinted at me. "What are you doing here?" Up close, she looked quite a bit like Dr. Hill—an angular slash of a face, thin-rimmed glasses that made her look far more rational than I'd been given to understand she was.

"I'm just watching," I said.

She looked at me like that sounded crazy, which I'm quite sure it did. She stood up. "What are you?" she said. "Some kind of security detail?"

I didn't answer that.

"He was my father. I can be here."

"We can both be here," I said, trying to sound reasonable.

"I'm just bringing flowers. Am I not allowed to bring flowers up here now?"

"Just the flowers," I said. "You're not messing with that thing."

"Messing, how?"

"You're just not messing. It's illegal."

"It's illegal for me to visit my father's grave?"

I looked down. "It's illegal for you to do anything." I was embarrassed to articulate such an outlandish, slanderous claim—and this woman, though unfriendly, did not seem to have the requisite level of derangement. "I'm going back to my car," I said. "But I'm staying."

I went back up the hill. In the car, Stephen and Andy were using Lorraine as the I Spy object—I Spy something tall; I Spy something partly white and partly brown. I watched her. She moved the flag from the family headstone to Dr. Hill's military stone—the one that told his war and rank and dates of service. Then she just stood there. It looked like she was waiting for something, though I supposed anything could look like waiting. If she was crying, I couldn't see it.

"Who's that?" said Stephen.

"I've told you a million times," I said. "Play a quiet game now. Grandma has to call her boss."

Angela wanted me to call every day to check in. She didn't like to come up to the cemetery herself—which was understandable, and also typical. There's an inverse relationship between the amount of time you spend at a person's sickbed and the amount of time you spend at their graveside—unless, of course, you're getting paid to do both. I figured this was as good a time as any to call—real-time reporting, and all. While the phone rang, I rolled my water bottle under my foot. There didn't seem to be anything left in it.

"Hi, Angela," I said when she answered. "It's Jo."

"How's it going up there?"

"It's going fine," I said.

Down the hill, Lorraine was still just standing there. She looked like maybe she was praying—though I supposed anything could look like praying.

"Has she come?" said Angela.

"She's here now," I said, shifting the phone to the other ear. "But she's just looking. She's just paying her respects. She's not trying anything."

In the backseat, Stephen or Andy started yelping about some offense the other had committed. I turned around to glare at them. There was a meaningful silence on the telephone.

"Do you have—is that a child you have up there?" Angela said finally.

"It's my grandchildren," I said. "Their mother isn't feeling well today."

"You're having them sit in a graveyard?"

I thought this was a little much coming from her. "We talk about history," I said. "We look at the dates. They think it's interesting."

"It must be strange for them."

"It's a little strange for everyone," I said. There was a pause, and I knew I shouldn't have put it that way.

"Yes. Well," said Angela. "Keep me posted." She hung up.

After ten minutes, Lorraine walked up the hill, carrying a welter of rust-colored flowers. They were probably from Angela. I felt strange letting her take Angela's flowers, though there was no denying they were dead. I wasn't sure if defending against this kind of action was part of my job or not, and I wasn't calling Angela back to ask.

Lorraine walked toward her car, then made a sudden turn and headed toward mine. She knocked on the window. I rolled it down.

"What?" I said.

"How much does she pay you to do this?"

"What?" In the backseat, Stephen and Andy had grown quiet.

"How much does she pay you for this?" she said. "To sit here and stare at an old man's grave, day in, day out?"

"I'm not answering that."

"Is it more or less than she paid you to change his diapers?"

"You're being rude," I said, as though this was the worst of it.

"I'm just wondering. Don't you think there are some things people should do for themselves?"

"I think there are some things people can't do for themselves," I said.

"You're not kidding," she said.

I rolled up the window and watched her walk back to her car. Angela's flowers swung upside down from her hand like small prey.

For four more weeks, she didn't come, but I was grateful for the work. Two of my evening clients had recently died back-to-back—one had been expected, but the other had been a man with only moderate dementia who had broken his hip and died postsurgery, and I hadn't been expecting loss of that income quite so soon. It was a relief to know that no matter what happened to my other clients, I would still have Park View. The dead would stay dead—and, in my experience, the feuds would stay feuds.

That month Penny needed my help with the boys almost every day after school. They'd watch TV in the evenings with the elders. And in the afternoons, at the cemetery, they'd make etchings of all the gravestones, and I'd tell them about the winners and losers of all the different wars. Sometimes they asked me about Dr. Hill—since he was the one we were up there to see—but I'm not the person to ask for fond anecdotes of the man. Most memorable, perhaps, is the day he grew inconsolably wrathful about one injustice or another—a disagreement over the shower, perhaps, which was always a source of bitter quarreling between us. He grabbed my arm and bent it back until it almost broke.

"You bitch," he'd said. "You bitch."

I'd disentangled myself from his grip and gone out to the car. I took off my sweatshirt. I was counting on him thinking I was a different person if I wore a different shirt. This is what they pay me to know. I waited three minutes. When I came back, he was holding a frying pan and looking nonplussed. I put on a bright smile and adopted a sweet voice. I usually try to avoid both of these things—personally and professionally—but it seemed wise, in this case, to make an exception.

"How are you today, Dr. Hill?" I said.

"I'm glad you're here," he said. "And not that bitch who was here before."

But that's not a story I would tell the boys.

"When Dr. Hill was younger, he went to twenty-seven different countries," I'd say. This was an oft-quoted statistic Angela told me several times while Dr. Hill was sick. And it was mentioned, of course, at the funeral. The boys were unimpressed.

There's an argument to be made that it's morbid to take little kids up to graveyards all day, but they didn't seem to mind it so much after the first time. And there's something to be said for early and practical exposure to the inevitable. The inevitable, after all, is not so terrible. I've watched more deaths than I can count, and though I've seen plenty I wouldn't want to sign up for, every death I've seen has seemed like an earned reward.

At any rate, Stephen and Andy didn't mind it so much. And they loved the ride down afterward. They'd scream when we rode down the switchbacks. The hairpin turns snake around with appalling sharpness, and they'd holler at me to speed up, speed up and then slow down, please slow down. Shale went tumbling down the cliff sometimes, and other cars emerged in front of us with the suddenness and manic barreling of rabid dogs.

The last time Lorraine showed up, I was alone. Penny had managed to pull herself together that week—she'd gotten out of bed and washed her hair and even made the boys cereal, though the milk smelled like it was about a day and a half away from going bad. I'd left the boys with half-filled coloring books and gone up alone. There were perks to the solitude, and I'd been slugging away at my flask for forty-five minutes before Lorraine appeared on the horizon. It's possible I had miscalculated some or not eaten enough for lunch because I was feeling more buzzed than usual—not drunk, of course, but very relaxed and too clumsy about the tongue to talk quickly or well. It was not a great day for Lorraine to visit. I'd gotten complacent, and I hadn't been expecting her. When I saw her, I slapped myself on the face and stuck three pieces of gum in my mouth. I put my bottle underneath the brake pedal. On her way down to the grave, she rapped on the window.

"Still paying you the big bucks, I see?"

I rolled my eyes, and then I rolled up the window. I didn't trust myself to speak. She walked down the hill and stood at Dr. Hill's gravestone. I smelled my breath against my hand, and it smelled mostly of mint. I figured you'd have to be pretty close—closer than this woman was going to be—to smell anything else.

Lorraine stood in front of the grave. Then she knelt and set down a bouquet of purple flowers. I kept my eyes straight ahead and tried to think focused, caffeinated, sobering thoughts. After a few minutes, she stood and started walking up the hill toward my car. I willed her to go away. She kept walking. I felt a surge in my chest and realized it was panic. She rapped again on the window. I rolled it down and said nothing. I looked at her.

"Hey." She looked genuinely sorry for me, and that annoyed me. "Those boys who are usually with you."

"Yes."

"Those are your grandchildren?"

"Yes," I said. "Obviously." I should not have said "obviously." I was annoyed that she had mentioned Andy and Stephen, but I still should not have said "obviously." Because when I did, there was a slight slur around the sibilant. Lorraine looked pleased.

"Look," she said, "you know what I want. That's why you're here."

I nodded miserably.

"Give me some of the ashes," she said. "And I won't tell."

"Won't tell what?" I said, though I wasn't optimistic about this approach. I'd caught a glimpse of myself in the side-view mirror, and I looked like shit—bloodshot eyes, flyaway hair. I was sure she could smell it in the car. I had not been careful.

"You're drunk," she said cheerfully. "And you're going to do this for me. Every time I'm here, that groundskeeper woman is watching me like a hawk. You're here all day, every day. They don't pay attention to what you do."

"I can't do that," I said.

"Because you're getting paid not to. Fine. She's not going to know."

"That's not the point."

"What's the point?"

"I don't even have any idea how."

"I do," she said. "You'd have to dig up the box. It's eighteen inches underground. It opens in the bottom. You unscrew the bottom of the box with a screwdriver. You put some ashes in a medicine bottle. It doesn't have to be much. Then you screw it back up and rebury it. Carefully."

I tried to arrange my face in an expression that captured how insane I thought this was.

"What?" she said. "You think someone's going to check to see if the ashes are all accounted for?"

"I'm not doing it," I said. "It's atrocious."

"I'm his daughter. I didn't exactly get much of him while he was alive. He was always gone. Then he left us for Angela. Then he lost his mind. I need something I can keep."

"That may be," I said. "But I'm not doing it. Not for this job." Even though she must have known how badly I needed the job.

She looked away for a moment, and I thought I might have convinced her. But then she looked back. "It's not just this job, though, is it?"

"What do you mean?"

She pointed to my water bottle—bright blue and visible under the brake pedal. "You drive up here," she said. "Obviously, you drive up here. Then you drink. Then you drive back down. With those boys? On that road?"

"I am very careful."

"Obviously, you have a problem. Obviously, you drink on the job. In fact, it makes me wonder if you weren't drinking some while you were taking care of my father. Can't imagine your other families would be thrilled to hear that."

I stared straight ahead. The ocean was a brutal silver, too bright to look at straight. I didn't want to discuss the violation of a grave with someone who looked exactly like the person buried in it.

"I'll come back on the weekend," she said. "And then I won't come back again."

She produced a medicine bottle from her pocket and placed it on the dashboard. I rolled up the window. In the hut, the groundskeeper was blinking at me worriedly. I watched Lorraine pick her way down the hill—delicately, as though she was afraid of stepping on the wrong piece of shrubbery. She got in her car and backed out of the cemetery lane. She didn't look at me again.

I waited an hour to call Angela.

"Angela, it's Jo," I said. I usually asked her how she was, but I was still being careful with my words.

"Are those children with you?"

"No," I said. "Not today." My hands were shaking, and I was feeling lightheaded now. I needed some water.

"Good," she said. "I've been thinking about it, and I'm not sure I like them coming up there with you." There was a sharpness to her tone, and it reminded me of how she had spoken to me at the beginning of my employment—back when she was so exhausted all the time.

"Oh," I said.

"Did Lorraine come up today?" Again that impatience—reminiscent of the way she spoke, sometimes, back before she knew to listen to me. Before she'd learned that I'd been down this road before, many times, and knew the way.

And before I knew what I was doing, I said, "No."

The first Christmas Dr. Hill was sick, Angela invited me to a party at their house. There were lights everywhere, and little bowls of green- and red-wrapped chocolates all over the house. It was the first party Angela had had in five years, and I guess it was like the calm before the storm—or the burst of energy before the suicide. With my help, she was starting to feel like her life was under control. It wasn't, and she'd know it before long. But for now she was into a schedule, and Dr. Hill was showered when she got home at night, and his medications were at a nice balance that kept him awake and gentle. She was sleeping a little more.

If things were more manageable for Angela in those months, they were less manageable for me. It had been a difficult stretch. Andy was a squalling newborn. Penny had just fallen into her first round of black depression and had stopped showing up to work and gotten fired for the first time. Then the muffler fell apart. Then we were told that Stephen needed glasses, though I wasn't sure what a two-year-old was going to do with them. All fall, I'd been thinking about the check that Angela might give me at Christmas. All my families gave me something at the holiday; well-off families like the Hills sometimes gave me a month's salary or more. Anything would make a difference. A month's salary would make a good deal of difference.

At the end of the night, Angela approached me holding a big box. I was drinking an eggnog—eggnog's a nice drink because nobody can tell if you're drinking and how much—and I tried to smile even though I knew it was the wrong thing. The package was square and hefty and not in the shape of a check. Still, I thought. Maybe inside.

"Merry Christmas," she said. "We got this for you."

She handed it to me. She was all done up that night—a black silk party dress, heels, mascara. When she sat next to me, I could smell her perfume—complicated and spicy and invasive. Her earrings were little bells, and they shivered when she moved her head.

"We wanted to get you something personal," she said. "After all you've done for us." She was still using "we" at this point; she was still signing cards "Love, Angela and Albert." She hadn't figured out yet that she was all alone.

"Thank you," I said, opening the wrapper paper. I saw an enormous expanse of blue sky and the top of an orange pyramid. It was the book about Egypt. I stared.

"I always find it out when I come home," she said gaily. "So I thought you should have it."

I stared. It opened naturally to that epic cemetery—the tessellations of tombs, the little bobs of light where people must be living, or trying to, in the great expanse of that breathing ossuary.

"Oh," I said. "Thank you."

I opened to the front of the book. I thought maybe there was a check in the front. On the front page it read, "Merry Christmas, Jo! We appreciate everything you do. Fondly, Angela and Albert." The book, I noticed, had been published in 1978.

She beamed. "It's quite the book, isn't it?" she said.

And I said, "It's amazing." Because really—I was amazed.

After three days I decided to do it, or something like it. It was a Saturday. Penny had the boys again, and the air was clear and thin. Lorraine was right that the groundskeeper was never watching when it was just me up on the hill; she went into her little office for hours at a time and shirked her responsibilities in whatever ways she saw fit. I'm not one to judge. So I sat in the car, and I got ready to do it. I thought about how Angela couldn't be hurt by what she didn't know and how Dr. Hill couldn't be hurt by anything at all. I got out of the car.

I walked down the hill, feeling queasy and hungover, though I wasn't. I approached the grave. "I'm sorry, Dr. Hill," I said. I knelt down, and I started to dig. I dug around on top and produced a handful of what was probably just grainy sand. It must have been just grainy sand, since the ashes were sealed up in that box eighteen inches underground, and I wasn't about to touch that thing. Still, I couldn't help but wonder if it counted the same—to muck around with someone's grave, to disturb and uproot it, to take away a piece that used to be a part of it. It felt wrong, and my hands didn't want to do it—I had to force them, and I started to shake so hard that my teeth chattered. "I'm sorry," I whispered again. I remembered apologizing to him when I took away the car keys, when I forced him into the shower, when I pressed a needle into his ancient vein. "I'm sorry, I'm sorry, I'm sorry."

I told myself it was okay. This was what was called a compromise.

I put the dirt in the pill bottle Lorraine had given me. I wondered what it had been a prescription for, but the label was peeled off. Under my fingernails, the earth of Dr. Hill's grave looked greenish-black and permanent. I despaired of ever getting it out.

The light was brittle now, coming down in rotating sheets to meet the ocean. In the pill box, the dirt looked like anything—sand from a sandbox, dust underneath a bed, the cherished remains of a charming and brilliant man. Lorraine would believe it was what I said it was. And who was to say that it was not?

I walked back up the hill toward the car. The ocean was a celestial gray, and it met the white, apocalyptic sky at an angle that didn't look quite ninety degrees. It looked more like sixty degrees—more like a half-open jaw. From the hill, it was easy enough to believe the world was flat. It was easy enough to believe the world was round. And the easiest thing of all, perhaps, was to believe you could spend your whole life being wrong, and it would never, never make a difference.

Happy Dust

Alice Fulton

In the twentieth century I believe there are no saints left, but our farm on Boght Road had not yet entered the twentieth century. At that time, around 1908 it would be, I had a secret I could tell to no one, least of all a saint or an arsenic eater. In my experience, it is better to keep away from saints unless you have business with them. The same backbone that makes them holy virtuosos makes them eager to mind other people's p's and q's. But some of the saints I knew were family, and this made them hard to fend off. Don't think I am speaking of my sister-in-law, Kitty. She was not a saint but a lost soul.

It was through Kitty that I first got wind of the spiritual genius down the road. My sister-in-law had mixed up a batch of French chalk and gumwater colored with Prussian blue and was using this to fashion veins on her face. I was washing the bedroom windows. As she painted, Kitty let it slip that she'd brought some extra milk from our dairy over to St. Kieran's Home. I knew the history of this "extra milk." And I knew only a lost soul would give it to an orphanage. That part of her saga rang true.

While searching for a foundling to take the milk, Kitty said she'd wandered into St. Kieran's garden. It was full of crispy white flowers, and in the midst of these blooms, a nun was standing with her arms outstretched "like an oaken figure on a cross," Kitty said. The nun had her back to Kitty, who was about to vamoose when the sister fell to her knees, kissed the earth, and commenced to speaking Latin.

I put no stock in this at first because Kitty had very refined nerves. I'd sized her up the minute I saw her alighting from our dairy wagon in full feather and needletoed kid shoes. My brother-in-law, Mike Flanagan, was holding a parasol dripping fringe like a horse's fly sheet over her head with one hand and steering her around cowflops with the other. My husband, Joe, tagged behind, lugging her trunks and looking dumbstruck. Oh Mary! I thought, what kind of rigmarole is this? Why would a fine tall man with Mike's black curls and his eyes like bachelor buttons hitch up with such a helplessness? "Enchanted," Kitty said in that voice you'd need an ear trumpet to capture. She extended her hand in glove to me in my leaky shoes and dress so mended it fell apart in the wash. I shook it thinking this girl's a lost soul.

When we moved to the farm, I was a young woman of twenty, hardy though never comely, with lank dark hair grabbed back in a bun. They called me Mamie Come Running because if anyone needed help, I was the one that would go and do. Now, at twenty-six, I was chapped and thoroughly sweated from the care of four children and the day-in, day-out labor of the place. The washing and mangling, blacking and beating, scrubbing and baking, the making of soap and babies had taken all the calorie out of me. I was thin as a cat's whisker. I had a hacking cough and pallor. My face had taken on shadows. Though I couldn't admit it, I was in a bad state of wilt.

Kitty's delicate ways had me all the more overtasked. She was supposed to do the sewing, but left to herself she'd make only belle-of-the-ball garments and nothing for everyday. And everyday was all there was on the farm. Our little brick house was neat as the Dewey decimal system but meager and common as could be. We had windows but no curtains, rooms but no closets, walls but no wallpaper. It was mostly brown and coarse, and Kitty shed tears when she saw it. She and Mike lived on the second floor. We took our meals together, and I soon discovered she could make a cup of tea at most. She'd drink it in little sips while Joe and Mike poured their coffee into their saucers and slurped. I don't know what she thought of them. She had that way of soft-soaping a man till he felt he was her all-in-all no matter what was in her head.

Her with her milk baths, saying we were a dairy and could afford the waste. We could not. Two quarts, sufficient for a sponge-down, was what we settled on. Then she wanted to sell the used milk to the poorhouse at a reduction. It doesn't take a wizard to figure what she gave the orphans. She and Mike had a childless marriage. If I was called to help Doc Muswell with a delivery, I'd return to a Bedlam of bawling infants, for Kitty was no good with them.

Now that I was expecting again, I wished we could pack up our home and roll it down Boght Road to Watervliet on a barrow. I would have liked to pull a shade on the past and have this baby in town. I had a superstition that a child's birth predicted the course its life would take. And I was determined that my fifth would be welcomed in perfect circumstances, without any forceps or cows in the house.

It was this secret intention that led me to take things up with Katherine Tekakwitha, the Lily of the Mohawks. Kitty begged to join my pilgrimage, and in early September we boarded a steamer for Albany, followed by a train bound for The Shrine of Our Lady of Martyrs in Auriesville. I had baby Edna in my arms, and the three runabout children, Helen, Dora, and my Joseph, clinging to my skirts.

The train left us off, dusty as coalmen, at the foot of the Hill of Torture. This long path wound grandly up through massive gates and meadows toward the sky. I suspected many pilgrims from the city never knew there could be such earth on earth. I shaded my eyes and gave the crowd a once-over but saw no sign of Sister Dorothea or Sister Adelaide. These relative nuns from New Jersey were meeting us and returning to the farm for their annual home visit.

Kitty put down our market basket and fanned herself with a holy card. I tried to keep baby Edna from grabbing it. "What are you going to pray for, Mamie?" she asked.

"That the nuns won't stay more than three nights," I told her. They had requested courtesy at St. Kieran's Home since their Rule required them to sleep in a convent. But yours truly would have to feed and entertain them. How to do that was the puzzle. I only knew they liked looking at the Sears catalogue to see how many things there were in the world they didn't want.

"You'll never guess what I'm going to pray for." Kitty gnawed delicately at the holy card. "But do try."

"A magic lantern and a switch of storebought hair." That was what she'd told me last night. Feeling a cough coming on, I set baby Edna down and fished a clean handkerchief from my shirtwaist.

"No. Something ever so much more important."

The cough changed its mind and I was grateful. "You wouldn't be wanting a little fountain in your room that shoots perfume before falling back into a marble basin, or white satin slippers, exquisitely fitted, that do not button or lace but are cunningly sewn on in the morning and ripped off at night? You wouldn't be praying that your name become Fannie Wellbeloved, Annabel Lee, Clara Lazarus, or Evelyn Friend?" Kitty's pipe dreams were famous to me. "Joseph, get over here while I clean your ears." He was a little redheaded dickens of five years. I went after him with my handkerchief. The girls were nicely turned out in their white pinafores and dotted Swiss, I thought.

"Dare I speak my heart aloud?" Kitty asked. "I'm praying to be accepted as a nontuition scholar at The Troy School of Arts and Crafts." She gave me a cow-eyed confiding look.

"That saloon run by teachers excommunicated from The Emma Willard School?"

"Darling Mamie." It was a sweltering day, and the party next to us had a coverlet fixed to four broomsticks raised above their hats as a canopy. "I wish I'd brought my sundown," Kitty said. Reaching into her purse, she found a little pocket mirror, a jar of finely powdered starch and orris root, and began dusting herself. "This weather is a persecution, is it not? I'm dying, I'm dying, I'm dead."

"You'll be a beautiful corpse," I told her. And she perked up. If she wasn't bleaching her freckles with borax in rosewater, she was applying solutions of corrosive sublimate, prussic acid, and caustic potash to her complexion. There was a tin of *Poudre Rajeunissante* containing ratsbane in her room, for Kitty had been an arsenic eater since the age of seventeen. She stayed pretty nimble despite this habit. But she'd experience the fatal symptoms and be carried off should she stop. Once begun, an arsenic eater is tied to that unnatural diet all her days. I never let the children visit her upstairs for fear they'd get into her poisons and destroy their lives.

I followed her eyes to six-year-old Dora. She was standing with her arms spread like wings and her head wrenched back toward the sky.

"That's cross prayers," Helen told us. "Sister Honoraria showed her." Helen was my eldest, an independent girl of eight years.

"The nun in the garden, I'll warrant," Kitty whispered. "That child has the most charming buck teeth."

The Hill of Torture was lined with hucksters pitching miraculous medals and phony relics, and I just then spotted our Brides of Christ standing in full poverty by a vendor's cart. Nuns had such dignity and difference, I always thought they should be introduced by a loud gust of trumpets. By the same token, ours were something of a Mutt and Jeff. Sister Dorothea was stately as a steeple, while Adelaide was jolly and stocky. Each had her hand concealed up its opposite bat-wing sleeve, and no peddlers were rushing them. Those men knew better than to pester a nun. I ran over to grab the little black satchels leaning against their hems.

"Good day, my dears. God be with you," Sister Dorothea said. The woman had a voice in her like a velvet counterpane. Adelaide was making an ado over the kiddies.

We saw the procession forming then for the march up the Hill of Torture to the park where Katherine Tekakwitha had been born and saints had been martyred in days of old. We fell in with the other parishioners on the upwards trudge, saying the rosary and singing Ave's aloud. Before long, we were wiping the dust off our eyes with holy water passed hand to hand.

Everyone had been fasting since midnight, and I'd all but lost interest in human sacrifice by the time we got to the top. The nuns were still full of tallyho, of course. The procession followed a dirt path through the Seven Dollars and the Stations of the Cross to the Martyr's Chapel. This was a rough-hewn log pavilion, open on all sides so overflowing pilgrims could hear Mass from the lawn—though being with two Mercy Sisters guaranteed us seats inside. Baby Edna was asleep, my Joseph was hoping for a sermon full of tomahawks, and the girls were busy with the pictures in my missal. In 1908, a wasting disease was a blot on the family name. Seeing as I could not confess my health to anyone alive, I roosted on the kneeler, eager to air my secret shame and heart's desire before God's saints.

I knew Katherine Tekakwitha, the Lily of the Mohawks, had recovered from smallpox. She had been an orphan. And she had been Godly without being martyred. I respected her for that. My prayer went, "If I was not worn out by the white plague, I would not worry about adding again to our household. But as I am poorly, I am sincerely sorry for it. I cannot go to a resort where the air is Adirondack and sleep on a screened-in porch. But help me be fit enough to give the child its life. Give me gumption. My spirit is gaunt." I told Katherine that if I died, my children would be half-orphans, halfway to St. Kieran's Home. As an orphan herself, she'd know that when a mother goes to bed and dies, her little children stand crying because no one is minding them. The father might try, but he is too discouraged and new to the work to be useful.

Since a feeble mother will have a weak infant, I prayed mine would not be a blue baby or an idiot. Let it be born modern, a twentieth-century child, with no muck or mire, no caul or purple mother's marks upon it, I prayed. Lily of the Mohawks, I said, let this baby have a decent, not a blind-alley life. I would not mind this baby being a saint, but I would not like it to be a martyr or a lost soul. A saint wasn't much of a livelihood, but it was better than farming. Farm life was what I did not want for the baby most of all. Last, I prayed it would be an ordinary child and have happy luck all its days.

I got so caught up I hardly noticed the incense and adoration. The next thing I knew, we'd genuflected and were out on the grass again. I spread the cloth and unpacked the bill of fare. I always cooked day and night before the Sisters visited, and then they'd peck away with their puny appetites, selecting a tidbit here, a morsel there. I'd made a round of beef, fricasseed chicken, potato salad, piccalilli, chili sauce, and rhubarb pie, all the same. I knew from last time they would not touch my homemade root beer because of the word "beer."

"Mother, is Sister Dorothea a saint?" Dora asked. She and Helen were braiding each other's brown straight hair. The sky had turned dreary, and the trees looked boisterous.

"A saint has to be dead, I guess." I handed Sister Adelaide a corned beef sandwich and began helping everyone to salad. I didn't know what to say.

"Sister Honoraria is a saint," Dora said. "She was struck twice by lightning, and now if someone sticks pins in her, it doesn't matter, for she don't feel it." I thought this must be a great gift to a Sister. I knew from washing our relatives' habits that nuns were mostly held together with pins.

"Some religious women fancy they are specially singled out for miracles," Sister Dorothea said, brushing crumbs off her worsted skirt.

I'd seen lightning split a crystal dish without a shatter. I'd seen it roll itself up in a ball before exploding. And I believed it could strike twice if it had a mind to. There were but two things I feared: lightning and a dark cellar.

"Sister Honoraria is Dora's teacher," I explained. St. Kieran's was the nearest school. The children went there to be educated with the orphans.

"The Presentation nuns are all very well," Sister Dorothea said. Veils were flapping, and I had to hold on to my hat.

"Their order is enclosed, and a few decades older in the faith than ours," Sister Adelaide allowed.

I told Helen and Dora, who were dandy helpers, to get a move on and find their little brother. He'd gone to watch some boys carve a cross in a tree, and now with a storm brewing, I'd lost sight of him in his everyday blue denim brownie suit.

"Mamie, I couldn't broach this with the children here," Sister Dorothea said, as soon as the girls were gone. "But it is my duty to warn you." She fingered her beads. Kitty leaned forward, egging her on. "It's passing strange how some vowed women believe they're doing God a great favor instead of thinking the world well lost."

"Obedience comes more readily to some than others," Adelaide explained.

"There have been allegations concerning Sister Honoraria," continued Dorothea.

"Concerning her past," said Adelaide.

"Don't be grabbing Sister's spectacles," I told baby Edna.

"It is said that Sister Honoraria was called back from a foreign mission, and that she engages in excessive penitential practices." Here Dorothea touched the big black crucifix shoved under her belt. "What's more, this sister's conduct with a priest was deemed—" she paused and puckered her lips. "Familiar. He was observed to impiously venture to touch her hand."

"It is said," Adelaide put in.

"You mean there was a scandal, Maggie?" The shock made me forget and call Sister Dorothea by her Christian name.

Kitty was in her glory. I could feel her nerves shaking next to me. "The nun in the garden," she said.

The girls came skipping over then, dragging my Joseph behind them, and we had to shush. There was no more talk of Sister Honoraria, though Kitty kept trying to sneak up on the subject. The storm held off, and we spent the rest of the afternoon strolling the grounds, greeting old cronies, and telling each other what a grand time we were having in this heaven on earth before the sun got low and the train left for home.

The nuns came and went without any uproar, and it must have been a week after their visit that Helen raced home in a great state of emergency. I was putting sheets out to dry on the lines and hedges when she skidded into the yard, out of breath, yelling Mother Come Running! Sister Has Fallen! "Sister is down?" I said, stopping my work to listen. When I'd heard enough, I left the little ones with Kitty and took off down Boght Road at a good clip.

Once we got to St. Kieran's, Helen led me through the high brick gates into a big garden patch out back. There was Sister lying down in the dirt. A blunt knife and a jar of water were on the ground nearby. She looked dazed but awake. "Was I struck by lightning?" she said, looking up at me with long gray eyes. I knew I had to get her out of that sun posthaste, but she proved hard to move as a trolley off its track. As I tried to raise her, I noticed an open can of gummy brown perfumey stuff fastened to her belt. When I saw her bare feet, I thought this Sister is a rugged little number—light yet durable, scanty yet galvanized. Once I got her up, Helen wedged herself under one arm, I got under the other, and we limped toward the convent.

As we stepped into the cool gloom of the place, I was struck by its smell of starched linen and dusty paraffin. Though it was a hotter than blazes Indian summer day, some frosty twilight poured from the high windows. Sister Honoraria (for she was our fallen nun) said the others were at prayers and must not be disturbed on her account. "Let me take up my cross," she said, "or I will never have my crown." She directed us through waxed amber corridors, up an oak stairway to the nuns' dormitory.

The sisters' beds were separated by sheets hung from poles to make cells the size of small box stalls, maybe six feet square. We entered Sister's alcove through a curtain and laid her down on her iron cot. The place was dark as an icehouse. It took a while to make out the white wooden box, straight plain chair, washstand, soap dish, and tin cup that were the furnishings. I told Helen to go rescue the kids from Kitty and ask Papa to fetch Doc Muswell.

I then set about pulling the heavy togs off Sister. She spoke of this and that she had to do, but I said the doctor was coming, and she was too listless to argue. When I unfastened the strings of her headpiece, I was surprised to find that the starched bonnet had prickers on its inside. I saw they'd left marks on the skin and stubby scalp of her. Under her habit was a muslin gown big as a croup tent, and as I wrassled with her outer outfit, this undergarment pulled in such a way that I glimpsed a scar, livid and cross-shaped, on her ribs. "You got a bad cut there, Sister," I said, just to keep the conversation going.

"Here cut and here burn, but spare me in eternity," she said.

"How'd you get a cut like that?" I had lockjaw on my mind.

"No doubt you've heard tales," she said. "People, even good people, are given to falsehood and exaggeration. And yet I would do wrong to say I did no wrong."

She asked about the can that had been fastened at her waist, and I said I'd put it out of the way, under the cot.

"If I had walked too heavily, or used my eyes with liberty, or kissed an infant for its beauty . . . for these sins, I might be forgiven," she continued.

"Nobody's perfect," I said.

"Perfection is a nun's purpose," she replied. "She must wash the taste of the world from her mouth with carbolic and sleep on thorns lest she sleep too well. If the chapel is cosy, let her kneel in snow. If for an instant she forgets Christ's suffering, let her take switches to her shoulders, brand herself with faggots, wear an iron chain about her waist."

I was beginning to think this Sister was a deep customer. "The worst sin is shiftlessness," I said. "It's better to shuck your blues and shake a leg."

"Perhaps tales have reached you. Vile accusations have been made," she said, "concerning the orphans. That I had them kneel like dogs and used their backs as writing desks, when in fact they are raised most tenderly."

"That I didn't know," I said.

"I was torn by a confliction of duty—" and she would have gone on but we heard footsteps. There came a light scratching of fingernails on the curtains, and Doc Muswell entered, along with the Mother Superior or some other bigwig, by the look of her.

In his single-breasted Prince Albert suit, I'd call Doc Muswell pretty nobby-looking for a country sawbones. Before I married, I'd worked as his housekeeper and assistant, so we were old pals. I knew his wife to be a malingerer, and he knew I had a wasting disease. He had trained me as his nurse, and many times I'd saved him the weary night work of delivering infants. As he saw it, childbirth was long hours for short wages.

"Does Sister suffer from any known disease?" he asked the Superior nun.

"Only the disease of scrupulosity," she answered back. She told him to report to her before he left and excused herself.

Once he'd overlooked the situation carefully, Doc asked Sister if she knew the day and place she was. She said, "I thought I was on the Ganges plain between Patna and Benares, but now I see I'm in Watervliet."

"That's right, Sister," I said, to encourage her. I didn't know where the Ganges plain was located. Somewhere near the road to Damascus most likely.

Doc Muswell took out his stethoscope, and I thought he'd see her scar, but he turned his head to one side and listened without looking, as doctors did in the presence of modesty back then. "You have heatstroke, Sister," he told her. "Forgive me for saying so, but you are chronically overdressed for garden work."

"Your rebuke is well-taken, Doctor. The great discovery is in the heavens above us, not the garden below." She liked to browbeat herself. I'd seen that instantly.

"Well, Doc," I said in her defense, "Sister's skirt, sleeves, and veil were pinned up, under, and back when she had this spell."

"In accordance with Protocol Number 17," said she.

The words no sooner left her lips than her breathing told us she was asleep. Doc Muswell asked me to stay awhile and see she drank all of the potion he'd leave. He inquired about my own health, and I told him I was expecting. "The married woman disease," he said. When I confessed to coughing blood, he shook his head. "Mamie, it's as I've said. You'll have to get by on one lung the rest of your life." Then he took a packet from his bag and pressed it into my hand. "As a sedative for coughs, this is five times stronger than morphine," he said. By the lion and globe on the label, I recognized it as Bayer Heroin Powder. "Use it sparingly, and you won't become habituated. You will have call for it, I think." I was grateful as this medicine was very dear, and the more costly the cure, the more effective. "With your constitution, you'd do well to avoid stimulating food and drink, heat and cold, singing, hallooing, and declamation." So saying, he donned his hat and took his leave.

Sister opened her eyes then, and I fed her the potion he'd left. She was looking more chipper. "I could not but overhear your conversation," she said. "You are in a delicate condition. I have a remedy that will damp the fires of bodily mechanism and shallow the breath, resting your enflamed lung and encouraging the cavities to close." Nothing could be more powerful than the nostrum of a consecrated virgin. This I knew. "It is Indian Perfection Medicine. Take it when your time comes, and the pain will not threaten you," she said.

Hearing this, my heart soared, for I knew Katherine Tekakwitha had answered my prayer. I figured Sister got the recipe from a Mohawk maiden with a difficult vocation, and I thanked her feelingly.

"There is no need to thank me," she said. "There is a giving that does not impoverish and a withholding that does not enrich. I have but one request." Nuns always want some little selfless thing in exchange for their favors, I find. God's the same way when you think about it.

"Everything in the convent is ours, not mine. To give property without permission is a form of theft. I have been chastised in the past for giving to the indigent. I have been called more of a chemist than a Sister, more nurse than nun. I battle for obedience. Yet Saint Dominic said he would sooner cut up the rule book than let it be a burden to one's conscience. I have taken you into my confidence. I ask only that you hold my words in trust."

"You mean keep mum?"

She nodded, and I didn't stop to dicker. Give me that remedy! was how I felt. She told me the way to the convent's medicine closet, a large room in the cellar that would be open at this hour.

"What if I meet up with one of your sidekicks?" I wondered.

"If questioned, you must tell the truth," she said firmly. "Tell the truth, and say Saint Gregory the Great directed us to dispense to all sufferers that which they need."

I set off for the medicine room on a trail that twisted through corridors of mostly closed doors. The worst of it was windows now and then threw rays on big framed pictures whose sudden faces scared the daylights out of me. All along, I worried some nun would creep up on the balls of her feet in high perfection behind me and ask my business. I had to keep thinking of the baby and of all the cures I'd tried to no avail. When I got to the convent's depths, which were dim and dank as a root cellar, I wished especially for a lamp. But I remembered "Tekakwitha" meant "she who cuts the way before her" and felt steadier. At long last, I arrived at the third left-hand door of the west wing. In the sincere hope that I had not gone off course, I stopped and turned the knob.

My eyes had a tolerance for darkness by now. I could make out a long table of ledgers and accounts, along with stacks of labels, stamps, and envelopes. It looked like a tidy business for the Sisters, and I wished them well. To my left, I saw shelves holding small white cakes and bottles. Seizing one, I read the Indian Perfection label thrice. I'd already knotted the Bayer Heroin in my apron corner, and now I rolled the remedy in this garment and tucked the hem at my waist. It was high time, too, for a bell was tolling. And since early and provident fear is the mother of safety, and I'd as lief have my wolf teeth pulled as be caught red-handed, I fled.

That fall was damp as a gravedigger's skin. By November I'd developed a hectic fever that left pink circles in my cheeks. Before the winter zeros struck, I thought I'd better mend my lacy lung with Sister's remedy. Whether it was her medicine or the disease itself, by some means I was lifted into the high altitudes of hope and held there. I somehow kept my cheer, and in April the last shrouds of snow melted. Though I was large as Jumbo by then, the work of the farm would not allow me to remove myself from view as some think prudent.

One Saturday, having finished the morning chores and served a bountiful hot lunch, I was on my knees scrubbing the kitchen oilcloth and thinking about Kitty. That one isn't one to make love to the corners! I was thinking. Why, I've seen her grab a pair of silk drawers and begin dusting if she heard a neighbor on the steps. When I opened her trunk to get fresh linen, a swarm of mothmillers flew out, and we had to fumigate. Such were my thoughts when I felt the first pain. I didn't trust it since the baby had been incubating only eight months by my reckoning. And even if it was not a false alarm, it takes time for pain to work itself into a birth. Joe and Mike were leaving for town, but reasoning thus, I said nothing.

Every week they went into Watervliet to buy our groceries at Dufrane's Market. While the clerk was making up the order, they'd go across the street to Sherlock's Grill. Once they'd left, I noticed the pains were coming closer. Mamie, I said, this baby is going places. I stopped scrubbing the floor and began scouring buckets and bowls. I pumped water for boiling and placed torn strips of cloth in the oven to bake clean. A woman in labor should have plenty fixed for others to eat, yet I was caught short. I could only put a big plate of bread and butter on the table.

In our bedroom off the parlor, I set out the spotless containers along with a bar of carbolic. I tied a twisted towel around the headboard rails and fastened two more, like reins, at the foot. Then I covered the room and the bed with old issues of *The Troy Record*. Some expectant mothers put their own laying-out clothes in a bottom drawer, but my warm hopes would not allow this. I was thinking of the here and now, not the always was and will be. If you go to bed, the infant sleeps and you have to start again. So I kept pacing.

After the third birth, things get riskier. I tried to keep my mind on the happy deliveries and forget the poor devils I had seen. I would not think of the abnormal presentations, hemorrhages, obstructions, retained afterbirths, blood poisonings, convulsions, milk legs, and childbed fevers. Working for Doc Muswell, I'd seen prolapsed women full of ironmongery, pessaries to hold their insides in. Childbirth left them wearing these "threshing machines" only hoop skirts could hide. Such trials swept through my mind in kinetoscopic flashes. Yet those poor devils did not have Sister's remedy. This I knew.

The children were outside playing pirate, and I called Helen in. "You're a young miss now," I told her. She was nearly nine. "You can be your mother's helper." I asked her to go upstairs and alert Kitty, who soon appeared and settled herself on the divan like a brooding hen. When a pain came, I shushed, and when it let up, I started bossing the job again. All along I was trying to gauge the labor's progress, whether I was at the dime, nickel, quarter, half-dollar, or teacup stage. At the teacup stage, I would be "fully delighted," as Doc Muswell said. I figured I was halfway there.

It was twilight, and I was lying down to catch my breath, when Kitty began hollering from the yard. Mamie Come Running! she said. The Team Is Back! Rushing out, I saw the wagon and lathered horses but no sign of Joe or Mike. By the ropes of green froth dribbling from their bits, I could see Ned and Susie had grabbed a bite to eat. "We'll have to unhitch the horses," I told her.

"They are such great brutes, Mamie. Do let's leave them as they are. But what of Michael and Joe? Do you suppose they were thrown and are even now lying in some dark spot?"

"Joe and Mike are skillful whips," I said. "If they got thrown, then they must foot it." I knew those brothers were not brawling or visiting sweethearts. "Nothing ventured, nothing lost," that was the Flanagan motto.

I watered and unharnessed the horses without coming to harm, and when I returned, Kitty was strewn across my newspapered bed in an attitude of weeping.

"Perhaps the dainty waist and deep full inspirations of some Watervliet wanton have commanded Michael's admiration," she said. I could hear Helen trying to convince my Joseph and baby Edna it was bedtime. Dora was singing them a little song. I scrubbed the horse dirt off and lit the oil lamps. Then I lay down on the divan. Now that the pain was mustering, I wondered out loud if I'd have enough of Sister's remedy.

"Mother, if you needed more, we could have made it ourselves," Helen piped up. Having settled the little ones, she and Dora were giving me big looks. I only half-listened as she prattled about *Papaver somniferum* and lancing the pods so sticky flower milk oozed out. She spoke of scraping, drying, beating, molding, boiling, skimming, and straining, but it wasn't till she mentioned covering the cakes with white poppy petals that I sat up and attended. The word "poppy" had roused me.

"Is this what Sister was doing when she took that bad turn?"

"Yes, and I was helping her," said Helen with a proud little smile.

"You were helping her harvest opium," I said. I got up and stood with arms akimbo, thinking. If Sister's remedy was mostly opium, like Black Drop or laudanum, I might have become a dope fiend. Hoarding the medicine for tonight's baby was all that saved me. Now I had to weigh the danger of opium against the danger of pain. Most of all, I wanted this baby to be protected by the power of good. And I thought Sister Honoraria was a good woman, even if she was a bad nun. As I stood thinking, my waters broke.

I marched into the bedroom where Kitty was sleeping. "See here, Clara Lazarus," I said. "It's time to rise from the dead. I need streetcar courtesy. I have to push this baby out."

"Oh, Mamie, I am a wretch. Forgive me," she said. I lay down in a sweat and would have taken Sister's medicine, opium or no, but I could not afford to be dopey until the doctor got here. It must have been near midnight. I sent Joe wireless messages in my mind: come home, come home.

Dora brought me a saucer of dark fruit. "What have we here?" I gasped.

"Kitty says they are little black-coated workers." She looked at me with her bashful, born-yesterday eyes. I set the prunes down carefully and told her to fetch the blessed candle from the parlor.

My mother, Peg Merns, had unfastened every knot or button, door or stall while I was having baby Edna. She supposed so much opening would help the infant enter the world. Thanks to her, baby Edna was welcomed into a household of men with their garments falling off and an old bossy in the kitchen. I wanted this child to be born newfangled and free of Irish hoo-doo. But I'd kept a copy of a prayer my mother had recited, and I asked Helen to fetch it from the dresser's depths. It was written on vellum older than Plymouth Rock. I used the oil lamp to light the candle and read the words to myself: "Anne bore Mary; Mary, Christ Our Savior; Elizabeth,

John the Baptist. So may this woman, saved in the name of Our Lord Jesus Christ, bear the child in her womb, be it male or female. Come forth." That's how it went. It ended with Latin words written so they'd read the same in any direction:

SATOR
AREPO
TENET
OPERA
ROTAS

Though she was no scholar, my mother, Peg Merns, said the Latin meant "I creep toward the sower and holder of the workings and the wheels." I placed the paper on my big belly, and asked Helen if she could see to read it. With a little prompting, she soon had it down pat. I told her I wanted her to recite the list of holy births in a saintly voice while Dora held the candle aloft. My lambs looked scared in the shaky light, but Helen set her balky tongue to the task. "Anne bore Mary . . ." she began.

She got no further because Dora yelled Papa's home! just then, and the spell was broken. A moment later, Joe was standing at the bedroom door. He had *mea culpa* written all over him, but I was happy to see him in good health. "How are you, Mamie?" he said, with hat in hand.

"I am fully delighted," I replied. His face was barn red, and he looked more at a loss for words than always. "Where are the groceries, Joe?" I asked.

"I guess we lost track of time in the grill, and the team got tired of waiting for us."

He was standing like somebody rusted in place, and I told him he'd better go after Doc Muswell. "If he's out on a call, don't write 'CHILDBIRTH' on the slate or he'll mosey along. Write 'FULLY DELIGHTED,'" I said. Joe repeated this. "You heard," I said.

After he left, I started to cough. Then, my stars! The pain changed in character. I thought I had a lightning bolt lodged in my spine, though I couldn't let on with the children near. I had been leaning on Sister's remedy to see me through. And if that failed, Doc's heroin. But how could I bear down if I was doped? I needed all my wits. And what if those medicines fatally depressed the baby? Once a heavy thought has a grip, it is hard to dispel. I knew labor proceeded at a pace and mine was stalled. I felt my efforts coming to naught. This is the reckoning, I felt. I'm flagging, I'm past repair. I'm at the last gasp. Soon I will not want my body or the breath I breathe. This is the end of the world.

"Go get Kitty," I told Helen, who was standing by. My sister-in-law had been delicately raised, that was evident. She was genteel and artistic, though the man in the moon would make a better midwife. The children could do worse in a godmother, I thought. She came in, and I showed her and Helen the basin on the chair for bathing baby, the penny and binding for its navel, the boiled scissors, baby clothes, and diapers.

"Mamie darling, don't be blue," Kitty said, in her namby-pamby way. "You must use the happy dust the doctor gave you. It is much favored as a stimulant, I've heard."

"You're a good sister, Kit," I told her. "If the baby's a boy, I want him to be called James, after my brother. And if it's a girl, you can call her Annabel Lee."

"Stop it, Mamie," Kitty said. "You're frightening me." Her hands were shaking like a palsy victim's.

"Ma, are you dying?" Helen asked, and Dora started to cry.

I'd seen women lose heart and die of exhaustion. I'd seen them die with babies half in and half out. They died because they were frightened. I fully understood it. But seeing those little girls with the solemn-waif look already on them, staring at their mother like she was a hobgoblin, I came to my senses. I realized nobody was going to help me. I was it all. And I told myself to get cracking.

"Don't be crying," I said. "Your mother is a fighter. How can I die when there's a baby coming?" Course I can grunt it out, I told myself. God send me a pauper's low Mass funeral with no solemn requiem sung by three priests if I cannot. And I pulled on the towels I'd rigged, and I bore down.

Suddenly it seemed my little shut-in had been cooped up long enough. Suddenly it wanted liberty. It was coming like a locomotive headlight. It was coming quick as scat. God Almighty! Now this baby was helping. Now this baby wanted to be born. "Anne bore Mary . . ." I kept praying, for that was the one phrase I could recall. The pain waxed as it waned, with no pause, and I let the head creep slowly into my hands, though Immaculate Mary, it must be easier to thread camels through needles. The head, the shoulders, then the rest!

I caught the baby and laid it on my stomach. It lay there like a red frog, belly down. I rubbed its back to make it breathe. I held it upside down and patted the soles of its feet. I wiped the blood out of its mouth and blew on its stomach. I dunked it in water. At last I tossed a pinch of Doc's powder over its head and dabbed Sister's soporific of vegetable origin behind its ears. It gasped and was alive. May God protect the child!

After I'd cut the cord and had the afterbirth, I got up and cleaned the room of gore. Kitty brought in my Joseph and baby Edna. "Meet Annabel Lee," she said. I was imagining what Joe would think of this name. Annabel Lee Flanagan? Sounds like a lost soul, he'd say.

"You know, Kit, now that I see her, she looks more like she should be called Anne." I had it in mind to name her after Anne who bore Mary. And Anne Sullivan who taught Helen Keller to read. And Anne of Green Gables, an orphan of renown.

"Anne is the perfect name," Kitty said. "Though I will always think of her as Annabel Lee." She said Mike would take my Joseph fishing later, and I told her to thank him. "Am I truly a good sister, Mamie?" she asked.

"You are one of a kind," I said.

About thirty minutes later, Doc Muswell and Joe arrived. Joe's face lit up like a jacklantern when he saw the baby. Jiminy Crickets! was all he could say. And he took her to the window to get a better look.

Doc Muswell, meanwhile, had walked right past the bedroom door toward Kitty. I figured she must have arranged herself on the divan in a pose she called a "tableau vivant." "What the deuce is wrong with the girl?" I heard Doc say.

"Oh, Doctor. I'm dying, I'm dying, I'm dead," said Kitty.

"That's impossible, my dear. Mamie would not allow it," said Doc.

Our little bedroom would soon be as full as The St. Louis Exposition with neighbors, nuns, orphans, and my mother, Peg Merns. And I would be unruffled, as if the whole matter had been an every- day affair. Only to myself would I admit there should be singing crowds and a parade. Like every new mother I thought there should be aerial fascinations—gyrating star mines, electric flowers, and Catherine wheels—to celebrate this birth. For it had been as pretty a fight as any sportsman could wish to see. And since my children now numbered five, I would have liked a display of five balloons from each of which depended a single star that changed its color as it burned.

Just then I heard a bird with a voice so rare it sounded like it had studied at a conservatory. The sun was coaxing the first dusty colors from the ground, and I lay there thinking it had been an ideal birth, after all. Everything went smooth as glycerin, I thought. I looked at the children dozing on the floor with their stocking feet flung over each other, and our Annie in Joe's arms, and I thought perfection is not what you imagine. Happiness is nothing but God's presence in the silence of the nerves. And though my children were sleeping the sleep of the just, I half believed my unvoiced thoughts would reach them across that room full of twentieth-century light.

Exit Seekers

Tamara Titus

Even before I open my eyes, I smell smoke. At first I think I'm still dreaming—too many memories of my time under the stars, when everyone smelled like smoke or sweat—but then I see Cecil's outline over by the open window. He's sitting in his wheelchair with a blanket over his legs, and I can hear the oxygen machine chugging even as the haze from his cigarette settles around us.

"Cecil," I whisper. The digital clock on my nightstand reads 2:13, and the hallway outside is quiet.

His head is bowed, and he doesn't answer. While I watch, the orange tip of his cigarette falls into his lap.

"Cecil!" I hiss, and his head jerks. He mumbles, and I pull my chair over to the bed. When I'm fully awake, I can transfer without assistance, but even then I like to know there's someone within shouting distance, just in case. I set the brakes and hoist my ass into the seat. Then I settle my left stump onto the pad. It only takes five seconds, but it's too long. When I look back at Cecil, his nightshirt is already on fire.

Cecil screams, and I press the call button clipped to the bedrail and wheel over to the door in nothing but my undershorts. The corridor outside is empty.

I yell "*Fire!*" twice before rolling back into the room and grabbing a couple of hand towels at the sink. Cecil flails with his good hand while I soak the towels. I'm wrapping them around my fists when the bedspread catches, and I have just enough sense to switch off the oxygen before I grab the blanket from Cecil's lap and press my arms against him.

At some point there is noise behind me—people yelling over the fire alarm. The light comes on, and someone blasts us with a portable fire extinguisher. Cecil howls. I hold up my right hand and squint. My skin is splotchy, and pain moves like lightning across my synapses. "Don't let them take us to Grady," I say to the nurse closest to me, but she's not listening. She wraps a clean towel around my hand and wheels me out the door.

When the ambulance pulls up at Grady Hospital, all I can think is it's a good thing they've already shot me full of morphine. Before I moved into Cedar Grove, I spent my share of nights in the ER here. Winter nights, mostly. I lost my foot to frostbite, and they tried hard to talk me into going to a nursing home. But I knew I'd have to clean up, dry out. And I wasn't ready for that. Not then.

Once we get inside, I can hear the EMTs bringing the staff up to speed. Cecil's next door in room seven, and I know they'll work him up first 'cause he's bad off. I close my eyes and see the blue print of the dressing gown seared into his flesh. Then my brain misfires, and pain licks me in places I no longer possess. I'm drifting when I hear the one voice I do not want to hear tonight.

"Ben Gibson. I thought you were done being a frequent flyer."

It's been almost four years since I broke Dr. Loflin's nose. I was high on a little bit of everything that night, and I had a seizure in the middle of Briarcliff Road. Apparently, when I woke up in the ER, I woke up swinging. I don't remember any of it, but I'm sure she does. "A little bird told me you'd been missing me," I say.

Dr. Loflin pulls up one of those rolling stools and takes a seat beside the gurney. "And a little bird told me you were smoking in bed."

I'd like to pinch her, grab the tender flesh on the back of her triceps and squeeze like my sister Angie used to do. But I know what that'll get me, so instead I flip the blanket down and point to my stumps. "I'm a diabetic, not a dumbass."

"In your case, Mr. Gibson, one diagnosis does not necessarily preclude the other. But I'll make sure your objection is noted in your chart." She touches my wrist with one gloved finger. "In the meantime, why don't you tell me what happened."

"Cecil set himself on fire, and I was trying to put him out."

When she lifts the dressing from my hand, I hear her suck in a breath. She scoots closer, and I examine her face while she examines my hand. Whoever fixed her nose did a good job; you can't even tell it was broken. She's changed her hairstyle, too. There's silver at her temples now, fine hairs that almost disappear into her blond bob.

"Are you burned anywhere else?" she asks.

"I don't think so."

"Okay," she says as she rotates my hand. "Okay."

I can tell by the lack of ill will in her voice that it's not okay, and for the first time in weeks, I feel a panic attack coming on. It only happens when I'm in close quarters.

"On a scale of one to ten, how bad is your hand hurting now?"

My palm is puckered, all bright red and weeping. "At least an eight."

She stands and presses a button on the wall. "Not for long," she says. Then a nurse steps in and hands her a syringe, and it's Dr. Loflin's turn to make my world go black.

When I get back to Cedar Grove the next afternoon, I notice right away that Cecil's things are gone. The big picture frame that said family. His wall calendar, his clothes. I'm lying in bed staring at my hand, which is wrapped so thick it looks like an oven mitt, when Marianne taps on the open door.

"Knock, knock," she says, and she waits.

Marianne looks a little like Liv Tyler, only with brown eyes, and she's wearing a dress that falls to the floor. It suits her frame—it softens her elbows and hips—but I withhold the compliment. Her smile is too tense.

I nod at the chair by the bed. "Is Cecil dead?" I ask as soon as she sits down.

"No." She glances at the empty side of the closet. "But they're going to keep him at Grady for a while. He needs skin grafts."

"I take it I'm in for a new roommate?"

Marianne pulls the tray table over to her and sets a folder on it. Normally we discuss my care in her office, which is really just a windowless closet at the end of the West Unit hallway. The folder is bad news.

"Cecil's daughters have filed a grievance with the state licensing agency. They want to know how their father, who is wheelchair-bound and partially paralyzed, could have gained access to cigarettes that they did not provide." She folds her hands in her lap, and I wonder for the thousandth time how she can do this. How she can come to work, day after day, with people who are batshit crazy and not wind up that way herself?

"Maybe he lifted them," I say.

"Ben." She peers at me over her glasses. A strand of hair slips across her shoulder and rests against the side of her breast.

"I shared a smoke with him twice out in the courtyard. That's it. Both times I gave him *one*, and he smoked the whole thing outside."

Marianne opens the folder. "We're instituting a new smoking policy."

I don't move, but the room does. It shrinks around us like something out of *Alice in Wonderland*.

"From now on, your cigarettes will stay in my office. You can smoke three times a day, but only with supervision. I need you to pick one time in the morning and a couple in the afternoon." She pulls a form from the folder and turns it around so I can see it. "On the weekends, you'll have to get the shift supervisor," she says as she sets a pen on the table.

"I'm grandfathered," I say. Smoking is the one vice they let me keep. I had to give up booze and drugs, but they promised I could keep smoking as long as I lived at Cedar Grove. It's written in my resident contract.

"That hasn't changed," Marianne says.

"Right. I'm just restricted to three a day, with you as a babysitter."

She pulls something else from the folder. "Maybe you could tell me what this is," she says, and as soon as I see the handwriting, I feel my sugar spike. She's got my list. Normally I keep it on me at all times, but at night I stick it in the Bible in my nightstand.

She points to Rose Green's name and reads aloud, "Wears Mardi Gras beads and a bad wig. Always has lipstick on her teeth. BSC." Marianne looks at me. "What's BSC?"

Keeping tabs on the people here is how I stay sane. It's how I stay separate from them. I pick up the pen with my good hand. "Batshit crazy," I say.

"That's not how we refer to our residents with dementia."

"Tell that to the CNAs." Cedar Grove has a politically correct term for everything. When somebody falls out of his chair and busts his head, it's a *bad outcome*. And the nutjobs who try to escape are *exit seekers*.

I push the release form away and turn to the last page of my list, to the newest admissions. Under Cecil Carter it says, *Emphysema. Stroke*. I add the word MORON in all caps.

Marianne closes the folder and leaves the form on the table between us. "I'm sorry about your hand, Ben. Angie said she'd be in tomorrow to check on you." She delivers that bomb so smoothly, it's like she's opening the cargo doors of a C-130 from an altitude of twenty-five thousand feet.

I tuck my list into my shirt pocket and press the nurse call button. "Do me a favor, Marianne. Come back when you have good news."

Cecil's departure means I have a room to myself until they get another male admission. There's a lot to be said for privacy, especially in this place, and I briefly consider masturbating. But I'm right-handed, and the pain is stronger than my desire to get off. That night, my hand wakes me up at three am, and I watch *National Geographic* and *Pawn Stars* until I can't stand it anymore. Then I hit the call button and ask the nurse for more pain meds.

"You're not due for another dose until seven. I can bring you a couple of ibuprofen," she says.

I rest my burned hand against my stomach and imagine the night sky. Orion in winter, Virgo in spring.

"How about a smoke break?" I say. "A quick one."

"I'm sorry, Ben. You know I can't." A minute later she brings the ibuprofen in a tiny white paper cup. She watches me swallow it before she steps back into the hall, and when I'm sure she's gone, I roll over and stare at the empty bed.

Cecil was a good roommate; he just got desperate. Right now he's probably alone in a third-floor room at Grady, staring at a window he can't see out of. I tuck my hand to my chest and wonder if he hurts as bad as I do. And if there's a part of him that would jump from that window if he could.

I'm still dozing the next morning when I hear someone settle into the armchair beside me.

"I brought coffee," Angie says. Waking up to my sister's voice is a little like waking up naked under a streetlight. When it happens, you know some seriously bad shit has gone down. Angie's thighs press against the seams of her slacks. Now that she's pushing fifty, she's starting to pack on the pounds. She sets the Starbucks cup on the tray table between us.

I take a sip of the coffee, and it's almost as good as the drugs they're giving me. She even put real sugar in it.

"Marianne said you had second-degree burns." She tugs on her earring, a nervous tic she developed when we got sent to foster care. Angie protected me back then.

"That's what they tell me."

"She also said your roommate's daughters are pretty upset."

I close my eyes and count to ten. I know what she's thinking. She's worried somehow she'll get sued. Angie's never screwed up in her entire life, and even now, even after I've been clean for two years, she still keeps me at arm's length. "He's not my roommate anymore."

"Did you give that man cigarettes, Ben?"

I didn't, but she won't believe me. Angie hasn't believed me since I took her Honda and totaled it when I was fifteen.

"I should have," I say, and I hold up my bandaged hand. "I'm paying for it anyway, aren't I?"

The West Unit corridor feels a thousand miles long now that I've got only one good hand. I tried to talk the physical therapy department into giving me a motorized chair, a hot rod to cruise around in till I heal up, but they said it would allow my upper body strength to degrade.

I pass Ella on the main hall. She's got one hand on the rail and one hand on the collar of her nightgown. "Bring me a drink of whiskey," she says, and for the first time in months, an ache comes over me, a need so strong it nearly blisters me inside.

Marcus is loading the vending machines when I get there, and he hands me a 3 Musketeers. "Your friend's back," he says.

"I try not to make friends in this place," I tell him as I hand him my dollar. "Everybody's got one foot in the grave already."

Marcus laughs. "Not you."

We both look down at my stumps. "No, not me."

"Seriously, though," Marcus says. "He's back."

"Who?" I ask.

"Your roommate. Sparky."

I'm pretty sure Marcus is the one who bought cigarettes for Cecil, and I'd like nothing more than to lay him out. Unfortunately, I can't even reach his head. "Where did they put him?"

"Over on South. Right next to the nurses' station."

I look down the corridor to my right. South is the dementia ward, a hellhole full of old women who scream and cry at all hours. Rose Green, of the Mardi Gras beads and the bad wig, lives on South. Cecil will never sleep again.

"The Dr Pepper's been empty for two weeks," I tell Marcus. "I'm about ready to call the ombudsman."

He laughs, and when I don't join in, he quits stocking the drink machine.

"What crawled up your ass?"

"Nothing. Open that door for me," I tell him, nodding toward the courtyard. When it slams shut behind me, I wheel myself along among the flowers: salvia and snapdragons, bergamot and butterfly bush. Plants I know only because Angie teaches me their names on Sundays when she visits. She could take me out of here if she wanted to, but she's never offered. She just brings plants and talks to me while she sets them in the dirt.

I stop when I get to the gazebo and tear open the 3 Musketeers bar. That's when I notice Cecil at the far end of the courtyard, on the patio, where I'm still allowed to smoke. He doesn't look too bad, considering. His face is swollen, and he's got bandages on both arms. I take a bite of the candy. The sweetness is excruciating; it reminds me of the phantom pain in my feet. When Cecil sees me, I wheel over to the patio and turn my chair so we're parallel to each other.

"You know you fucked us both pretty good," I say. I glance at him, but he's staring at his hands. They're wrapped in gauze all the way to his fingertips. "Marianne's got my cigarettes now. I can only have three a day, and she has to sit with me while I smoke."

"I'm sorry, Ben," he says, but on his tongue the words have too many syllables.

"Yeah? Well, at least they didn't move me to South." I turn my chair around and tap on the window until one of the CNAs opens the door. Inside, Marcus is closing the drink machine, and when I roll by, I give him the finger.

The next morning, Marianne is late. I've been sitting on the patio for ten minutes, watching Marcus drill holes in the brick wall, when she finally shows up with her hair still damp. "Morning," she says, and she hands me a giant gray bib.

"What's this?"

She puts on her sunglasses and pulls one of the rocking chairs off about ten feet so she won't catch the brunt of my smoke. "Part of the new regulations," she says. "It's fire retardant."

The bib is heavy. Not as heavy as a flak jacket, but I know I'll be sweating before I can take two drags. Marianne pulls my Camels and my lighter from the pocket of her dress. "We're admitting a new resident this afternoon. His name is Gus."

I take my time lighting up. This is her backassward way of telling me I'm getting a roommate. "Is he a lifer?"

"I hope not. His family wants him home before Thanksgiving."

I pull smoke into my lungs while Marcus hangs a bright red bag that says *Emergency Fire Blanket* on the hooks he's just installed. It's got a black strap at the bottom that you can pull to release the blanket. I exhale toward the sky. "When are the state inspectors coming?"

Smoke drifts Marianne's way, and she makes a face. "They won't tell us. But I'm sure they'll want to talk with you when they get here."

I turn the lighter over in my hand. "If you bump me up to four a day, I'll sing your praises."

Marianne's perfectly sculpted eyebrows rise above the top of her sunglasses. "I've heard you in choir practice, Ben." She holds out an ashtray. "Let's leave the singing to someone else."

After lunch, I figure I'll take a quick nap before the new guy comes in, but when I get to the end of the hall, I hear people talking in my room. They're not speaking English, and I notice the nameplate by the door says, "Konstantinos Papadopoulos."

I start to back up in the hallway, but it's too late. One of the women sitting on the bed has spotted me. "Come in. Please," she calls. Inside, there's a kid—seven, maybe eight years old—using my bed as a trampo-line and an old guy in a wheelchair over by the sink. His English isn't any better than my Greek, so his daughters and granddaughter fill me in. They talk over each other, and the granddaughter keeps grabbing her son by the collar, saying, "Park it, Nick!" It's all I can do to get out of the room before I hyperventilate.

"Leave the door open," I tell Marianne when I get to her office.

"Okay." She smiles calmly, like a veteran teacher on the first day of class.

"There's seven people in my room right now," I say. "That's got to be a code violation."

"It's his first day, Ben. Give him time to get settled."

"I won't even be able to turn around with all those people in there. Much less take a piss in private. And you know how I feel about tight spaces."

Marianne folds her hands together. "Yes, I do."

"It'll never work. I already need a Klonopin."

"Well, there's a private room available," she says. "Do you want me to talk to Angie about it?"

We both know it's an extra thirty dollars a day for a private room, and Medicaid won't pay for it. Angie can afford it, but I'd rather eat broken glass than ask her. "I'll get someone to pick me up a Powerball ticket," I say. "But thanks anyway."

Marianne opens the file cabinet and takes out my cigarettes. "How about we go sit in the courtyard awhile," she says, "and I'll walk you back to your room when you're ready?"

Outside, I chain-smoke three Camels, and Marianne sits by the herb garden, running her hand over the rosemary. She brings her palm up and inhales, and when she sees me watching her, she looks away. "Catnip," she says, embarrassed. "For people."

"Careful," I say. "That stuff will make you crazy."

"Batshit crazy?" Her smile takes her from pretty to knockout, and just for a second, I imagine touching her nipples. Feeling them harden under my hands.

I want to stay pissed at her. I really do. But I stub out my cigarette and grin.

The only time I see Cecil is at dinner. He sits on the other side of the dining hall, and it takes him forever to eat. I nod at him on my way out each night and hold up my bandaged hand in solidarity. But Cecil is no longer my problem.

I've got new stressors thanks to Gus and the Greek chorus. People from his church come in and out all day, and his granddaughter shows up every morning to supervise his physical therapy. She brings her son, and while she's in PT with Gus, the kid wreaks havoc. He's supposed to stay in the activities room, but the minute she walks out, he's off climbing the medication carts and pushing buttons on the photocopier behind the nurses' station. Marcus even busts him eating Klondike bars from the freezer in the staff lounge. "And they think I'm trouble," I say when he tells me. "That kid's a Tasmanian devil. On speed."

On Tuesday I catch Gus's grandson on his knees in front of the vending machine. He's got one arm up inside the plastic door, angling for a pack of Oreos, and his face is beet red from the effort.

"It's a long road to juvie, kid, but you're off to a great start."

He pulls his arm out of the machine and walks over to me. "What happened to your legs?" He stares at my stumps.

"Same thing that will happen to your arm if you don't keep it out of there."

Cecil rolls out of the therapy room, inching along with his good foot, and I meet him halfway. The kid follows me.

"First you leave," I tell Cecil, "and now I have to put up with this hellion." I gesture beside me, but I'm pointing into space. The kid is over by the fire extinguisher, sizing up the glass cabinet.

"Nick!" his mother yells from the door to the PT room. "Don't touch that."

"Gus's grandson," I tell Cecil.

The kid takes off down the hall, and I follow as fast as I can. When I get to my room, he's going through Gus's dresser. "Find anything good?" I ask.

The kid squeezes past my wheelchair, sizing me up as he slinks out the door. He's wondering if I'll tell on him. And I'm wondering if I'll ever have a moment's peace. I pull the top drawer out of Gus's nightstand and flip it over on the bed. Taped to the bottom is Cecil's pack of Marlboros. Right where he left them. I bet Marianne never even thought to look. I tuck the cigarettes into my fanny pack and take out my list. At the bottom, I've written, *Gus Papadopoulos. Fought with Greek resistance in WWII. Hip fracture. Has night terrors.*

When I pass the therapy room a few minutes later, I stop and watch Gus through the window. He's doing weight-bearing exercises while his granddaughter takes notes. The kid is in the corner, pedaling the little device they use for diabetics with foot ulcers. Gus waves, and I give him a thumbs-up. At Cedar Grove, half of the admissions with hip fractures are dead within a year. If nobody tells him that, he'll be home eating baklava before Christmas.

Gus's family takes him out early on Sunday. I feel like I've won the lottery, and I spend the morning watching *American Pickers* and reading a Carl Hiaasen novel. Angie shows up after church, bearing the Atlanta newspaper. "Coupons," I say. "Just what I need."

"You want me to take it back?"

I roll my eyes. "It's a joke, Angie."

She sits down on the edge of my bed. "How's your hand?"

I rotate it for her inspection. "Not bad," I say. "Another week and I'll be back to popping wheelies in my chair."

She shakes her head, but I can tell she's trying not to smile. "And how's your roommate?"

I look over at Gus's wall of pictures. "He's great, actually. It's his family I can do without."

Angie picks at a spot on the bedspread. "Some people actually like their families, Ben." Her expression is part hurt, part anger. It's a look she's perfected: she's been wearing it since we were kids. "And I meant your old roommate," she says. "Cecil Carter."

I'm about to say "He's alive" when Angie reaches for her earring and presses her thumb to the back, checking it.

"I didn't give him the cigarettes, Angie."

"I know you didn't," she says softly. "He told Marianne he got them from one of the maintenance guys."

It's as close as she's ever come to saying she's sorry.

I busy myself with the newspaper, flipping through the sections like I'm looking for something. I want to beg her to take me out of here. Anywhere, even if it's just around the block. As long as we're moving and the windows are down.

I set the brake on my chair and slide into it. "Let's go outside," I say. "The lantana looks terrible. Maybe you can tell them what to do about it."

I take my last smoke break after dinner, and when I get to my room, Gus is back. With his entire family. There are four people sitting on my bed, and there's a Dr Pepper and a 3 Musketeers on my tray table. "Who left that?" I ask.

Gus's granddaughter hands me the candy and soda. "The man with the bandages."

I back out of the room and head toward South. This time of night it's deserted, and for once, it's quiet. Cecil's got a private room, and I'm thinking he's a lucky bastard when I find him half out of his chair, clutching the bathroom doorknob. "Cecil?"

The look on his face is pure anguish, and there's a broad stain across his lap. "Hang on. I'll get somebody."

At first I think there's no one at the nurses' station, but then I see the guy sitting behind the desk. It's the second-shift supervisor. The one Marianne has a crush on. "How long has that call light been blinking?" I ask.

He glances at Cecil's door. "I have no idea."

Saliva floods my mouth. "Christ on a fucking cracker. Cecil's pissed himself because y'all just let him sit there."

"Language, pal," the man says. He pages a CNA, and a minute later, an aide comes around the corner, swinging her hips slow and easy. "Twenty-two needs attention," he tells her.

I'm trying to decide if I should wait for Cecil to get cleaned up when I notice Rose Green at the end of the hall. She's wearing two strands of Mardi Gras beads—one red, one purple—and when she stops by the door to the parking lot, I hear it click, locking in response to her ankle monitor. "Let me out," she says, leaning over her walker to push the door handle. She'll be at it all night.

"Could you have someone bring Cecil down to the main hall?" I ask the supervisor.

"Sure."

"Tell him I've got something for him," I say, and I pat my fanny pack just to be certain.

When the big-hipped girl rolls up with Cecil, I'm finishing off the 3 Musketeers. "Thanks for the present," I say, and he nods. Then we both go quiet. Cecil stares out the window, and I watch Gus's grandson ricochet like a pinball from one doorway to another, looking for entertainment. He stops in front of the fire alarm, rocking heel to toe while he reads the instructions.

"Hey, Nick!" I yell, and he jumps like I've popped him with a pellet gun. "Come here." I tell him to push Cecil to the courtyard door, and he licks his lips, considering it. His tongue is purple. "Help us and I won't tell your mom you've been trying to rob the vending machine."

That gets him. He pushes Cecil and comes back for me. "Now hold the door open. It's heavy." Cecil inches his way through, and the kid makes a face when I reach the threshold, his purple tongue snaking out to touch his chin. I put a hand on his shoulder. "You ever pull the fire alarm at school?"

He squirms away. "Nope."

"I did." I make a show out of glancing up and down the hall, like I'm about to divulge classified information. "The firemen let me sit in the truck while we waited for my mom to come. I got to work the siren and the electric ladder."

Outside, the air smells like ozone and scorched concrete. I pull Cecil's Marlboros from my fanny pack. "I believe these belong to you," I say.

Cecil looks at me like we're seventeen and I've just handed him the keys to my Camaro. Then his head overrides his heart. "They'll catch us," he says.

"And do what? Take away our bingo privileges?" I turn off his oxygen and roll over to the red bag that Marcus screwed into the wall. When I yank the black Velcro strap, a blanket falls into my arms. It feels like steel wool against my skin.

"What's that?" Cecil asks when I hand it to him.

"A smoking jacket."

Cecil takes off his nasal cannula. "This is a bad idea," he says, huffing, as I unfold the blanket and tuck it around him.

"You got a better one?"

Cecil shakes his head.

"Me neither. We can smoke one before they miss us. And I have a feeling they're about to have their hands full," I say, pointing inside at Nick. I light two cigarettes, and we smoke, and watch, as the kid swoops up and down the hall with both arms out like an airplane. With each pass, he gets a little closer to the alarm.

"You think he'll pull it?"

Cecil asks. "God, I hope so."

The wind kicks up, and everything green bends and bows around us as Cecil takes a drag and taps his cigarette carefully into a plastic ashtray. "Not much left without this," he says, laboring over each word. He stares at the Marlboro between his bandaged fingers. "What do you miss?"

Bourbon. Barbeque at Fat Matt's. Lullwater Park in winter. My vision blurs, and I tell myself it's just a sugar spike. I nod at the long wall of windows. Inside Cedar Grove, Gus's grandson steps up to the fire alarm.

"Being him," I say, and we both lift bandaged hands to our ears as the kid reaches out and pulls the lever.

Nine Worthy and the Best That Ever Were

Austin Ratner

1. The Last Days of Sir Israel Schelde, 1968-1974

That there lived a man named Israel Schelde, there can be no dispute. There is the reflex hammer with the reddish rubber tomahawk head bearing his initials. There is the red shirt, thick and coarse like Indian jute, with black buttons, that Israel was known to wear as a coat and in which he appears in many photographs. And in many other places there are many other things, and many people will give accounts of him.

William Caxton said in his introduction to *Le Morte D'Arthur: It is notoriously known through the universal world that there be nine worthy and the best that ever were.* Three pagans—Hector, Alexander the Great, Julius Caesar; and three Jews—Joshua, David, Judas Maccabaeus; and three noble Christians—King Arthur, Charlemagne, and Godfrey of Bouillon. There are many stories about these men, but we know that they lived in this world. It must be so with Israel Schelde.

OF THE EVIL KING ON THE GREEN BICYCLE

Hershey the Vise squeezed your arm in an iron grip, pushed your face into the mattress, damp with your urine (what was wrong with you, anyway?), and if you spoke his name he slapped you in the face with Webster's dictionary, then opened it up to "father" and read you the definition: "the MAN who has engendered the CHILD! PROTECTOR of the child! Deserving RESPECT or REVERANCE!" (But he did not read the last sense of the verb, "to father": *to impose improperly as a responsibility.*) Slowly, deliberately, Hershey came up the drive on the green bicycle, knees rising slowly under the greasy apron, and Israel could see himself there, standing on the asphalt that smelled of hosewater—and knocking his father over onto the lawn.

HOW ISRAEL SCHELDE WAS CHASTENED AND BADE ANON FORSWEAR HIS PENNE BY JAMES HELPERN, THE GHOST BOY

The candle that burned for his mother flickered on the sill, and raindrops traveled slowly down the dark pane. On days like that Israel read Keats from a wine-red book that still had the Harvard Coop sticker on the back cover, and he copied down a few phrases, which he would toss into a briefcase with poems he had written on prescription pad paper. *Seashouldering whales, vision of greatness, a new thinking into the heart.* Israel grabbed his rough red coat from the hook and said, "Did you know Keats' girlfriend was named Fanny Brawne?"

"Will you stop wasting your time with that stuff?" James said. "Read *The New England Journal of Medicine.*"

"Fanny Brawne. It sounds like a gluteal condition," Israel said.

"Speaking of gluteal conditions, how're the anal fissures? How's your ass?" Ghost Boy pointed to his own ass and wrinkled his nose.

"Yeah, I'm presenting it at this month's M and M. My Ass: What Went Wrong."

HOW ISRAEL DRANK STRONG DRAUGHT AND MADE A SHOW OF HIS GREAT APPETITE BY DEVOURING AN ENTIRE COW; HE ATE THE PRIME RIBS, THE SHORT RIBS, THE SHORT LOIN, THE CROP, THE WITHERS, THE HORNS, THE POLL, THE BRAINS, THE MUZZLE, THE TONGUE, THE CHUCK, THE DEWLAP, THE BRISKET, THE FORESHANK, THE ENTRAILS, THE KNEE, THE PLATE, THE MILK WELL, THE FLANK, THE UDDER, THE HOCK, PASTERN, AND HOOVES, THE HINDSHANK, THE STIFLE, THE THIGH, THE TAIL, THE PINBONE, THE ROUND, THE RUMP, THE SIRLOIN, AND FOR DESSERT, HE ATE THE EYES

Dinner was a tempest. James' girlfriend, Amanda, accidentally knocked a glass of water off the table, and James sent his salad back to the kitchen. James said they were living in the age when all the heroes had been destroyed. King and Bobby Kennedy were both dead. Amanda derided James for his adoration of Burt Lancaster, and James said an imaginary hero is as good as any in this day and age. And he added that McLuhan was a charlatan, not a prophet. Israel's date, Danielle, produced a litany of alarmist pronouncements (the deputy chief of Cleveland police was another Bull Connor), and each time, she pursed her frosted lips and jutted out her jaw as though she had just captured the travail of her whole generation. Israel devoured a steak and fries and drank two beers in short order, and leaned back with satisfaction, so that all three of his dinner companions were in some contact with his splayed and bearish form. He breathed deeply and thought of Cape Cod: the cold drops on the red-gray chitin of a lobster and a conch's turreted lime, concretion of the ocean.

Finally Amanda burst into tears and pushed past James, who clutched his head in both hands and, looking wild and helpless, his hair standing up in a black sheaf, followed her out of the bar.

HOW THE GHOST OF DR. AUSTRIAN APPELLED JAMES OF MISCONDUCT, AND HOW ISRAEL SMOTE OFF ITS HEAD

James the Ghost Boy's eyes were red, and the collar on his white coat stuck up on one side. The rubber loops of his stethoscope drooped and bobbed over the edge of the chair, in danger of spilling out of his coat. A penlight, dog-eared index cards, a laminated Snellen eye chart and a green minibook on antibiotics bulged in his breast pocket. "What was the potassium?" James said again. They huddled together over a patient's chart in the back of the nurses' station, pointing at lab values on the wavy pasted printouts.

In the quiet, darkened doorways were patients in stockinged feet, sometimes reflecting one's passing look on their dark and still faces in a way that reminded Israel of Dante: Hades-dwellers peering out of the cracks in their hive. Sometimes the patients sat before windows of square twilight with steaming tubes in their mouths. "Mr. Healy was really, really short of breath this morning," Israel said. "They should have got another blood gas today."

They met for rounds in the Austrian Room, a surgery conference room that the fellow had got the key to. Dr. Anoyen produced his stack of blue index cards and prepared to hear lab values on his patients. High on the wall behind him was a portrait of the leaden-eyed surgeon, Dr. Austrian, in a cracked frame. When James said Mr. Healy's CBC was missing and would have to be ordered again, Dr. Anoyen's head shot up, and his eyes broke from their card-reading squint into an imperious stare. "Well, we need to know that white count right now," he said.

"Well, it will have to be ordered again, then," James said.

"Well, you better go get a stat blood draw right now," Dr. Anoyen said.

"Well, okay then," James said.

"I'll go do it," said the disheveled pulmonary fellow, who smelled of aftershave.

Later, in the hallway, tireless Dr. Anoyen and the tireless pulmonary fellow drove onward from room to room while the fatigued medical students hurried after them.

It was half past ten by the time they dragged themselves to James' car in the dank parking structure. Water was dripping from the concrete ceiling onto the hood of the car. "Fuck that fuckin' motherfucker in his fuckin' asshole. Motherfuckin' fuckface. Fuck," Israel said.

Before going to sleep, Israel jotted down a line—*faces in the cracks in hell's hive, they reflect your passing inquisition, and damn YOU*—and a poem in irregular feet, which he called *The Austrian Room:*

Dr. Austrian:
Would you have said
(if you weren't dead)
Do you like surgery?

Would you have spoken?
Or, manly, gave your silent token,
Condescending vision
In your eyes of molten lead.

HOW ISRAEL LONGED FOR A WOMAN WITH WHOM TO MAKE A HOME

Oh, what the hell, he drank down another, and asked her, "Do you want to go back for another drink?" Then he squinted and took a drag on a cigarette. In the morning she plucked her bra from the nightstand and inquired where the bathroom was. When she came back to his room, he offered to walk her out; she declined, and he stiffly kissed her serious round face.

He had been to a strip joint half-jokingly and flirted with strippers, tormenting in their ersatz stop-short business-deal nonsexy sexiness. He had dated women with blond hair, with brown hair, women in chartreuse miniskirts, women in dresses that flowed to the ground and who had moles on their necks, women in flower-embroidered bell-bottom jeans with unshaven armpits who sucked misty bubbles through purple-tinted glass bongs and wore quartz amulets, women with inappropriate laughter, women who bit and scratched him, insane women with frecklefaces whom he had had to push out of his lap, voluptuous women with strongly held though largely incomprehensible structuralist beliefs, truculent Friedanists and brainwashed prehousewives who wanted to marry a doctor or a lawyer, angular black-spectacled pedagogues who didn't get it when he spoke of anger and saucy street-smart ladies who guessed his thoughts accurately but didn't care for Shakespeare, beautiful women whose families had been touched by illness but who believed in mental telepathy, women with raspy voices whose words were tersely jettisoned in packets of smoke, women with hopeful eyes whose dreams would have to be fulfilled by someone else.

He wrote in a letter to his brother, "I can't find anyone that's right."

HOW ISRAEL WAS APPROACHED BY THE GHOSTLY LADY, WHO WAS HIS GOD MOTHER FROM BEYOND THE PALE OF LIFE, AND HOW SHE SPOKE TO HIM THROUGH CURTAINS OF LIGHT AND HE PLIGHTED HIS TROTH TO HER REMEMBRANCE

He could hardly remember his mother's face.

OF DIANA, WHOSE FAIR CLEAR SKIN AND DARK HAIR AND LIGHTEST GREEN EYES LIKE GEMS WASHED IN A FOREST STREAM MADE WONDERMENT INSIDE HIM, AND WHOSE SUNDRESS HE BELIEVED SHE HAD WORN JUST FOR HIM UPON HIS RETURN FROM THROWING OUT A WATER HEATER

The patio was full of bees, oscillating violently in the air among the blooms as if straining to escape the flower heads to which they were invisibly tethered. A yellow jacket landed on the back of his wrist, extending and retracting its stinger before cutting a frenetic serpentine path over the driveway.

Her face was light-soaked: fair skin, dark hair, light light green eyes. Her father, Dr. Neuwalder, was still at the hospital, and there was a touch of pride in her voice when Diana told them that her father went in to the hospital seven days a week. He was chief of medicine.

While discussing a movie or drinking ice water and standing in her garage in dusty pants, they found they agreed on many things. Elementary school was resurrected for both by an odor, a melange of chalk, older women's perfume, and old metal pipes—the third of the scents issuing from the drinking fountains' warm water, dribbling out of patina-crusted spouts, they remembered, into bowls of white porcelain. There was always a boy who put his lips to the spout itself, and then the water would have to be run for half a minute or so to flush away the germs. Sometimes the elementary school included freshly cut grass, and sometimes the odor of rubber—either that of the green springy oily seats on the buses or that of the red rubber kickballs whose hollow bellies were ready with tympani should they be bounced or kicked. How cruel children could be at that stage of life! And there was the smell of old library book pages in bed—for her, *The Secret Garden*, for him *Half Magic*. And the gutta-percha dolls in her grandmother's cedar wood attic and his army men who made long expeditions across the broken terrain of the pillow-strewn living room floor. When running through the kitchen he had accidentally knocked a tray of sliced onions off the counter; his father had taken away both the army men (gift from a cousin) and the favorite book by Edward Eager, which he had won in a third grade math contest.

He admired her father's ship's clock, she his bulky Seamaster quartz watch that his brother had bought for him before he shipped out on the S.S. *Annie Marin*. She opened the window wide to the night sky, put on a record of Vivaldi's *Nulla in mundo pax sincera*, and they drunkenly climbed onto the roof of her apartment and leaned against a broad vent-pipe. She hooked her ankle inside his, and they saw earthshine on the moon. I bet you think of your mother all the time, she said, and he said he did. He said, "This reminds me of one night I spent in Martha's Vineyard, the summer of the March on Washington." They had both been there and heard Dr. King say to them, I have a dream . . . "There were torches on the beach, and a girl wearing my sweatshirt, and the sound of the waves, and song rising up the dune with these red fireflies from out of the bonfire," Israel said.

HOW ISRAEL SPAKE TO BILLIE HARPER IN THE KINDERGARTEN SOCIAL WORK OFFICE, AND HOW HE BEHAVED HIM THERE; HOW HE WENT WITH HIS LADY INTO THE COUNTRY WITHOUT REGARD FOR POSSIBLE REBUKE

The children Diana counseled were a pleasure. She brought Israel many moving and delightful stories—the boy whose tears had plopped on the floor in the hallway because the turkey he'd drawn for Thanksgiving decoration had come out so much smaller than everyone else's; the boy who said his parents had allowed him to ride a roller coaster and asked Diana, "Do you think it's appropriate for me?" But Diana's new boss, Billie Harper, a squat and flat-faced woman who wore dresses with enormous yellow flowers on them, was a constant source of complaint.

"She needs to hire a secretary," Diana said. "All this endless paperwork isn't my job and it hardly needs to be done in the first place. She actually returns all these forms to the state—*in triplicate*. Nobody's ever returned them and we've never had a problem with our grant because of it. She's ridiculous."

"Tell her you won't do it," Israel said, squashing a handful of green grapes in his mouth and spitting out a stem. The wet grapes were soaking through *The Cleveland Press*, which was spread out over the breakfast table.

"I did. And can you believe this: she told me she'd fire me. She's anxious, so she needs to make other people anxious. Ugh, she's an impossible woman!"

On Saturday night, when Israel came through the door, he stamped his feet, which rattled the picture frames along the hall, and bellowed, "Going to the country with my lady!" He dumped his white coat and stethoscope on the low table under the coat rack. Sunday would be his first day off in more than two weeks.

But Sunday morning the phone rang at eight o'clock while Diana lay with a hand across Israel's chest. Israel turned over and the box spring creaked underneath him.

"Go away, intruder!" Israel said from under a pillow.

It was Billie Harper calling.

"She's at the school. She needs me to help her finish off the filing before Monday."

"Why?"

"I don't know." Diana sat up, sighed and tugged her nightgown down over her underwear.

"Oh, you're not going to go," Israel said, rolling over to face her, squinting in the light. He took the square black clock from the shelf behind the bed and looked at it.

"She'll force the issue. Look, I promise I won't be there past twelve. That still gives us plenty of time to drive out to Chagrin Falls."

"You've got to be kidding me," Israel said. But she was already running the faucet in the bathroom.

Israel stood before the frosted glass of the window on the office door. He called: "Mrs. Harper?" and rapped on the glass. "Mrs. Harper! Open up! I need Diana." Israel threw the door open. "Ah, there you two are! Hiding!" They were sitting on the floor with file folders all around them. Billie Harper frowned and looked at him. Israel had a red-and-white scarf around his neck and the collar was turned up on his red shirt. He extended a hand to Diana. "Come, lady!" Turning to Billie Harper, he said, "Madam, I'm sorry I haven't more time or I'd chat."

The two women didn't move.

"Ah! I'm afraid we have an appointment in the country that can't wait." He strode over to Diana and lifted her up.

"Izzy! What are you doing?"

He threw her over his shoulder, and turned around. With his free hand, he pulled a rose from the vase on the shelf and handed it to Billie Harper. "Madam. Goodbye. And I love your dress," he said. Then he carried Diana out.

In the car, she laughed and said, "You're crazy!"

He drummed his fingers happily on the steering wheel, rolled down the window and leaned his head out. "It smells like the country! Ha ha!"

OF DIANA'S FATHER, THE GREATEST MAN IN RECORDED HISTORY, KING DOCTOR LEONARD NEUWALDER, HEALER, SAILOR, SCIENTIST, LEADER, AND CONFUCIAN PHILOSOPHER; OF ISRAEL'S RECOLLECTIONS OF THE MERCHANT MARINE IN MALAY (PENANG)

Diana often produced her father's aphorisms in conversation. When they spoke of medicine—my father says that you must respect a patient's denial concerning his diagnosis; that new radiologic techniques are the future of medicine; that insidious illness is the worst sort; that most ailments take care of themselves. When they spoke of fruit and politics—that a peach is best slightly underripe; that McCarthy took all the brains on the Far East right out of the State Department (Owen Lattimore's *Ordeal by Slander* was among the volumes in Dr. Neuwalder's library). When he or she was hungover—my father says that olives are a remedy for a hangover and that aspirin is the wonder drug. Occasionally one came out of the blue—that the Shaker Heights Zoning Commission was anti-Semitic. Dr. Neuwalder had been prevented from building a dormer on his home on Laurel Road. When they strategized against hard times, her view included a citation of her father's belief that the key to life is recognizing what you can't control.

Israel and Dr. Leonard Neuwalder first met on South Bass Island. Dr. Leo—the name the other suitors to his daughters used for him—was standing in front of the greasy flames of the grill, gazing distractedly out at Lake Erie. His three daughters and the other boyfriends were lounging on the two picnic tables in the yard. A jug of red wine and paper cups were handed between tables.

"Let me get a good look at you," Mrs. Neuwalder said, and put her glasses on.

"The famous Israel Schelde," Dr. Leo said, and his eyes glinted with a smile. He was gray at the temples, tall, with tan arms that were naked of hair, and chapped lips. He looked a little like Gary Cooper. A skinny kid strode up beside Diana, shook Israel's hand firmly and disappeared into the house with Israel's merchant marine stuffsack.

"I missed the early ferry," Israel said. "Terrible traffic."

Diana nervously took Israel's hand, then said, "That was Harvey. He's a friend of your little brother's, I think."

"Well, I'm going to put you to work right away, Israel," Dr. Leo said, handing over tongs and an oven mitten. "We've still got hungry mouths, and I have to get a shower. Would you like a beer? Or some original South Bass wine? Diana, get him a glass of wine; he looks like he could use it." Dr. Leo smiled again and winked, then followed Israel's bag into the gray-shingled three-story house.

Israel spent an hour sweating over the grill and the plates of sauce and raw salmon, of hamburgers and hot dogs. If Ghost Boy could only see him: medical student on duty on South Bass Island.

Jenny sprayed perfume onto the inside of her wrist and held it out to Anne for a sniff.

"Would you like some?" Jenny said, and she sprayed Israel's arm. The air was full of the minty scent of the hedge, and citronella, and the perfume she'd sprayed from the yellow bottle. The sisters had bright clear faces and pale green eyes just like Diana's; all were of the same lithe and beautiful species. "Didn't you go to Harvard?" Jenny said. "Harvey and I are in Trumbull at Yale."

"Did you go to any of the Harvard-Yale games?"

"No, I never did."

Clouds drifted unfettered across the sky, and sailboats crossed below.

After dinner, while the girls were upstairs washing up, Dr. Leo and Israel sat in the living room with the faded Audubon merganser duck and the doorway with the west-facing entablature, all lit up with red light from across Lake Erie.

"Diana tells me you're a sailor."

"Yes sir."

"You took door knobs to Malaysia?"

"Door knobs, pillows, blankets, grain, all kinds of things," Israel said.

"Ordinary seaman?"

"Yes sir."

"My brother sails in the merchant marine," Dr. Leo said.

"So you must know something about ships."

"Something," Dr. Leo said. He smiled and swished the ice cubes around in his Scotch, drank the last of it. His eyes twinkled.

"What's this?" Israel asked and crossed the Persian rug. On a peeling gray bookcase loaded with hardbound volumes, between books on the Second World War, stood what looked like an old sextant.

Dr. Leo approached the bookcase. "It's an antique sextant. This one belonged to Oliver Hazard Perry," he said. "You probably never heard of him, but he repelled the British in the Battle of Lake Erie in the War of 1812. It happened right but there." He stood with his back to the window and tapped on the windowpane with the knuckle of his middle finger.

"Where did you get it?" Israel asked, and picked it up. "Do you mind if I handle it?"

"It was given to me by a patient, one of Perry's descendants."

"Amazing," Israel said, and tried to look through its lens.

"The sea is really something to experience, isn't it?"

"It certainly is. Everything is there. The whole story," Israel said. He carefully replaced the sextant. "Has your brother ever taken you aboard one of the big ships? Would you ever want to ship out yourself?"

Dr. Leo smiled. "Oh, I was in the Pacific Fleet in the Second World War." Israel looked at the titles of the books in front of his nose: *The Axis 1945, Iwo Jima, Survival in Auschwitz*. "Would you like the sextant?" Dr. Leo asked.

"What? To borrow? I couldn't."

"To keep. It's beautiful, and I know you'd take care of it. Between sailors," Dr. Leo said and winked.

At dusk, Dr. Leo led Israel out onto the coarse wet grass. Square windows full of yellow light shone up and down the side of the dark house. Someone was playing records, and there was a silhouette in the window on the third floor. Israel scratched his ankle on the pricker bush as they walked out into the yard. Dr. Leo held up the sextant to the royal hue of the late evening and said with a cigarette clamped in his mouth, "Arcturus."

He handed Israel the sextant and Israel peered through it uselessly.

Israel said, "You could have sailed the *Kon-Tiki,* Diana says."

"I could have. Thor Heyerdahl wanted a doctor along."

"You knew him?"

"I saw him as a patient once."

"What was wrong with him?" A stupid question; Dr. Leo was not at liberty to say.

"If you ask me, he was nuts."

"Did you consider going?"

"To sail across the South Pacific on a balsa raft with a bunch of crazy Norwegian ethnologists? I had enough excitement in the navy."

Israel sat on the end of the picnic table bench, but Dr. Leo remained standing, exhaling a stream of smoke with chin uplifted. Israel stood again and asked, "What was the war like?"

"Just like life, Izzy." Dr. Leo looked at him. "Only more concentrated. I saw my buddy blown through the neck with shrapnel"— Dr. Leo pointed to the hedge— "standing that far away. Now, this mess in Vietnam is a whole different war. But you should be glad to be away from any war there ever was."

"I guess I can't even imagine what it would be like," Israel said.

"Sure you can. Don't misunderstand me; in my opinion, there's nothing in the world like coming under artillery fire—it's like getting a speeding train thrown at you from out of the sky, at you personally. But I think combat is just like life. More concentrated, but the general character of it—the way it separates those who've been in it from those who haven't, the way it puts the facts right in your kitchen, death, right in your face—it was familiar to me already, in a general sense. I know you lost your mother when you were a child. You probably know what I mean."

Israel hesitated, then said, "Maybe so."

"The navy was unrelenting pressure." Dr. Leo pulled down the lower lid of one eye. "I was bloodshot the whole time. You felt the pressure of the constant threat of extinction. Just like life. Just like life . . . Have you ever seen an eagle in the wild? You know why an eagle is considered a war-like bird? Because it's a goddamned sober-looking animal. When I was in the state of Washington, I saw an eagle eating a fish on the limb of a tree. I'll never forget him, the way he straightened his plumage and refolded his wings when he was done pulling at the fish carcass, how he retested the wind and prepared himself for the next thing. An eagle is an expert. That's all expertise is, you know? It's training and knowledge you get because you need it to survive. Nature makes an expert out of you if you want to survive. That's a war. Just trying to survive. You know, I don't feel awe when I see an eagle. I feel sad. I feel sorry for him. There he is, him and me and you, experts in our jobs, because of the constant threat of extinction." Dr. Leo pulled the ash off the end of his cigarette with his fingertips, the same way sailors had done it on the *Annie Marin*. "Well, that was a speech!"

Now he sat down on the picnic table, and Israel sat down too.

"Would you like a job in my lab?" Dr. Leo said.

"What? Well, that's a nice offer. But I'll be applying for residencies this year and . . ."

"I know you're applying. I can get you on a paper in a few months. That can't hurt," Dr. Leo said.

"Yes. Thanks. But it's my fourth year, sort of my only year to relax—"

Dr. Leo laughed and patted Israel on the back. "All right," Dr. Leo said.

"All right. Sounds good. I'd love to. Thank you," Israel said.

Dr. Leo laughed again and said, "It'll be good for your career, chief, I promise."

"Thank you."

Dr. Leo squished his cigarette on the table, lit up another one, and handed one to Israel. Israel relievedly drew the smoke through the red ember. They sat in silence and gazed into black Lake Erie. A flock of geese passed overhead, honking, and offshore a buoy clanged.

The *Annie Marin*. The sailor with the missing fingers, on one hand the middle, on the other the ring finger, lost to the winches. "I got a speck of a tattoo on my dick," the sailor had said in the wheelhouse glow of the cathode ray tube screens. "When it's hard, the tattoo says, 'Josephine Cunningham.'" On the watch there were lights blinking on and off at the horizon. If you felt spray on your face, you had to leave the bow because the water had to be big. Once he had felt the spray across his face and removed to the fly bridge. From there he saw the boat pitch down, and a swell washed over the bow deck where he'd been standing minutes earlier. They were skirting a typhoon. And in the huge waves and rolls, fixtures were ripped from the bulkheads; men lashed themselves down on the bridge after others had broken their bones, and cargo tore loose.

In the morning he'd sorted through all the spilled pillows and socks. That people—everywhere on earth—required pillows, cushions on which to sit because their nerves would grow pressed and numb and the blood would be squeezed out of their limbs! That a mere pricker could make one dance to avoid its slash through soft skin. Careful! Because people were soft.

After the storm he had not wanted to leave port and get back on the ship. Then he had seen the Plimsoll mark on the side of the ship, a big blue circle with a line through it that set the maximum height to which the ship could safely be loaded. He had looked at the circle, the mark of some protective influence, and under the view of its circular maternal eye, he reboarded.

On second thought, in the morning, though it made Diana crazy, Israel turned down the lab job.

HOW ISRAEL SUFFERED

They were still celebrating the wedding more than a year later. At dinner, Dr. Leo accidentally kept reaching over to pour Israel wine and had to be reminded that Israel was working as night float at the hospital. After dinner, Israel told Dr. Leo a joke he'd made up: "Knock knock."

"Who's there?"

"Surgeon."

"Surgeon who?"

"Let me in. This is surgery, not a joke, dipshit." Dr. Leo laughed mightily, and Mrs. Neuwalder, who had just had some minor surgery, laughed loudly too. Israel nudged Mrs. Neuwalder and added: "You know why surgeons always stop elevator doors with their heads, don't you? Their hands are too important to their work." Dr. Leo howled and wiped a few tears from his eyes. He carried his plate to the kitchen and walked out onto the patio with his wife, whistling happily.

Overnight, Israel's patient crashed while Israel was putting in a central line. The medical student worried it was his fault; he hadn't mentioned that the lung exam sounded a bit murky. Israel told him it was nobody's fault. Israel told the same thing to the family; nothing more could have been done.

At home he was awakened after an hour by a phone call. He flung off the pillow he'd laid on the telephone to muffle its ring and swore. "Come to Laurel Road." It was 11 a.m. He ran up the drive. On the kitchen table were the remains of breakfast: a cold cup of coffee, the scoria of eaten toast on the china, an orange peel. Someone said, "When Neuwalder lectured the medical students, he used to write on the chalkboard with an antacid pill and then say, 'This is what we give to people.'" Someone else mentioned his "scorched-earth policy for his few enemies."

Four years later, Israel remembered the charred crusts of toast. He remembered that a peach is best slightly underripe and that the key to life is recognizing what you can't control. And when he first saw Diana: in the garden full of flowers. And when he last saw her smile, standing in her raglan coat in the snow with his son, Leo, little Leo. What a perceptive little boy he was! And his own bold and perceptive face, the way it had been only a year ago. Two old, old people, with mottled dry-corded faces, he and Di—what he had expected. Keats, if he'd had time. And of course his mother, and his bastard father, knocking his father off his bicycle, the last time perhaps that they had physically touched. And his brother, and the baby, Matthew—his second son, a treasure before him he would never get to touch. And sailing with 10,000 pounds of doorknobs to Malaysia. The sun was like a red gong over the South China Sea.

At last the name "Lefty Paradise" came to him out of a fog and a great distance, like an ambassador from a magic land. Lefty Paradise: a pitcher in the dice baseball league he'd run with his brother when eight or nine years old. "I loves those combed cotton sheets of yers (I feel like I'm in a hotel)," he had once said to Diana. That was a while ago.

Then, like Dr. Leo, he was dead.

II. Letters and Notes, 1974

A LETTER TO MISS FRANCES DELUCA

Miss Frances Deluca
Chief of Nursing
Department of Nursing
NIH

Dear Miss Deluca,

As a hematology-oncology fellow I had a brief experience with you in which I found you to be a strong advocate of the patient. Therefore, I am writing to you at present to apprise you of certain complaints generated by my own stay as a postlaparotomy patient in the NIH surgical ICU during the period of August 23-25, 1974.

In comparison with the nursing care delivered to me personally on floors 5E and 4W during a two-month hospitalization, the care in the ICU was an absolute nadir. I was repeatedly made to feel as though I were a nuisance, and the clear preference seemed to be for comatose or semiconscious patients who apparently presented less disruption to the order of the unit than I.

It was, in fact, reported to a nurse on 6E (a friend of mine) by an ICU nurse that I was a "terrible patient"; I was not aware that postoperative (or other) patients were required to conform to behavioral standards defined by the nursing department.

I was ignored when calling for a nurse on numerous occasions when I could see at least one nurse sitting in the nursing station. My earliest response to the ICU nurses' efforts to help me in and out of bed was fear that this would cause increased pain, and I therefore resisted. As a result I was assisted with ambulation, but no one had the patience to teach me the easiest way to enter and exit the bed. On 5E I was finally shown how to minimize pain in doing these tasks; I was no less fearful of second-party intervention at that point, either.

Furthermore, my bed curtain was often pulled halfway closed for no other ostensible reason than to obscure my view of the ICU clock. I was using the clock to judge the time for delivery of pain medication and was clearly annoying nurses by reminding them early of my need for it; however, the clock was also the single device by which I was able to orient myself in the most dehumanized and disorienting setting I have experienced. The clock was an essential companion in the face of the extreme dearth of human interchange provided by the ICU nurses. There were, in fact, only three nurses (whose names ever reached me) from your ICU that I would allow to care for anyone who meant anything to me, given any choice. The rest were fit for the care of the half- and near-dead only; i.e. those patients beyond placing any direct emotional demand on nursing.

My experience on the ICU will linger in my mind for years as a nightmare. I am, by the way, not the first person to observe these things regarding these highly trained "angels of mercy."

Thank you for your attention. Hopefully you will be able to bring some changes to bear in what I feel is a weak link in an otherwise strong nursing department.

Most sincerely,
Israel Schelde, M.D.

ISRAEL'S NOTES

12/73 Behaved beautifully at Dr.'s for 2-yr checkup—listened to preparation, said, "I'm scared" but let pediatrician examine him, etc. Opened mouth on request for oral exam. 1 and 2/74 Says, "It's too dangerous" to certain prohibited activities. Now tells of need to make poop or pee pee and gets both in potty regularly. Accidents are rare. Says, "Daddy's doctor, I'm big boy." Says, "Mommy's big, I'm just yittle, Daddy's biggest." Noticing hairs on my arms and legs—wary of it. Does not like my developing beard—tries to avoid kissing me directly—says, "beard scratches." Creating imaginative stories from pictures and objects. Handling separations and fears better—pulls self together after initial tears and says, "I feel better." Reassures self that we "come right back." Now can identify objects himself as "just part of bed; just pretend; just a friend" to reassure self against fears. Starting to draw recognizable objects (barely). Has been drawing faces for months. Criticizes own drawings—"not good owl; not good plane." Whispers and says, "Ssh, be quiet" with finger over lips. Tells time—it's "free clocks" all day. Asks me each morning "Daddy go work?" If yes, he is visibly disappointed and withdraws. Responds with glee at my returns—running to me saying, "Daddy, Daddy" over and over. When I tap on his back, he says, "Don't knock me, Dad." Very sensitive to others' feelings—if you look sad etc. he says, "You're mad" or "You're sad," "Don't cry, Dad; feel better in your eyes." Says, "I need a hug; lemme give a kiss." Memory fantastic—occasionally reminisces about things that went on months ago. Imitates well—makes sounds of many animals—e.g. squeak-squeak (mouse), hoo (owl), hello (parrot = carrot), caw (crow), roar (lion, tiger—we told him he was named Leo for lion, roared like he was a lion), growl (bear—high-pitched growl for "yittle bear" which he thought of by himself). Brought me imaginary "candy turtles" to feed me yesterday. Often says Jenny and Harvey and Grammy are in planes he sees in books—says they are going "zoom" from "runway" coming to see him. To my declaring my mistake in putting "jammies" on backwards, he said, "Not on purpose." Gets control of tears quickly now, rubbing tears away and saying, "I feel better in my eyes" as he struggles to maintain control. In response to my continuing to sing after his demanding I stop, he said, "I mean it!" in exact imitation of my words and tone to him on other occasions. Interprets table's being set for evening company as "Happy Birthday" someone. Takes any opportunity to sing Happy Birthday song ("to Leo") and claps afterward in quietly pleased glee. In response to being told it was the wind whistling in his bedroom windows (which frightened him), he said, "It's not wind, it's snake in the window." Described a mouse being chased by a cat in a book as "cat frightening dat mouse." Knows meaning of number two, full, empty (close and far) and identifies "engine" and "caboose" ("parts of train"). Calls eyebrows "eyebrowns." Opens his mouth and shows you how "Doctor looks in your FROPE (throat)." Able to thumb through pages of books in perusal for items or subjects he likes (like "lotsa cars"). After tripping on shoelace, said, "Oops, Daddy, better tie my shoe!" While thinking of things to draw with me he said, "I got a idea." Of a bump that continued to hurt, he said to Diana, "Dat's a problem." Poses for camera, smiling sl. artificially on command. Blows kisses, hugs and kisses friends spontaneously now. Says, "bless you" and "gesundheit" to sneezes. On 2/10/74 handed me an old letter and said, "Sign your name." 2/16/74 learned to use drinking straw. Referred to self as "a little guy." Copies pediatrician in playing doctor—examines your mouth ("open mouth"), says "you're fine," offers a lollipop. Says, "I'm de doctor"; "I'm big boy doctor, you're daddy doctor." Takes his toy tool box and says, "I'm going to work"—returns in a few seconds, running in with arms wide, hugging us and saying, "I missed you, good to see you. I wove you. I come back, see?" Pretends to exercise on living room floor, demanding our participation and saying, "like Grammy." Puts a plastic cup over one eye, squints with the other and says, "Smile for the camera." His imitations show amazing attention to detail and nuance. 3/4/74—Says, "I'm so pretty and proud"; "I keep my pants dry and warm and comfy"; told me while sitting astride me on the floor, "I'm imagining I'm riding a horse." 4/74 Says, "Mommy bought me a wonderful present." Frequently ends requests with "or sumptin"—e.g. "Daddy, give me a ride, or sumptin." In car says, "Oh God, de traffic." Makes faces to scare me. Says, "I fink we going outside" as a hint; or "Maybe we'll go for a walk or pway in puddles, or sumptin." Says words with great animation and inflection. Using complex sentences and questions, with many inappropriate "ands" and "buts." Realized he couldn't see his eyebrows on 4/18/74 and thought he'd lost them—cried till we showed him he could feel them with his fingers; his joy was immense. In response to being told we'd have a baby someday by Diana said, "You will change the diapers, and I will go to work, but don't worry, I will come home for lunch." Said to a neighbor girl, "Larissa did you know I can go to school and I can read?" 4/29/74 Leo asked Diana, "Mommy, is there a baby growing inside of you?" [Yes.] "In your tummy?" [Yes.] "I got one too," he said, pointing to his tummy. Says, "see dat" finally as he explains things to you. Appropriately identifies TV characters as "wonewy (lonely)." Tells us when we or others (even on TV) are "upset"—wants to know "what's matter." Says of scary TV scenes, "It will frighten you away." 5/7/74—Told me this a.m. that "I dreamed a man was scaring me." Says, "Be gentle with me." Refers to "our mommy" (mine and his). Almost able to ride his new (used) tricycle. Said, "Mommy you're special." Learned to put his hands in his pockets; stands around like one of the Dead End Kids now. Sits between and hugs both of us together around the neck, showing great pleasure to have us close in a trio. Making real buildings with blocks—builds carefully and when very tall, squeals to us with glee and pride, "Isn't it beau'ful?" Enjoys knocking down his "buildings" or "towers." Says of many things, "It's so funny." Said on my accidentally bumping him over "dat rockled me over." 5/24/74 "I used to be a doctor; now I'm a cowboy!" In response to request for a kiss said, "I'm too busy now; I'm too tired." 6/74 Said, "I want to be a fire engine when I grow up, and help people." Rode tricycle well and alone for first time. Says "upside-up" as opposite of upside-down. Told me, "Trees are made of wood." Says, "Hi, lady" to Diana and says, "Hiya Dad, how ya doin'?" to me. Calls either of us "young man." In tub said, "I found the ocean." 7/74 Put his hand on Diana's belly and said, "Don't worry, Mom, I won't hurt the baby growing in your breast." Knows whole alphabet and counts to 20. Calls me "sir" jokingly on occasion and "Daddo" (assimilation of my name to his, Leo?). Told Diana that "whoopsie daisies are flowers." Diana had hair in pigtails after swimming. Leo said, "Oh Mommy, you look like a girl." Told us a few days later, "Mommy got her hair wet and then looked like a girl." Was using 2 hands as puppets, with one saying, "I will help you up the hill, Daddy." When he saw I was puzzled he showed me: "This is hand Daddy and this is hand Leo." Says, "A monster makes me mad at John (next door 2-yr-old)." 8/74 Now says L's correctly (instead of like W's) and relishes repeating L words correctly. Says, "Sorry you yelled at me, Dad"—a left-handed apology. Says, "I yelled at you and you yelled at me. Sooooo shut up." Grammy showed him places on the globe. Next day he pointed to Turkey, asking, "Who lives in that chicken?" Has developed his own words to use when angry at someone: "I scrumped you off, Bummo." Describes dreams now, usually regarding witches and "gophs" (ghosts). If our hair is wet or rearranged slightly differently he says, "That's not you" and gets upset until correction is under way. Then says, "Now it's you!" After months of resisting my kissing him due to beard or mustache (12/738/74) his first comment to me when I shaved my beard was, "Now you can kiss me."

DIANA'S NOTES

Says, "I'm sad about Daddy. I'm mad about Daddy." Strokes my cheek. "Remember when Daddy used to do this to you?" At night crying that he was sad about Izzy. When I told him I was too, and that he had me and I would always take care of him, said, "And Uncle Harvey cause he's a men." I said, like Daddy was? He nodded. Swings his arms "like my Daddy does." Wants to be like him. One night, crying, he said was afraid if I rocked too hard in the chair the house would break. I reassured him and he said, "But who will fix it? My Daddy could but he's not here." When I cry sometimes he gets very upset; often tries to comfort me. One night, "Soon it will be late and the people I love will come home." When asked who he meant said, "I love my Daddy but he's not here. But there are other persons that I love—like Uncle Harvey and Aunt Jenny—and soon they will come." Talks about being like Daddy who is "the biggest." Said, "If my Daddy was here I would play tackle with him." Said, "When I'm bigger I'll dive in the water and my Daddy will watch me."

III. The Bear, 1984

James Helpern had come to stay with them on the weekend of Leo's birthday. He squatted before a fern in his madras shorts and said, "Your mother never could take care of a plant." He had hard-cut, piston-like calves that looked as though he'd pulled a rickshaw all his life, and wild black hair and a wild black satanic mustache. Leo's mother and Nick, his stepfather, had gone to buy a new set of glasses before the party. James plucked out a brown frond, dropped it in the plant bed, and sat down on the gray porch couch, which was slightly damp. He looked at Leo as if he were peering inside him at the back of his skull.

"They used to call me Ghost Boy, you know," James said, lightly stroking his mustache. "I was pretty fast when I was in school. A kid named Freddie Rudig—your father knew him—Freddie Rudig named me that—he said, *The Ghost Boy, so fast he wasn't even there.* I ran the 100 and 200. Of course, in those days, we didn't have good shoes."

Leo had seen Rudig's note in his father's yearbook, a green book on the shelf next to the window where the icicles always hung down: *Izzy. Your humor, your wit, your brains, your brawn, you've got it all. You are better than all of us (but not at basketball at which I will kick your ass everyday). Good luck with the rest of the best at the big H.* And James the Ghost Boy he had met a few times before. He was a cardiologist in Connecticut. Was it Ghost Boy who had given him the doctor's bag?

"You know, your father was one of the great men, better than any of us," James said, poking his finger into the soil in the fern pot. "We had never seen anything like him. I always thought, he was *roughhewn by life,* that's how I always put it to myself. I was nothing compared to him. These other guys, they had money, they had family. But he didn't. He had his character. He did it all purely by the force of his personality." He stared at Leo again as if he were looking into Leo's soul, and shook his head. "And he was as strong as a bear." Ghost Boy grinned like a devil, and concluded, "You look more like your mother."

There be nine worthy and the best that ever were.

Before bed, Leo looked at the picture of his father: the arc of his great torso and powerful arm, his wistful expression in the August heat over the lake, the perimeter of trees behind him, fading sky everywhere, a green-gray fuzzy twilight full of tiny insects, maybe, deflected off barely damp skin, deflected off his pressed clean white shirt. The lake was a great dark mirror, ticked over with fine rings because of the commerce of flying insects. In the other picture: the toasted-bread stubble over his square jaw, his pipe and his dark hair. That picture was kept in a frame with chipped silver paint.

Leo brought up to his room the stethoscope, medical book and pathology journal that James had given him, and the card with red balloons on it that said, "Happy Thirteen!" He lined up the milk crates and boxes on the floor of his room in two rows. The row of blue plastic crates started at the base of his actual-size poster of Marilyn Monroe, with whom he had recently become infatuated. She looked at him askance in black-and-white profile, standing up in high heels and a dark maillot. She held her down-turned hand under her chin like *The Thinker,* except only touching lightly with the ends of her extended fingers. A poster of Einstein had also recently gone up; the hoary-headed genius had replaced Aquaman, the orange and green superhero of the sea.

In the first crates went the *Star Wars* toys from his closet. The Millenium Falcon, the X-wing with trusty droid R2D2 in the back (R2D2 could be pushed down to open the spaceship's wings into the X formation) and all the miniature *Star Wars* people, whose ability to bend at the elbow, knee, or waist had to be imagined: orphaned hero Luke Skywalker, who came with a yellow light saber even though none of the light sabers in any of the *Star Wars* movies were yellow; old Obi Wan Kenobi in an unrealistic chintzy plastic cape; Darth Vader, whose light saber was an evil red; two Han Solos, one with a huge head, one with a normal head, now hard to find in the stores; a bunch of Princess Leias in her various outfits—rarely used. The Legos, once dismantled, would have to go in the boxes. He broke apart the spaceships he had built, and the interconnected space stations where the Lego spacemen had made their home, bravely huddled in the heart of lonely crepuscular moonscapes and black empty space—small defense against the wild expanse of the universe. When Leo was done, the shelves where the space installation had been were barren. The crates and boxes were loaded with a rubble of toys.

He hung his father's old stethoscope in the closet next to the black belt and the rough red shirt. He took down the blue box from Higbee's that had in it his father's sweat-stained T-shirt (HARVARD in block letters like a badge at the breast), and the hospital I.D. card and the merchant marine license. On top of those things he lay the pathology journal. James said his father's pathology report was written up in it because the doctors had never seen that type of lymphoma before. Immunoblastic sarcoma. James said the doctors looked at the pathology and they didn't know what the hell his father had.

Leo opened the dusty medical book and saw where his father had written ISRAEL SCHELDE, M.D. He put the book on the shelf that had just been vacated by his Lego spacemen.

What must I do? Leo thought, giving a last look into the closet. What do you do? You make a black leather belt in the hospital playroom with a black lady with a pick in her hair, a stranger—fitting each soft leather piece into the next in a daisy chain; and you hang that belt in your closet like the shed skin of a black snake and let it hang there forever. Next to the dusty red coat.

Unintended

Yuko Sakata

Shinji arrived at his cousin's house early Monday afternoon after a four-hour train ride from Tokyo. His cousin's wife, Yumi, was the only one home. Despite short notice, she immediately made Shinji feel welcome. Over some tea and home-made apple cake—she said she taught cooking classes at a local cultural center—they had their semi-introductory conversation. They had never had a chance to sit down and talk one-on-one before. And in the course of this initial chat, she told him about an incident involving her son, Kazuo.

"Incident," they called it, because they had never found out what exactly happened. When Kazuo had come home one night a few months earlier, he had seemed a little quiet. He'd called out from the front door that he was home, gone up to his room to change out of his school uniform and come down for dinner. While he helped set the table, he only gave halfhearted responses to Yumi's questions about his day. But then again, at age thirteen, he was becoming less enthusiastic about sharing his thoughts with his mother in general. Shinji's cousin Akio had been working late, as was often the case, so it had been just the mother and son at the table. Kazuo wouldn't look Yumi in the eyes as they ate from the simmering *nabe* hotpot between them, but he didn't seem to be consciously avoiding her, either. Then, midway through dinner, he'd said, "I was wondering today, why are manhole lids usually round?"

"Manholes?" Yumi had halted her chopsticks probing the contents of the steaming pot and contemplated for a second. "I think I've read it somewhere. Isn't it to prevent the lid from falling down into the hole? You know, if it's square or any other shape, it could fall through when the lid isn't placed perfectly. Or something like that."

"I see," Kazuo had said, without particular appreciation. Yumi went on to pick out some more vegetables into her bowl.

After eating in silence for another minute or two, Kazuo had asked again, "So I was wondering, why are manhole lids round?"

Yumi blinked and looked at her son's face through the inviting steam from the *nabe*. He was still looking at nothing in particular, now poking at the food in his bowl with his chopsticks. She had not been able to detect any irony or irritation in his voice.

"Well, so you see, if a lid is square, for example," Yumi said, drawing a shape in the air with her chopsticks, "and if the lid for some reason came down not horizontally but tilted"—she tilted her palm to illustrate—"then because the diagonal opening of the hole would be longer than the width of the lid at this angle, it could fall through. Whereas with a circle, the widest part of the opening, the diameter, is always the same as the diameter of the lid, whichever way you turn it, so it can never fall through. Right?"

"Uh-huh," Kazuo said.

"Is something wrong?"

He continued to poke at the now mushy food in his bowl. Then Kazuo's eyes started to swim a little, as if searching for something to focus on. And as he repeated his question for the third time, his eyes settled straight on Yumi's face, and he was finally there, looking at her. He finished his sentence and sat there blinking, as if he had suddenly come out into the light.

"But Kazuo, you just asked me the same question three times." Yumi placed her chopsticks down in quiet alarm.

"So it turns out that he didn't remember anything about the two or three hours leading up to that," Yumi said to Shinji now, pouring more tea into his cup.

"Thank you," he said. "The cake is delicious, by the way."

Yumi gave him a smile that took over one side of her face slightly more than the other, then got up to boil more water. The warm smell from years of cooking, both sweet and savory, seemed to have seeped into the walls of their house. Sitting in the midst of it, Shinji felt comforted by this mark of domestic life.

"He didn't remember coming home or changing his clothes or eating," Yumi went on, talking over the kitchen counter. "And the more I tried to make sense of it, the more upset he got. I called Akio and made him come home early, but in the meantime Kazuo fell asleep on that couch over there. When we tried to wake him up, he wouldn't budge. Boy, that was scary. We took him to the emergency room, but we couldn't really explain what had happened, and he slept for three days straight at the hospital. Just slept."

"Did they find out what it was?"

"Not really," Yumi said and slipped back into her chair. "At least, they found nothing physical. We were worried that he had been hit in the head or something—bullying at school, hit-and-run, you never know these days—but nothing. They said there was no trace of injury, and he was in perfect health. There was no reason he shouldn't be awake."

Then, she said, he'd woken up on the fourth day as if nothing was wrong; he ate up the whole hospital meal and, after a few more tests, was released the same afternoon. He'd seemed fine, but he couldn't remember those few hours leading up to the manhole question.

"The doctors thought it could have been a short-term memory loss called temporary amnesia—or is it transient amnesia?—that has something to do with the hippocampus. They said it's something very rare for a young person, but not unprecedented. But have you ever heard of such a thing?"

"No, I don't think so," Shinji said. "But I have to say it's kind of fascinating."

"Fascinating, yes," Yumi said and poured more tea into Shinji's cup. "But you don't want your child to have anything to do with such a thing."

"Of course. Sorry."

Yumi smiled and gave a dismissive wave of hand. "Anyway, thankfully that was the end of that mysterious incident, and everything seems to be fine since, so no worries."

"Well I'm glad to hear that." Shinji meant it because he hadn't planned to impose himself in the middle of a complicated family situation.

Later in the afternoon, Shinji went to meet Kazuo at his school. Kazuo was walking across the schoolyard with a small group of lively boys, but he wordlessly separated from them to come and meet Shinji at the gate. The group kept on without taking note of his departure. It was difficult to tell if he was actually part of the group or if he had just happened to be following it.

"So you had a fight with your wife?" Kazuo said, once he and Shinji had sat down next to each other on the soft, grassy slope of the riverbank near the school. The wide river flowed at a leisurely pace in front of them, and its smooth surface looked silvery in spite of the clear sky it reflected.

"Who told you that?" Shinji said.

Kazuo shrugged and squinted at the sun. "My dad, I guess."

"Hm."

"He didn't tell me, exactly, but I heard him talking to Mom," Kazuo said and pulled at some grass near his right foot. "Is that why you are staying with us?"

A sweet scent wafted from the ripped grass and made Shinji wonder when he had last sat on the ground like this. On the other side of the river, a little downstream, cherry blossoms along the path had just passed full bloom. Shinji could see some young mothers pushing their bicycles with small children on the rear basket seats. On the baseball field to the left, kids were practicing batting, and once in a while a nice, crisp sound of the ball meeting a metal bat would ring through the air.

"Well," Shinji said, "long story short, I guess that's it."

"What's the long story?"

"What?"

"You said, 'long story short.' What's the long story?"

Kazuo was mindlessly ripping at the grass. He was short for his age, and his oversized school uniform seemed to assert more presence than the body inside. There was a softness to him that didn't have much to do with his physicality. His bangs were a little too long, hiding his eyes when he looked down.

It was Yumi who had suggested that Shinji go for a walk and meet her son. Shinji couldn't tell if she just wanted him out of the house for a while or if she was hoping for his perspective on Kazuo in light of what she had told him. Shinji hoped it was the former, as he wasn't good with kids Kazuo's age. Especially now. They seemed tactless and brutally honest, and yet he had no idea what went on in their heads.

When Shinji didn't respond to his question, Kazuo glanced at him sideways without fully turning his head.

"It's really boring," Shinji said. "You don't want to know."

Shinji had lost his job the week before. He had taught English grammar at a private cram school in Tokyo for seven years. The school took anyone from five-year-olds trying to get into prestigious private schools to high school seniors aiming for top universities. Shinji mostly taught those in between, which included kids Kazuo's age. Though he had never outgrown his discomfort with the pubescent kids, he liked the late hours that allowed him to take on freelance translation jobs on the side. That was what he had meant to do after college. He had once intended to become a specialist in film subtitling.

One afternoon, he had been called into the division manager's office. The HR manager was there as well. A student—or her mother, it was never made clear—had apparently accused him of sexual harassment. Right there in the manager's office, Shinji was presented with a retirement sum and an offer for impeccable recommendations on the condition that he leave quietly. "We're sure you understand," they said. "A scandal of this nature would be disastrous for our type of business." Shinji could guess who this student might have been: a girl who had had a blatant crush on him, one from whom he had done his best to keep a polite distance. She wore just enough makeup not to be called out, curling her long lashes and constantly reapplying her lip gloss. She kept her skirt short and frequently stayed behind after class to ask questions. It was a completely groundless accusation, but the manager didn't even attempt to confirm its veracity with him. Shinji sensed this wasn't really just about the accusation and understood the futility of defending himself. So he took the offer and left.

In truth, he was ready to go. It was a ridiculous place anyway, and he had felt increasingly alienated from its aggressive culture. In recent years the school, struggling to keep its competitive edge, had started making younger instructors practice enthusiastic, scripted lectures in front of a camera in empty classrooms. They had vigorous training camps. There was a lot of competition among the teachers under the performance-based salary. Penalties were posted openly in the teachers' lounge. Shinji had been doing okay number-wise, but he'd quietly evaded all the absurd trainings, retreats and drinking that went with them. Maybe he had stepped on someone's toes. The retirement money wasn't insignificant, and he still had his translation jobs. He'd decided to lie low for a while.

But to his amazement, his wife had been skeptical.

"With a fifteen-year-old?" she'd said. She had been surprised to find him in the apartment when she'd come home from work. "That's clearly underage, an obvious crime, isn't it? Was it even legal for the school to handle it internally?"

"What are you talking about?" Shinji said, standing beside the kitchen counter in his apron. He had been cooking when his wife had come home. "I can't believe that's what you are concerned about. I told you, it's totally bogus, it's groundless. My point wasn't even that."

"You're sure it was groundless?"

"Excuse me?"

"I don't know—these things are really complicated. The subjective experiences of victims and offenders often don't match up. I'm just saying."

Shinji stared at his wife. She was half reclined on the couch, still in her well-tailored suit. She looked smart and professional but tired.

"What are you accusing me of?" Shinji said. "You are the one who's actually had an affair. With someone much younger. Your subordinate. That's textbook sexual harassment right there."

"But it's the criminality," she said. She sounded like a teacher dealing with a slow student. "Mine was consensual."

"What criminality?" Shinji took an indignant step forward, but then heard the pot boil over and hurried back to the stove. He was boiling water for pasta. The savory aroma of salmon slowly cooking in the oven permeated the apartment. He had a bottle of white wine cooling in the fridge. "Of course it wasn't consensual. I'm the one who didn't consent."

"Then why did you give in so easily? It's such a dishonorable accusation. You could have sued."

"You know, I was happy to leave that job," he said, releasing some linguine into the boiling water. "It wasn't something worth going through a legal nightmare for. And of course they knew I wouldn't fight them. Why would they make such a ridiculous accusation otherwise?"

"They knew you well."

"What's that supposed to mean?" He came back out around the kitchen counter. "Just think about what you are saying. You did have an affair, you screwed this coworker, and I forgave you. We put that behind us. And you are accusing me of what? Something that never even happened."

"Forgave me," his wife said. She had her elbow on the back of the couch. She looked strangely relaxed. "Why do we even talk about forgiving? Who's in the position to forgive?"

"We are married," Shinji said. "Aren't we in the position to forgive each other, if anyone is? And to stand by each other in a moment of hardship like this?" He paused. "What am I even talking about? I didn't *do* anything."

"I didn't ask you to forgive me," she said.

"What?"

"You probably shouldn't have forgiven me so easily."

Shinji stood there. The familiar apartment seemed foreign, as if someone had moved each piece of furniture just by a couple of centimeters this way or that.

"I'm still seeing him," his wife said.

The kitchen was getting hot from the oven. A burned smell was starting to replace the savory aroma. Shinji realized he had forgotten to set the timer for the pasta. He hated overcooked pasta. But he couldn't move.

"Why are you telling me this now?" he said.

"I just wanted to be truthful." His wife remained in the relaxed posture. But then she pinched the corners of her eyes with her fingers for a good three seconds, and the gesture made her look older than her age.

"Why are you suddenly being truthful at this particular moment? Couldn't you keep it to yourself? I mean, at least for now. Until we got through this crisis?"

"I thought it would only make things worse if I waited," she said. "The whole thing would get drawn out, and there would be more hard feelings in the end. It's better that we deal with all these things at once. Maybe it's all for the best."

"Wow," Shinji said.

"Besides, this is not really my crisis."

"Wow," he said.

Since the apartment belonged to his wife, Shinji had to find a place to sleep that night. She repeatedly said there was no need, but of course there was. He quickly packed his small overnight bag and left. Later he remembered he had not bothered to turn off the stove or the oven.

"What's she like?" Kazuo was asking on the riverbank. "Your wife?"

Shinji thought about it for a moment. He no longer knew. "God, you just ask these questions." He tugged at some grass. The stalks were tougher than he'd thought, and he couldn't pull any off at first try. "Let's see. She's the kind of person who at a restaurant orders a huge sandwich, picks it apart, eats bits and pieces of things between the bread and, leaving most of it uneaten and dissected, absentmindedly pokes at the remaining food mash on the plate with her fork for the rest of the dinner, while talking."

Kazuo kept looking downstream for a second, but then he turned to Shinji and raised his half-hidden eyebrows.

"I know. That was mean." Shinji sighed. "No, she's very smart. Intelligent. She's pretty. She works out and stays in shape. She makes more money than I do. Or did. She has a great sense of humor when she chooses to. She has lots of interesting friends. I guess she's just a better person than I am. I don't know."

"So are you getting divorced?"

"Jeez, is that what your parents said, too?"

"No. I'm just asking."

"Well don't talk about such disturbing things," Shinji said. "I don't know yet."

Akio owned a small printing business in town, and Yumi said he was rarely home. Shinji didn't see him until Wednesday morning, just as Akio was leaving for work.

"Oh, you're here, good," Akio said when Shinji found him putting his shoes on at the entrance. "Sorry, but I have to run. Make yourself at home."

"Man, you must be busy," Shinji said. "I never even hear you come home at night."

"Well, can't complain in this economy. It's a blessing to be busy." Akio smiled, and wrinkles softly gathered at the outside corners of his friendly eyes. "Stay as long as you like. We have plenty of space."

"Thanks. I really appreciate it," Shinji said.

"You're unemployed or freelancing or something, right?" Akio said. "In a way, it's a luxury that you don't have to be in any one place."

Shinji didn't know what to say to this, so he just nodded.

"Ask Yumi how to get around. Movie theaters and such, you know. Well, then." And with a little wave of hand, he was out the door.

"He just loves what he does," Yumi said later, when Shinji told her about the exchange. "I don't think he even thinks of it as work. It's like playing with a toy, always experimenting with new techniques."

From the kitchen table Shinji watched her come and go in her green indoor slippers, watering the plants and picking up misplaced items. There was something fluid about the way she went about her tasks. Their house was never immaculate, but it was kept at a comfortable level of clean untidiness. Observing Yumi's movement, he realized that she was fit and maintained a shapely figure. Her round eyes curving down at their corners, together with her full cheeks, had given him the impression that she was much softer and plumper than she really was. He found himself enjoying this discovery.

"But don't you sometimes wish he was around more?" Shinji said. "Hasn't it ever been difficult for you?"

"Oh, please, it's not like we are newlyweds." She laughed. "We make do with what we have." But then she halted in front of the table and rested a hand on the back of an empty chair. "Are you thinking about your own situation?"

Shinji looked up and was met by her gentle, lopsided smile.

"You are wondering if it would have made any difference in your case?" she said.

He blinked. "How did you know?" he said.

"It's the wisdom of age," Yumi said, and winked with both her eyes. That is, although she blinked both eyes, Shinji could tell it was meant to be a wink. "Just give it some time," she said. "Come help me with the plants in the back. I've been wanting to move those heavy pots around for ages."

"What do you think is the meaning of life?" Kazuo said as he carefully peeled the asparagus stalks. "Do you think there is a meaning?"

He and Shinji stood together in Yumi's kitchen, preparing dinner in her place because she had an unexpectedly late meeting at the cultural center. People arranged their kitchens differently, and using someone else's would normally pose a slight inconvenience even if it were well organized. You would have to look for the measuring spoons or spices, inspecting each drawer and cabinet before finding them, for example, in the fridge. Even in his own kitchen, Shinji was often frustrated when his wife "misplaced" items according to her own logic. But Yumi's kitchen was extremely functional, and he felt right at home moving around in it.

"It depends on what kind of meaning you have in mind," Shinji said. "I tend to think there is no particular meaning, so I don't look for one."

Shinji was chopping off bits of vegetables to make the soup base for risotto. Kazuo had volunteered to help and obediently followed his instructions. Shinji could see it fascinated Kazuo that they got to mess with his mother's domain.

"Not that you should listen to my silly opinion," Shinji said a little later. "I don't quite have what you would call a respectable life. Do you discuss these things with your parents?"

"No. Not really." Under Kazuo's careful labor, the asparagus stalks shed their fibrous skin. He inspected each of them before placing it neatly in the skillet. "Do things get easier when you get older?"

"Easier?" Shinji put the vegetable bits into a pot of water and turned the heat on. "That also depends on what you mean by 'easier.' From my personal experience, as many things get easier as get harder."

Kazuo sighed, and put the final asparagus in the skillet. "Now what?"

"Pour the water just enough to cover them, and put the lid on."

"I meant like dealing with friends and worrying about, you know, things." Kazuo wiped his hands on the towel and stepped back.

"Well, I would never want to be a junior high student again, so you can take that to mean things get better after that. I think relationships at your age are generally excruciating." Shinji chopped up some mushrooms and then took an onion from a basket. "Is there anything you want to be?"

"I don't know," Kazuo said. "I'm kind of interested in geography. I think."

"Yeah? Good. That's more than I ever knew at your age."

Leaning on the column at the kitchen entrance, Kazuo scratched his ankle with socked toes. "When you look at a map, you see all the roads and city blocks laid out, right?"

"Right."

"And all the man-made things like streets and bridges and canals were planned by someone at some point, intentionally, right?"

"Right." Having finished with all the chopping, Shinji placed a saucepan on the stove. "You can turn on the stove for the asparagus, too. See, like this."

"Okay," Kazuo said. "But when a city or town develops over a long period of time, it doesn't only expand outward, but things get changed, right? Like new layers rewriting parts of the old layers, but not completely? So maybe sometimes things get left out. Like underneath where highways and train tracks intersect or where a street gets cut off on both ends. Places no one ever visits or thinks about anymore. I think about these spaces that weren't in anyone's plan."

Shinji glanced at the boy. He heated some olive oil in the saucepan and started cooking the risotto. That familiar smell of garlic and onion wafted off the pan and filled the kitchen. "Well," he said, "so maybe you are interested in something like urban planning? You want to plan out city streets and public spaces and stuff like that?"

"I don't know. I don't think so. I don't think I want to build anything."

"Oh."

"I'm just curious about these unintended places."

"Huh," Shinji said. "What about your dad's job?" He wasn't sure how much longer he could keep up his end of the conversation. "Does he want you to go into printing? Take over the family business? You can turn off the stove and dump the water now."

"I don't know much about Dad's work," Kazuo said, following the instruction. "He's always off in his own world. We don't really talk much. When I was small we'd hang out a little more. You know, like playing catch."

"You want to play catch? Shall we?"

"I didn't mean it literally. I'm not good at sports, anyway."

"Oh. Good. I'm not good at throwing and stuff, either."

There was a sound of the front door unlocking, and Yumi sang out, "I'm home!"

Shinji was more relieved than he thought he would be. "Here, let's roll the asparagus with prosciutto."

They started on their last project. The risotto was just about *al dente*, and the dinner was almost ready. It was nice to cook for somebody. The meaning of life, Shinji thought, could be something as simple and small as being able to cook for someone else.

Despite the clumsiness Shinji felt with Kazuo, Yumi seemed to appreciate his presence at their house. It was great to have company, she kept saying, especially for meals.

"I'm really sorry to burden you," Shinji said one afternoon. "I promise it won't be too much longer. I just need to get my bearings."

They were both doing some work on their laptops in the living room, Yumi making the handouts for her next class and Shinji working on a new translation job. The monotonous sound of the raindrops outside seemed to make the colorless scenery even flatter. But it made the warmly lit indoor space all the more cozy.

"Are you kidding me? You cook, you do the dishes, you lift heavy things, you hang out with my teenaged son—oh, you're such a burden." She laughed but then put her folded arms on the coffee table and leaned over a little. "I'm very glad you are here. Especially for Kazuo. With him being so quiet these days, I can never be sure if it's just the age thing or if there's something we should be worried about. I'm glad he's taken to you."

Shinji felt awkward about this assessment. "I don't know if you can say he's taken to me, but . . ." He saw Yumi's expectant eyes. "I mean, I think he's a great kid. A smart kid. A lot seems to be going on in his head, for sure."

Yumi smiled, satisfied. "Really, take your time. Don't rush." She reached over and squeezed his wrist. Her hand was surprisingly soft and cool on his skin. "Akio says so, too."

"Shinji-kun, shall we go out for lunch?" Akio said.

It was late Saturday morning, and the two of them were reading at the kitchen table. Yumi had gone out already to prepare for her class, and Kazuo hadn't come downstairs yet. It was apparently a rare occasion that Akio was home on a Saturday; he and Shinji were sitting down together for the first time. Outside the window, the light rain from the day before was still moistening the trees.

"What's that?" Shinji put down the international section he was reading and looked up.

"There's this coffee shop that serves great lunch food. Especially curry. Would you like to go?" Akio said. "Two or three days ago I suddenly had a craving for curry. Don't you get that sometimes? It's almost lunchtime, too."

Shinji stroked his stubbly face with his palm. He was still in his pajamas. Akio, on the other hand, was already dressed and clean-shaven. He looked like the kind of person who wouldn't do anything before he had made himself presentable, even if he had nowhere in particular to go.

"Sure. Let me go get ready, then," Shinji said. "What about Kazuo-kun?"

"Hmm, I wonder," Akio said. He went back to reading his newspaper, but when he realized that Shinji was still looking at him, he got up and walked off toward the staircase. "Hey, Kazuo," he called upstairs without going up, "Kazuo, are you awake?"

"What?" Kazuo's voice replied from above.

"We're going out for lunch. Do you want to come along?"

There was a bit of silence, and then Kazuo said, "I'd go if it's ramen."

"I don't think they have ramen. It's a coffee shop. They'd probably have pasta, though."

"Okay," Kazuo called down.

"So are you coming?"

"All right."

Akio came back to the kitchen and settled into his chair.

"I guess he's coming." He picked up the papers but then put them down on the table again. "The thing is, actually, I was sort of thinking we could go out and have a little chat, you and I. Since we hadn't had a chance yet."

"Oh, sorry," Shinji said. "You should have just told me."

Akio smiled and shrugged. Shinji thought there was something charming about this gesture. "No, you're right, he should come. It'll be good, the three of us together," said Akio.

The coffee shop was old, but it was filled with abundant natural light. The front portion of the store was a bakery, and the sweet, buttery smell permeated the modest space. Behind the counter a small, elderly woman stood by herself, wearing an apron with pink vertical stripes. On a small display table sat a few dishes with plastic wraps over them, indicating the day's lunch menu. There were only a few tables and chairs set up along the windows in the back, and a young couple with a little girl was having their lunch at one of them.

"You'd think they can't possibly be good, right?" Akio said, pointing at the sloppy, not particularly hygienic display. "But you'd be pleasantly surprised. Their food is amazing. Especially curry."

When the three of them sat down at one of the empty tables, the same old lady came out from behind the counter to take their order. After hearing Akio praise it repeatedly, Shinji had to order the curry as well. Kazuo made it known that he still wanted ramen but settled for spaghetti *carbonara*.

Even with his raised expectations, the food was delicious. But Shinji felt awkward sitting with the father and the son as they ate quietly. Akio repeatedly made an admiring sound in his throat and shook his spoon at his curry but didn't elaborate on his thoughts, so it never developed into a conversation. Kazuo kept his head down, his bangs hiding his eyes. He bounced his knee under the table nonstop. Shinji thought about asking Akio some printing-related questions, but he wasn't interested enough and didn't know what to ask. He found himself looking forward to dinnertime, when Yumi would be home, leading the conversation.

Halfway through the meal, Akio's phone rang, and he flipped it open after a glance at the caller ID. "Hello? Yes, so you got it? You're sure you can open the file this time? Okay, start rendering. I'll head over now." Akio stood up, pulling out his wallet from his back pocket.

"Work?" Shinji said.

"Yeah. Sorry, I have to run." He placed a few folded bills on the table, then put his hand on Kazuo's head and patted a couple of times. "Take your time. Their pastries are great, too."

Akio went out the door, and the bell attached to it tinkled in his absence. Kazuo fixed his hair where his father had apparently mussed it up, turning it back into an intentional mess. Classical music was playing at a low volume. The young family had left a while ago, and Shinji and Kazuo were the only customers in the store. Kazuo finished his *carbonara* and went on to work on his father's half-eaten curry. Shinji wondered where in his small body all the food went. It was so calm that the clinking of cups and dishes as the old lady rinsed them in the sink started to sound hypnotic. Shinji wished he had brought the papers with him.

"You know, I actually know a place like that," Kazuo said, as though picking up a conversation where it had been left off. He was still chewing, but he had his elbows on the table now, resting his cheeks in his palms. His voice came out muffled.

"What's that?"

"The kind of place I told you about. Near my school."

"What do you mean? What kind of place?"

"One of those unintended places. Don't you remember? The spaces that weren't planned?"

Shinji thought about it for a second. "Right."

"I go there sometimes," Kazuo said. Without changing his posture, he looked at Shinji, searching his face. "And sometimes, I leave things there."

"Like what?"

"Just things. I don't know." He slurped up the soda at the bottom of his glass with a straw. "Do you want me to show you the place?"

They reached a street with heavy traffic and walked along the narrow sidewalk for a while in single file. Then the sidewalk ended abruptly.

"Hey, should we be walking here?" Shinji called out to Kazuo's back a few paces ahead. "Isn't it dangerous?"

Kazuo kept on walking. The two-lane traffic became heavier as they went, and under an overpass even the shoulder disappeared. They had to walk almost brushing against the damp concrete wall. Several cars honked as they sped past. Just on the other side of the overpass, there was a small public playground. Kazuo went in, and Shinji followed, glad to get off the road.

The stench met him immediately. Almost completely in the shade of the highway overpass, the air of the park smelled musty. And there was an assertive undercurrent of something chemical mixed with the bitter-sour fume of a garbage dump. The last time Shinji had smelled something similar was when he was in kindergarten and visited his grandparents. There had still existed near them an open sewage canal where a local factory dumped its wastewater.

It was an oddly shaped piece of land. The busy road and the tall wall of the overpass formed its two sides, and a long chain-link fence cut across diagonally to close off the triangle. On the other side of the fence was a gray, windowless building that looked like a factory. Although the basic amenities such as a swing set, a jungle gym with a slide and a sandbox indicated that this was a playground, everything looked dejected. Here and there some bright yellow and red paint chips clung to the rusted structures.

Kazuo walked to the far end of the playground and turned to Shinji with his fingers hooked on the fence. Shinji went over and stood next to him. There was a deep trench between the fence and the factory grounds, and its bottom was covered with trash of all kinds, soaked in foul-smelling liquid.

"So this is it," Kazuo said.

"Wow," Shinji said. "It stinks."

It was as if all the trash people had ever littered in this town had ended up here. There were plastic bottles, diapers, broken umbrellas and food packaging. Disintegrating plastic bags clung to other objects like tattered rags, making it hard to tell what the objects were. There was something that looked like a bicycle frame, and Shinji saw a leg of a chair sticking up. Underneath the busy road was a barrel-sized opening from which the murky water trickled out into the trench, but there was no indication of how these objects might have ended up down there. It was arguably the least suitable location for a playground Shinji could think of.

"You said you come here often?" Shinji said.

"Just sometimes."

"Why?"

"I don't know. I just do," Kazuo said and pulled at the fence a couple of times. "I guess I'm interested in this kind of place. Like, conceptually."

"Man, you know difficult words."

Kazuo rolled his eyes. "I'm almost fourteen."

"Right, right. Sorry."

"Anyway, like I said, I sometimes leave things here," Kazuo said. "I thought you could use a place like this, too."

"What, like throw a piece of trash in there?" Shinji said. "Is that what you do?"

"Of course not," Kazuo said. "It's conceptual. You know, you can leave things, like, behind. Because no one cares. No one wants to think about a place like this. It basically doesn't exist in anyone's mind, so whatever you leave here doesn't exist, either."

"Okay."

A plane flew across the sky overhead, trailing an unusually loud, roaring engine noise. When Shinji looked up, the plane itself was far-off and tiny, and it seemed ill-matched to the sound it made.

"I just want to ask," Shinji said, looking at Kazuo again. "You're not saying that this has anything to do with that memory incident of yours, are you?"

They stared at each other for a second. Shinji could actually see Kazuo's eyes from that angle. They were round and turned down slightly at their edges, like his mother's. Suddenly becoming aware of the silliness of it all, Shinji shook his head. Why was he playing along with Kazuo's make-believe?

"Well, okay. What have you got that you'd want to leave behind?" Shinji said. "For god's sake, you're thirteen. Do you have problems at school? Do you want to talk about it?"

"You don't have to be middle-aged to have problems, you know," Kazuo said.

"Well, sure. Thanks. It's just that—man, you were just born around the time I met my wife."

"And you two have problems, don't you? I've been alive the same amount of time."

Shinji thought about it. "I guess you're right," he said. "But you're just not my idea of a troubled youth, you know? You have a great mom and dad who care about you, who seem to understand each other so well. I almost wish I had a family like yours."

"Please don't sleep with Mom," Kazuo said.

"Excuse me?"

"You're sad because you had a fight with your wife. You can leave that here."

"What are you—"

"My mom sometimes goes out with these younger men. I've seen them," Kazuo said. He spoke straight into the fence and the ditch beyond. "Because Dad can't sleep with her anymore. It's what they've worked out."

Shinji stood there, one hand on the fence.

"They think I don't know these things because I'm thirteen," Kazuo said. "But it's really screwed up, and I don't think you should sleep with her." He looked at Shinji. "I think you are a good person."

A small truck honked at a car slowing down in front of it, and a flock of sparrows took off from the overgrown bushes.

"Kazuo-kun," Shinji said, but then had to lick his lips. He must have had his mouth open, and now it was dry. He could taste the foul air on his tongue. "I'd never in a million years even imagine such a thing." But then he wondered if he sounded convincing even to himself.

Kazuo relaxed his shoulder and let out a small sigh. A smile formed just on the edges of his mouth. "I have to run," he said. "I have a piano lesson."

Without waiting for a reply, Kazuo walked away from the fence. Shinji, left standing in the stench, watched his cousin's son disappear under the overpass. He seemed so small. He wondered if this was Kazuo's act of leaving; if he, Shinji, was the thing being left behind.

On Sunday morning Shinji went downstairs and found the kitchen and the living room empty. He had never been the first to come down, and he felt like an intruder moving around in the quiet house. The curtains were drawn, shutting out the sunny day outside, and the dim, empty rooms looked as if they were holding their breaths. He made some coffee in the large coffee maker, but he wasn't sure if he'd used the right amount of grounds. Being used to making coffee just for himself, he always messed up when he tried to make a larger amount. While it brewed, he went to the front door to retrieve the newspapers and brought them back to the kitchen table.

He opened the curtains, and the sunlight spilled onto the floor, making the different textures of the wood flooring and the carpeted areas flat and uniform. A bird kept chirping right outside the window in regulated sets of three high chirps, then three counts of rest. It was so regular that after a while it started to sound like a truck backing up. Shinji felt a little sorry for the lone bird, who called and called without being answered.

As he sat trying to read the papers, Shinji wondered what he might say to Yumi when they found themselves alone at the kitchen table. Before coming downstairs, he had packed his overnight bag again. He couldn't be sure whether he really hoped for an opportunity to be alone with her. Because what could he say, really? That he was leaving because they might sleep together?

But it was Kazuo who came down after an hour, still in pajamas, hair pressed up on the side where his head had been against the pillow.

"Morning," he said and lifted his palm toward Shinji.

"Good morning." Shinji lifted his in response.

Kazuo walked over to the TV in the living room, rubbing his eyes. He set up his video game right in front of the large screen and started playing an elaborate shooting game, with 3-D graphics that moved seamlessly. The volume was turned low, and the image of Kazuo sitting quietly on the carpeted floor in the morning sun, shooting down the realistic-looking zombies, was oddly peaceful.

A few minutes later Akio came down, as if drawn out of bed by the electromagnetic wave of Kazuo's game.

"Morning," he said to Shinji and poured some coffee for himself. He sipped at it and grimaced a little. It had come out a bit too strong. Akio was also in his pajamas today, and his hair was flattened almost at the exact same spot as his son's. He went over to Kazuo with his coffee.

"That's too close. How can you see? Let's bring it back here so we can sit on the couch."

They reconfigured the machine and the cords, settled onto the couch side by side and started to play a racing game. They played together quietly, both absorbed in the computer-graphics world on the TV screen. Their matching bedheads sometimes bobbed with a slight time lag as they manipulated tight curves and involuntarily tilted their bodies. Watching the pair, Shinji felt he belonged to a generation that had been accidentally skipped over. The bird outside chirped an irregular set of two and then stopped.

Lastly Yumi came down, already dressed and with her light makeup on.

"Good morning!" She flip-flopped into the kitchen with her green slippers, and the house came to life. The water ran in the sink, the fridge door opened and closed, pots and pans clattered. There was chopping on the cutting board, ticking of the toaster and sizzling on the skillet. The downstairs was no longer the same, quietly sulking space Shinji had found earlier in the morning. The life of this family took over, and the space that contained it receded into the background to play the supporting role.

"Breakfast is ready!" Yumi called out half an hour later toward the living room. She set out on the table the plates of omelets and toast, bowls of cereals and yogurt, glasses of juice and milk, butter and jam and, finally, the utensils. The father and son didn't budge.

"Come on, guys, eat while they are hot!"

"Just a minute," Akio called back, without taking his eyes off the screen.

"We're about to finish this level," Kazuo said.

Yumi sighed theatrically, but she was already in her chair. She passed the butter to Shinji and winked with both eyes. "There's nothing to be done with those two," she said. "We'll just go ahead."

He could see traces of faint lines at the corners of her eyes, which would only solidly materialize when she smiled her full smile. He suddenly felt the oncoming loss, although nothing in this picture was his to lose.

Shinji bit into the thick toast and let the buttery warmth spread in his mouth. The sky outside the window was so clear and so uniformly blue that it almost looked fake. The potted flowers on the windowsill were bright and fragrant. Together they seemed to be conspiring for the impression that the world was completely peaceful, that everything was just as intended and would stay that way.

The blood was the mountain and the mountain was the bear

Rachel Yoder

Eliot had wanted to hike in deep, but the trails were all closed that day, and clouds were blowing in fast from the west, whole countries of weather that slid over Whitefish and roiled there in the sky. Even the mountains felt small.

He was hungry. It had been weeks of beef jerky and trail mix from the panniers on his bicycle. His legs had stretched out taut and ropy from the miles of pedaling through the Montana mountains, and then the early spring prairies filled with pink flowers, past a river jammed with logs, on that stretch of road where it seemed as though his bike would nose up from the pavement and fly him over the meadows and mountains and, further south, to the red soil of the canyon lands. He carried with him a pinecone big as his foot and a smooth white rock he'd pried from the mud at the edge of a clear lake. He carried with him the space of big sky country. He had taken it into his body. But come Whitefish, come the national park signs and printed regulations and asphalt, come the ponderosas spiking up into the expanse of blue, he had, against his will, shrunk back down to the size of a common man. By the time he reached Osha on the porch of the visitors' center, he fit perfectly inside a familiar idea of himself.

"Can't believe you didn't read about it, hear someone talking, something," Osha had said as they stood there on the porch of the visitors' center looking out over the near-deserted parking lot. "Took the hand of one hiker and the thigh muscle of another. Protecting its cubs, they think. They got it today but still have to confirm it's the right one. A team is coming over from the university in Bozeman for the dissection."

"Can I see it?" Eliot asked. Osha laughed a little. He squinted at the sky.

"Yeah, but we should go now. Before they get here," he said. They walked around the building and then down the back stairs to a service road that cut through the trees and further back into the woods.

Eliot hadn't seen Osha in ten years, not since college. He'd only heard updates from time to time: Scandinavia at a Norse shipbuilding school. Traveling with sherpas to the Tibetan interior. A monthlong hike through the Chilean rainforest for a single day with some neural science guru. He ran the ecopsychology program now at the park, dressed in cleanly pressed government-issue beige-on-green.

"Never thought I'd see you in a uniform," Eliot said.

"Right?" Osha said, laughing and touching the metal on his chest. "I get a badge."

Eliot tried to run his hand through his hair, which had clumped in dark, greasy hanks. Stubble sanded his neck and sunken cheeks, and it was almost as if he could feel his skin wrapping around the contours of his ribs and the ropes of sinew running through his legs. As if he'd been shrink-wrapped. As if all the air was being sucked from him by an invisible machine. He could smell himself. He knew there was an insanity to the way he appeared. His thoughts that day had been of blood and damage.

"So you started in Idaho, man?" Osha asked. "How long have you been riding? And why? I mean, just for fun?"

Eliot made a laughing sound. They walked in silence, watching the long legs of light stretch between the boughs.

Before the bike trip, he'd been on vacation with Becca. Idaho, at his dad's cabin. A last go of things. One more honest attempt. Canoeing and long afternoon walks, lovemaking in and out of sleep, late breakfasts with small white cups of strong coffee and runny eggs. But it hadn't worked, hadn't even been meant to work if Eliot was being honest with himself. More like leave things on a high note. More like Eliot had been hopeful, but he just couldn't anymore.

She had gotten on a plane back to Arizona, silent as he hugged her in the airport. She wouldn't look at him and turned, stripping herself of her belongings, sliding her belt out of the loops with one hard pull. Her long hair swung blackly as she walked away.

He rode over a hundred miles that day and then stepped off his bike to feel his knees bend, muscles voided of strength. There was a soft give to the earth as he landed and stayed that way for some time, unable to rise.

"I've been planning it for a while, but then Becca and I broke up, and I extended it," Eliot said. He rubbed his palms over his eyes and felt the grease on his face. Osha leaned back and turned his face to the sky, letting out a ribbon of breath.

"What was it, ten years?"

"Eleven. Yeah."

Osha nodded. They walked in silence. The day was sunny but held an undertone of coldness left over from the long winter.

"I don't know where I'm going. I just know I'm headed south. Is that crazy?"

"It's good."

"Sure," Eliot said. The sounds of birds rang like bells far above them, and in the darkness beneath the trees, the way the clean light sliced and flickered in blinding lines held the feeling of water, of a cold church.

Osha unlocked the door and swung it wide for Eliot as he entered.

Eliot had ridden all the way out to the park because he wanted high, thin air, to hike up to the edge of a cliff and then have one of those moments where you find yourself stunned by what's spreading out for miles and miles all around. An unplanned moment. Proof of grace. He had needed to feel the acid burning in his muscles and to walk beyond it, to keep going until all that mattered was breath and a rhythmic thud, until his thoughts became soft and muted, summer clouds suspended far out at the horizon.

What he got, though, was a musty little outbuilding, fluorescent lights, a metal table pulled in from the staff kitchen, the pungent smell of hair and oil and something more, something sweet and rotten. A blue tarp barely covered the body.

Its hind paw slipped from beneath the tarp, and Eliot paused. The pads were callused and dirty and black like worn shoes. Its claws had the look of something prehistoric, something made more of rock and ore than of flesh and blood. This was a creature forged from the remains of other animals, from beaks and teeth and hides. It could not have not been born.

"So in Scandinavian folklore, they think people can turn into bears," Osha said, standing at the head of the covered pile, motioning to Eliot. He raised the tarp to show him the bear's face. "They used to have these ceremonies after a bear was killed where the fur was treated with herbs and oils and then given to warriors. It was supposed to make them able to chew through shields, stuff like that. That's all I can think about when I see something like this. Such a shame."

Eliot turned to the body as if in a dream. Its head rested on a pile of dirty towels seeping gore, the fading edges of which formed a pink corona around the animal's skull. A clean hole broke through the head just beneath the ear in layers of dark fur and bright bone and, further in, shades of red and gray and beige. The fur covered it, shiny and thick and soft like a toy. The bear looked nothing like the idea of a bear.

"Could you imagine if this were a person?" Osha said. "Imagine."

Eliot nodded. The claws. They could go straight in your arm and out the other side.

"It doesn't really seem . . ." Here Eliot paused. Could a mountain die? Could gold? "It doesn't really seem dead, in a way."

Osha looked at him, then took the tarp in silence and raised it higher to reveal the trunk of the animal.

"They'll cut into it and try to find the remains," Osha said. "But the body has to be under lock and key, you know, since there's such a demand for black-market gall bladders. Like any of us would do such a thing."

Black teats peeked through the fur. Eliot took a step back.

"What about the cubs?" he asked. Osha winced.

"They'll fend for themselves as best they can, I suppose. Worst-case scenario a male finds them and eats them. But that's worst case."

"Jesus," Eliot said, staring at the animal's coat, which shone almost red in the downing sun. The luxury of its colors and furs and snout and tongue all descended on Eliot at once, and quite suddenly it was as if the queen herself had been laid out here before him in her heavy pomp. It was the end of everything. The kingdom was set to storm, or at the very least turn dark and strange.

This. All this. And somewhere in Arizona, Becca was bleeding on a couch. "Pregnant," she had said in the message that morning as he held the grimy payphone receiver away from his face. He listened to their old answering machine play her voice with all the resonant emptiness of a woman calling from the bottom of a dark well. "Abortion" reverberated toward him, the sound waves almost visible. "Two pills and then it's done. Come now. I'm fucking serious."

Osha insisted he stay the night, but Eliot wouldn't.

"Beer," he said to Osha, who nodded.

"But before you go . . ." He motioned to the cluster of cabins set back in the woods as he locked the shed door. "I actually can't believe I still have it, this letter I wrote you when I was in India. I didn't have a mailing address—I think you had just moved or were going to, something. It's a *good* letter, man."

Of course he had an old letter. Osha of the late-night stories and wrinkled letters from around the world. Eliot waited outside as he rustled around in his cabin. Early-season birds called to each other. Through the trees, the cabin with the bear pulsed with a sickening gravity.

Osha emerged with an envelope in hand, striped blue and red around the edges.

"This," he said, holding it up in the air with one hand. "I've been carrying it for, what, six years? Not until this very moment was it supposed to reach you. That's how things work."

Eliot took the letter and grabbed his hand, pulling Osha to him and slapping his back.

"You are a goddamn hippie," he said. They laughed, and Eliot thanked him, thanked him for showing him the bear and thanks but he needed to go, he needed to be gone, and he went as quickly as his legs could manage, back to his bike and then pedaling on the hard asphalt, away from the park and the bear and out into the cold, clear air where he could finally breathe again. He had been holding his breath for what seemed a very long time so as not to awaken whatever it was that was sleeping, and now he breathed and pumped and breathed and breathed and breathed.

He was overcome by his hunger. Even though he couldn't afford it, he wanted a steak, purple rare, with cheap beer he could buy by the can. Back in Whitefish, he wound up at the Moosehead, where a jukebox played songs about sangria and perfection over and over again as he folded himself into a booth.

He ordered from a burnt blonde with a long braid down her back.

"Rare," he said.

A few minutes later she put a beer down in front of him.

"First one's free," she said without smiling, then turned and, as she walked away, moved her ass in a manner so as to suggest she knew he was watching.

He sat and he drank. Two dusty cowboys murmured at the bar as a young, freshly washed couple in expensive belts and ugly ergonomic shoes politely examined photos on the walls, then the cowboys and the longhorn skull behind the bar. They sat with their hands clasped in front of them on the table and held themselves in deliberate postures.

Somehow all this—the day and Becca and those clean, happy people—he blamed on his father. Actually, it wasn't the day exactly that he blamed on him, but what he would do next, go to Arizona and be with Becca, even though the bike trip and the distance had all been to finally get away from her, make the break, end the hulking thing that had been their relationship, a thing they had both counted on as being forever but which had finally turned heavy and dark.

He wasn't like his father. His father had left his mother with five kids and a teetering house at the ocean's edge in the cold and the wet of Washington-state winter. His father was a cliché, off with the legal secretary to leave Eliot, the youngest child, the only one to listen as his mother rambled to herself behind her bedroom door night after night. All the others were off at college or married. Eliot had been the mistake and remained the mistake, the awkward giraffe of a boy who watched silently as his mother folded and unfolded cloth napkins at the kitchen table for hours.

"Mom," he would try.

"I had no idea I'd be this busy," she would say.

He switched to whiskey. The steak tasted of blood and he ate.

Some places, people could really respect a piss shit of a mood on a man. Some places, a man could actually feel like a man instead of the memory of one, where the meat was cooked right, which was nearly not at all, and beer was cold and shitty and canned and you could open a door and walk outside and everything spread away from you like a beautiful goddamn kingdom.

When he was done, he pulled the crumpled letter from his pocket with a wave of nostalgia and warmth and brotherly love. He should have stayed at the park with Osha, should have stayed with him and shot the shit, played cards, listened to his stories about bear men. The light of the bar had turned golden, and the blonde moved silently among the tables, bending across the wide planks of wood to move a cloth slowly against the grain, her long braid rubbing against her back and falling over her shoulder in a choreography that made something deep in Eliot move and stretch.

Trails of blood pooled in the ring of his plate, swirling with grease. His focus sharpened and blurred, sharpened and blurred, until the blonde was there and smiling, can I take your plate? He wanted more whiskey, and she brought him one along with a tall glass of cold water. He looked down, and the letter was still in his hand.

Osha's longhand was elegant and faded, and Eliot blinked and then blinked again to focus on it. *Eliot,* he wrote. *I have to tell you what just happened.*

He said he was in India, on his way home after a year studying at a monastery. He had been on retreat, translating Sanskrit texts. He'd lost his confidence in the modern world, in the idea of personal agency, in technology, in free will and family. *I don't even know how to think about love*, he wrote. But the translating hadn't really worked. He was still miserable, way out in the western hills of India. *Cosmic darkness,* he scrawled at the bottom of the first page.

> *Over the mountain in the next valley, there was this tribe of wild monks and they were, you know, dirty and naked and had these unbelievable dreads. I never actually saw the monks, but I heard enough about them. They were devoted to overcoming disgust. That was their pursuit, to not be disgusted by anything, and they spent their whole lives doing this. The main way they practiced was by eating human flesh. Acolytes would walk for hundreds of miles to get there and be sacrificed. I saw a few of these guys walking past the monastery on the road that ran over the mountain.*

> *So I've been silent for three months and watching these guys walking to get sacrificed and trying to dig out from this feeling of being buried, and then I come to Delhi for a week before going home (tomorrow), and in the market tonight, with all these smells and the lights. How can I explain? There is no comfort there. And I'm walking back to this shitty room I've rented on a narrow, dark street—I'm sure I'm going to get killed—and I just happen to look down through a bright basement window. Inside there's a woman who's naked and bathing. She was washing her hair, I think, with her back turned to the window. I stop and stare at her, because it's the most beautiful thing I've seen in a year, in my whole life. She brought me back. This just happened moments ago.*

He lowered the letter to the table with an unsteady hand.

He'd caught a fish. It was in Idaho. A silver flash of scale and sunlight breaking through a cold stream. But it wasn't the fish. It was air becoming water then movement then scales then light. Alchemy, he had thought. And now he knew there was not some sort of separation, that estrangement was not essential. He could nearly touch this thought, so palpable and plain. He would never be able to explain it to anyone else.

He wondered if he was too drunk. He decided that he simply couldn't be. Everything was as it was, as it should be. And the blonde. He was certain she wanted to fuck him.

She watched him from behind the bar, drying pint glasses with a dirty towel.

"All good?" she asked, approaching the table to take his plate. "Another drink?"

"What are you doing tonight?" he said.

"Oh, you know." She glanced at the front door.

"I'm on a bike trip," he said. "A long one."

"Sounds fun," she said.

"My body is eating itself," Eliot said, clutching his hands to his chest. He meant this as a joke or banter, as lightness. "I can feel it eating everything away."

She shifted her weight to one hip and pointed again to his empty glass.

"You know, my friend, he used to live in India, and one night he saw this beautiful naked woman through a window, and it restored him. I mean, it was this miraculous experience. She was so beautiful." He held the letter out to her.

She tipped her head to one side. "You're saying your friend was leering at some naked chick through a window?"

"Well, yeah," he said, drawing the paper back to himself. "I mean, no."

She tilted her head back. She laughed.

"You don't *get* it," he said.

"Dave," she said, turning to the bartender, and it was over then.

Outside, he stared at the pay phone across the street with the wavering concentration of profound drunkenness. Chin tucked, breathing through his mouth, he swayed like a white aspen in a high wind. He could hear his mother. Not his fault—no one's fault, really—but definitely his responsibility. She had always been his responsibility.

And then he was on his bike. The air was cold and awoke in him another person. He tried to think but soon forgot the question. Soon all that mattered was speed and darkness. He pedaled blankly. At some point he became chilled and began shivering. He had to piss, so he did. It coursed hotly down his white legs.

It was late and the moon was nearly full when he stopped by a sloping tallgrass meadow. He bent in the ditch and vomited.

"Fuck," he said, running a hand through his oily hair.

The ride had not done him well, especially the last sobering leg of it, as Becca edged her way back into his mind, their final year together living in an Arizona hotel her father owned, an Old West place that perched on the very top of a mountain in a tiny, defunct mining town–turned–tourist trap. One narrow road wound through the galleries and knick-knack shops and biker bars crowded on the narrow, tilted skid of rock. Eliot had thought this would work. Becca could make her jewelry to sell to tourists and work part-time at the one diner in town, a precarious place built on a wedge of land.

It had started off fine, with Eliot driving down the steep switchbacks each day to any number of odd jobs, temporary construction or lawn care, whatever he could find, Becca making shimmering necklaces and coming home with a pocket full of tips. But soon enough, she couldn't leave the hotel without him.

"This is the kind of town you can fall off of," she had said, ripping at her nails and cuticles, her face wet from crying.

"Stop," he had said, putting his hands on hers to calm them. "Just stop."

The steep stairs, the supposedly haunted houses propped on the side of the mountain, the road that threatened long, arcing descents at every turn. It would be so easy to just keep your foot on the gas and launch, a slowly turning body against a wide swath of blue. She was in bed when he left in the morning, and she was in bed when he returned in the afternoon. The velvet curtains stayed drawn. She became the very idea of weight, a statue of a woman, something too heavy to live in such a high place.

"You need to imagine you're a cloud," he would tell her, stroking her head as she leaned into him. "A bird."

He was responsible. For the good days, the bad, and she did not disabuse him of this thought that yes, he was responsible, for everything, always. "Eliot, I mean it," she would say, pleading with him from bed, her hair mussed and T-shirt falling from one shoulder. Pleading don't go and stay and I'll make you breakfast, then jumping from bed and pulling eggs from the minifridge, turning the dial on the hot plate. Just stay with me and stay and stay. . . .

It all came back to him with a moment of thought, a moment of lapsed discipline, and then he could feel the pall of it enshroud him. He loved her.

The light from the moon cut deep shadows in the ground around him. He pitched his small tent there in the grasses and, inside, sipped water from a bottle that smelled of citrus. He had no strength.

On the ground he turned and turned and fought his way into a restless, half-drunk sleep. In the twilight between the night outside himself and the night within, a picture materialized of a pale acolyte, barefoot, walking a dusty road through green hills that rolled and extended inside a lushness that made him want to cry out. He understood the desire, pulsing and horrible, a near-sexual urge to be consumed for the sake of something outside yourself, for this wisp of color and light. Against the darkness of half sleep, the wisp moved like breath.

When he finally fell away, he dreamed he was riding his bike back and forth between two distant dark canyons. He kept leaving behind his food, and he'd have to turn around to go get it only to realize it was ahead of him, so he'd turn back around and try again. All the while he felt his body shrinking and worried he would become desiccated before he ever found something to eat. He pedaled harder, but the shrinking only sped up. And then his mother was serving him oatmeal with no taste in a chipped bowl, and he was back in the cliff-top house in Washington, and she told him about the placenta that came out after him. It looked like a tree, she said. It was thick and deep red, laced through with veins. She held both her hands up in front of his face with her fingers spread: a tree, Eliot. A beautiful tree.

He awoke cold, in the deepest part of the night. He watched his breath billow in the full-moon light filtering through the thin tent, trying to will the urge away. His head was thick and eyes smeared with the dregs of drink. He felt his way to the tent opening, crawled out with his eyes closed, a hard thunder of pain swelling in his head. He stood and pressed his palms to his temples. Gently, he opened his eyes, then froze with the ice of adrenaline.

There, so close he could see its filmy breath, an elk, steaming in the moonlight, its black eyes reflecting lakes of mirrored ice. It stood even stiller than the night around it. A calf moved between its legs, bucking its head against the underbelly.

In the meadow behind it, an entire herd, lit with the light of the full moon in a tableau otherworldly and terrifying, so beautiful for its strangeness he wondered if it was possible this was some hallucination: a message or a sign. The hundred elk had been feeding, all of them now perfectly still in the sloping meadow. A massive bull stood at the edge of the herd, his rack spread above his head like giant hands. His skin rippled, and the muscles between his front legs tensed.

But it was the mother that made the wave of cold roll through Eliot. Beads of sweat bloomed on his forehead and lip. He'd heard stories of springtime mothers charging and trampling men trying to take photographs, brash men who had edged too close without understanding the danger.

He did not move, nor did the mother. The calf suckled beneath it, nosing its face into the musky warmth there, then turning to look at him. He could see the foggy breath of the beast moving around its nostrils, could see the contained chaos in its eyes, its head turned just so, ready to run at him, or away.

But it wasn't the mother. It was the bull. The animal took off in a moment so swift and wild it was as if the entire world around Eliot was pulled up by the roots and launched into the sky. The herd lumbered away from him, the sound of them hitting deep inside his chest. They disappeared into the pale trees, the beat of their canter growing soft, until Eliot was alone again in the meadow, shivering, cold with sweat.

Eliot awoke with one thought that started softly as he sat up and remembered the elk, then grew rapidly, like cells multiplying in the air. A flight to Arizona would more than max out his credit card. He had no money for an abortion. He had already borrowed money from everyone else, owed more than he'd ever be able to repay. Christ. He was going to have to call his dad.

He unzipped the tent and stretched his legs in the grasses of cold dew. His head balanced heavily on his body, and the coldness of the morning stung his eyes. A train would be cheaper. Slower, but cheaper. And maybe deliberateness was what he needed. A purposeful movement with a sense of an ultimate direction. He would need to call Becca, pack up his bike, get a ticket, figure out the train schedules, find the goddamn depot itself. He had a sense of the right direction, so that was where he went.

Smokestacks rose in the distance against a pink early-morning sky painted with still, white clouds masquerading as mountains, what looked like a faraway range brought into being as if by a giant, long-felt yearning. A chill breath of vertigo swung through him: this false range of mountains, a sense of distant protection that, all at once, became nothing more than a beautiful illusion. He pedaled toward it, toward Becca and the blood.

As he pedaled, though, his thoughts turned not to Becca but again to his father, a father who had not wanted to be with Eliot's mother, and still he'd stayed. She'd gotten pregnant and then they had Eliot and his father stayed, for thirteen unlucky years he stayed. Eliot closed his eyes and felt the wind. You have to imagine you're a bird. He pedaled and breathed and thought and couldn't place what it was, the feeling he had, something about his father. It kept rushing away from him.

The *Fantôme* of Fatma

Otis Haschemeyer

A bell made from one piece of hammered steel hung outside the Chief's door. Inside, they sat on pillows, with a silver tea tray in front of them. The Chief wore an embroidered white tunic and black headscarf, had clear eyes and a trimmed gray beard. Miles thought him beautiful but then felt guilty that he'd objectified the Chief in a way that he wouldn't objectify a white person. Then again, so many of the Malians were beautiful. They drank tea together. Miles glanced at Wolfy as she brought the teacup up to her lips and wondered what she felt, if she was as happy as he was being here in the intimacy of the Chief's hut. Beyond Wolfy, Deon sat with legs folded under a loose skirt and fidgeted with its hem. The Chief glanced at her often, speaking in a French made more exotic by his sonorous and clipped pronunciation. Miles heard the words *escarpment* and *attention*.

Karl, leaning over his folded knees, gestured with one hand. "He says if we want to climb on the rock, we have to be respectful of the spirits that live there and the ancestors of the people who lived there from before, in villages in the cliffs, and that we should not damage or take anything we find." Karl turned back to the Chief. "Also, he says to have good experiences."

"Ask him where we can put up a new route," Rodney said.

"I don't think he knows about the climbing," Karl said.

"Ask him anyway," Rodney said, flexing his wrist back and forth, stretching his forearm muscles.

Karl asked, and the Chief responded. Karl said, "He says it is all new."

Quietly and away, Rodney said, "Well, we know that's not true."

It had been Miles's dream to come to Mali, and he'd done the research. He knew that the fingers of Fatma had been climbed before, before Europeans, before Dogons, before people who had come from elsewhere, before history. The people had used sticks braced in the cracks to negotiate difficult sections, had villages and sacred places on the peaks to worship and follow the stars, to remain safe from their predators. At that time, the flora and fauna had been more dense. The *harmattan* had not yet come, and more rain had fallen. But Rodney was concerned with recent history, with climbers bagging first ascents and naming their routes.

They drank more tea. Karl talked with the Chief, and Miles tried to understand. Rodney and Wolfy talked about getting on the rock, what grades they might want to start with. Wolfy was the best climber among them and a large reason Rodney had wanted Miles and Wolfy along.

Now the Chief addressed Deon. She smiled and then laughed, jutting her chin out. "What does he want?" she asked.

Karl said, "He asks why you are here."

"Why is he asking me?" she said, laughing again. "Don't I look like a rock climber? Tell him I'm just here to see."

The Chief spoke to Karl, and Karl asked Deon, "Are your people from Mali?"

The Chief smiled.

"God, no," she said. "They're from Oakland."

When they'd finished their tea, the Chief stood at the door and looked only at Deon. Miles caught the word *fantôme*. After addressing her, Karl interpreted, "He says there is a ghost who frequents the rock."

Driving in a *bachee* to the camp, they commented on the quaint and superstitious Chief of the village.

Their first night in the Spaniard's camp, Miles scanned the crags with Rodney's image-stabilizing binoculars. Le Main de Fatma turned out into the desert like four fingers and a thumb, the buttress as the open palm. The Hombori Mountains, the rising escarpment, and the spires of Le Main de Fatma pulled what little moisture there was from the air, and the villagers in Hombori pumped up the ancient waters that had leached into the aquifer. But at the Spaniard's camp there was no water, and they'd had to bring their own.

Not many climbers came to the Sahel, and very few Americans, so they were alone coming to the Mali desert at the end of the season. Soon the *harmattan* winds would blow day and night. In the center of their enclosure was a platform and thatched hut, and Miles and Wolfy sat on a rock wall, one of a maze of stone walls set against the persistent evening wind. Miles laid the binoculars down. As the sun set off to their left along the orange desert floor, he whispered, "You excited?"

"Totally," she said. They stared into the Sahel and the hand rising from the sand and scrub brush. Echoing faintly in the wind was the song of the *mu'addin*, the call to prayer, and on the road, some distance away, a bus stopped, allowing passengers to exit and pray under the gaze of Le Main de Fatma. After talking to the Spaniard, Rodney returned to tell them he didn't think the man would help them find a new route. "He wants them for himself," Rodney said. "That's what I think."

"Sounds paranoid," Miles said.

"We're nobodies. That's the thing."

"Maybe we can't just come in here and colonize the place," Miles said, looking off at the two-thousand-foot quartzite towers, red and pink with iron oxide. "Personally, I just want to climb."

"That's the way things are done," Rodney said. "The way life marches on. This into that. Colonizing. It's pretty basic."

"Yeah," Deon said, rising from her suitcase on the platform. "Just like fucking."

"I heard that," Wolfy said, imitating Deon's black English, which Deon herself imitated. They smiled at each other and hooked each other's little fingers and pulled them apart.

For a divinity student, Deon swore a lot, but when Karl mentioned it, she said, "What? I can't believe in God and say 'Fuck'?" Karl was flirting with her but Deon didn't notice. She was interested in Rodney. Miles rubbed Wolfy's knee, thinking first that it was nice not to worry about such things, then thinking just of Wolfy's warmth, then of their circle of light and the desert, of Rodney, of the difficulty of doing anything, of sand and ancient people and time and of a colossal stone head lying in the middle of nowhere. The face, with blunt features, had eyes without lids. Once he recognized that he was thinking of "Ozymandias," he struggled to recall the words of the poem but couldn't.

The next night, around the fire, Deon told them that while hiking she'd come to a pass between two boulders when she'd heard a call that she couldn't identify. When she'd looked around, she hadn't seen anything or anyone. She put her hand on one of the boulders to step through and then heard the cry again, and small rocks scattered about in front of her. This time when she looked up she saw an African boy leaning out from a crevasse. She stopped, and then the boy came down. She wasn't frightened because of the loose, nonthreatening way the boy moved down from the rock and toward her. From a distance, he urged her to go around the boulders by another way, gesticulating with hands and arms.

Rodney and Karl said they'd seen an African boy climbing on the cliffs too. Rodney said, "All free solo. No rope. We trailed him, and then he disappeared. I mean, I saw some of the things he was climbing."

Rather than scout lines, Miles and Wolfy had climbed on the western edge of the formation and hadn't seen anything except desert, sun, giant birds hovering in the thermals and bats, cooing aggressively in the cracks where Miles and Wolfy had to wedge their hands to climb.

Now Miles drank wine from his purple-stained plastic cup. Wolfy leaned her head against his shoulder. He stretched out his stiff legs.

Karl said, "I've seen free solos."

"Would you do it?" Rodney interrupted, taping a cloth around a stick and taping a carabineer to that, making a tool he'd use to push bats further into the cracks.

Karl continued, "He was climbing only in leather shoes."

Later, sharing Tasty-Bites—vegan Indian food in plastic pouches—with their hosts, they asked about the boy they'd seen. The Spaniard's wife, a Peul woman, had cataracts in her left eye that occasionally flashed opal white in the glare of the fire. With a hood over her head, she spoke in a mix of Fulfulde Massina and Spanish, and her husband translated in his lilting English. She said the boy had appeared several years ago on the cliffs, that he lived in the old caves and hid at night. Some villagers left food for him tied to a post, where the dogs would not get it, or at the base of the rock. Mostly he survived like the ancient people, pulling bats from the cracks, or birds' eggs, taking water from the cisterns in the rock. Once, the village people had tried to get him out, but they couldn't, and they saw his presence as the will of God. "Now," the Spaniard said, translating, "he steals in the village and is treated with reverence. It is the rumor his sister is sold in slavery."

Rodney said, "There isn't slavery anymore."

The Spaniard, in brightly colored parachute pants, crossed his legs. "It is here. It is in your country. Sex slavery. Agricultural slavery. People promise dreams," he said. "If that."

Miles was the first one awake and out of his tent the next morning to see the *fantôme* of Fatma crouching on their wall, overlooking their camp. He was folded up upon himself, noticeably lean and squat, about the size of Wolfy. His arms were long and embraced his knees, and he wore shorts and a dirty red T-shirt. His toenails poked from the holes worn at the tips of his shoes.

Miles said, "Hello. *Bonjour.*"

The *fantôme* didn't say anything. Miles noted his elastic ease, his dark skin, chalky with dust, his thick, cracked hands, and strong forearms. Miles approached and held out his hand. The boy unfolded one arm and placed his hand in Miles's. The boy did not grip with his hand at all but only let it lie there. Miles felt the dry, callused skin.

He could not discern the boy's motives for crouching there and left it at that. "Okay," he said. Strange things happen, Miles thought. He pumped the fuel canister to start the stove for tea. When the others emerged from their tents, Miles remained quiet and nodded in the direction of the wall and the boy. Miles then fixed a bowl of granola and soymilk and brought it over to the *fantôme*. The boy did not take it, and Miles put it down on the stone wall next to his feet.

The boy remained motionless, taking them in, until Deon emerged. Then, just discernibly, his eyes followed her. "I think he likes you," Karl said.

"At least someone does," Deon said and laughed. "He probably just wants a glass of water." She poured water into a used plastic cup and rubbed the inside with her finger, tossed the purple liquid out onto the sand. Then she filled the cup with fresh water and handed it to the boy. He took it, watched her, then drank. When he was done, Deon filled the cup again and gave it to him. His eyes showed no emotion, but the corners of his mouth turned very slightly upward.

"You've made a friend," Wolfy said. She approached the boy and hoisted herself up onto the wall to sit next to him. She ate her granola and then motioned for him to eat his. After she placed it in his hands, he did begin to eat, pushing the oats into his mouth with his fingers.

Karl tried speaking to the boy in French and then Spanish. The boy didn't respond. Rodney said someone should get the Spaniard's wife. "Maybe she can talk to him."

Miles ran to the Spaniard's hut. The Peul woman and her husband were already up, and Miles motioned for them to come quickly, using the word *fantôme*. Though they didn't seem interested, they came along, and the Peul woman tried speaking to the *fantôme* in Fulfulde. The boy turned his head at a few words. Then she spoke to her husband.

The Spaniard said, "A great many languages are spoken in the Sahel. He doesn't speak her language, she doesn't think so. Maybe he may not speak." Then, pointing at scar tissue on the boy's shoulder, he said, "He has come from a war. Straight, deep. A machete."

"He called to me yesterday," Deon said, and she told her story of the boulders. The Spaniard asked a question or two and then said a mamba snake had a territory between those rocks.

"A black mamba?" Deon said.

"I brought antivenin," Rodney said. "I'll leave it here if we don't use it."

"A lot of good that would do me," Deon said. "Out in the middle of fucking nowhere. Anyway, I'd prefer not to get bit by a fucking black mamba."

"But there is no reason to go over there," the Spaniard said.

Deon tilted her head. "Well, I was lost, then. Wasn't I? I suppose that's my fault."

When they hefted their gear and headed for the col between the two spires, Suri Tondo and Wamderdou, they were surprised that the *fantôme* got up too and came with them, sometimes following and sometimes leading as the group worked its way around Wamderdou. Miles trailed, marveling at what was occurring. The boy wanted to be with them. Finally they ascended a scree field and arrived at the east face of Wamderdou.

The *fantôme* stopped at the base of the rock, where a chute led to a chimney and then out to a ledge. He motioned with his hands. Then he began to climb.

"Hold on," Rodney said, but it did no good. The boy slunk up and around the quartzite crack, quartz sand and silica fused under tectonic compression, fine-grained and smooth. He wedged his feet and ascended, more graceful than even Wolfy, and he did it without a rope. Rodney backed up from the cliff and scanned with his binoculars. "Is this an unknown line?" he asked.

Karl looked over his French climbing book. "I don't see anything," he said.

Rodney looked up. "It's beautiful. A natural." And then he said, "But see that roof?" He passed the binoculars to Karl, and then Miles and Wolfy had a look. Toward the top of the climb, a thick slab of rock edged horizontally out from the cliff face. For the climber it would be like a roof edge; from the base, the roof appeared to Miles substantial, jutting out maybe fifteen feet.

"What do you think of that?" Miles said.

Wolfy said, "Let's do it."

Miles and Wolfy unpacked their gear and stepped into their harnesses, and Wolfy clipped gear to her loops.

"So that's it?" Deon said. She took out her Emerson and found a place to sit in the shade.

"You knew we'd be climbing," Miles told her.

"But who could imagine it would be nothing else?"

"Maybe tomorrow, after we bag this," Rodney said. "We'll take a trip. Maybe the next day."

The two pairs followed the *fantôme* past a crack and through a bulge. Wolfy led the pitch as Miles belayed. Every now and again she'd scream as her hand brushed a bat, but she pushed on and finally stopped screaming. Wolfy built her anchor on a ledge some 150 feet off the ground and tied into it. Miles followed, yanking the placed gear from the cracks as Wolfy belayed from above. Miles could follow this route, but the climbing was at the edge of his physical and technical limit. He marveled again at the boy's grace and his ease at climbing without a rope.

Miles's pitch moved through a deep red-colored stone. The climbing was less strenuous, hand-sized cracks, larger holds. He moved onto a face with several small roofs, edged between them and made a solid placement, compressing a cam and letting its wedged teeth expand in the crack. He then moved along and built an anchor with placements of nuts and cams in a flake and a crack. Finally he rested on a double hump covered in bird and bat shit. When Rodney arrived at Miles's belay station, Rodney took over the lead. Miles cautioned him to shorten up the pitch when he found a good place to set an anchor. "Three pieces in different features."

"I've logged more face time than you," Rodney said. That was probably true. Though Miles had been climbing for many years and had introduced Rodney to climbing only several years ago, Rodney had a trust fund and could climb whenever he wanted.

Rodney's pitch and then Karl's were easier still, passing over a black slab at midafternoon. Above was their first major roof, some six hundred feet above the desert, under which the *fantôme* traversed left, following a ledge that led away from the roof and around. To see him climbing without a rope so high off the desert floor made Miles shiver. But Miles understood that the *fantôme* knew exactly what he could do and what he couldn't, and he only did what he could accomplish, unlike Miles and the rest of them, trying to accomplish something beyond their ability.

Rodney stood out from the rock, laying his weight against his anchor, clipping pro onto his gear loops. "I've been thinking," Rodney said. "He's taking the escape to the right. We'll go straight up and over that roof. That's the natural line, and that will be our first ascent. Straight up the east face of Wamderdou."

Wolfy was game. She took the lead, and Miles belayed. He watched her and then looked off into the distance for a moment. The sun had come around, and the heat rippled off the desert. Above, a marabou stork floated in a thermal. A dust devil swirled at the desert floor, rising a hundred feet, well below. Sweat dripped down Miles's back and pooled at his harness. The stork's shadow rippled across the rock and passed over Miles, a moment's relief from the African sun.

Wolfy found a cam placement above in the crack, clipped the rope in the carabineer and then made her way up twenty-five feet and approached the first crux of the climb, a blank section without visible handholds in the shade of the roof. Miles leaned out from the rock so he could watch her, clenched the rope in his right hand, pushed down and away from the belay device. He fed rope as Wolfy moved, keeping a little slack in the line. If she didn't have the rope just as she liked it, she would have trouble. The hardest moves required perfect technique but also total body control. If a move was hard enough, Miles knew, Wolfy would search for a way to fail. In those milliseconds, if she found that something was not right with Miles's belay, she could blame him rather than rely on herself.

The muscles in her shoulder and back striated, then spread as she manteled off an edge; her fingers curled and turned down and away on the small crimp of rock. She extended her shoulder and arm and stretched her other hand to a smooth bulge of stone, blindly finding it with her fingers as her face pressed the rock. Her fingers walked over the bulge, and Miles was aware that her balance shifted.

She'd woven her blond hair in two pigtails, and they hung down. The crux move was only a question of balance, and Wolfy, if she got her head straight, could do it. Wolfy's fingers hesitated as they tried to gain purchase on the sloping rock. "Watch me," she yelled.

Miles's nerves jumped. She was getting mental. He leaned out and shouted into the air, "I am, baby. Stay focused. Eye of the tiger."

Wolfy yelled, "Are you watching?"

Miles saw that she needed to get her core muscles involved in the move and try to gain momentum from the right toe, which she'd left dangling. That was the way to handle the move. Miles was also aware that he'd never be able to make the move himself. He would not be able to follow her.

Once she'd edged her fingers over the sloping rock, she swung her leg below it and found a toehold. She pulled, stuck her hand into a finger-sized crack and was up. She set two pieces below the great roof that now loomed over her head, but the sun was getting low, and the wind began to come up. A few bats had crawled from the cracks; they flapped and squeaked in their erratic spirals. She and Rodney decided to leave their anchor placements and try the roof the next day. Miles would have agreed if he'd been consulted. His legs were stiff with the tension of standing out from the rock. Rodney said he would rappel down from the top to look at the great roof tomorrow, see if there was any way they could get over it.

They took the *fantôme's* escape route right, rappelled one length down the north side of the rock and then down-climbed into the col between Wamderdou and Suri Tondo. They found the *fantôme* sitting with Deon in front of the east face.

"There you fucking are," Deon said. They made apologies, explained their troubles.

"What were you doing?" Wolfy asked her. Miles glanced around and saw that the *fantôme* had climbed away.

Deon said, "He just sat here. I don't know. I read him Emerson."

The next morning the *fantôme* was again on the wall overlooking their tents and hut when Miles got up. When he saw the boy there, he said hello, poured him a glass of water and handed it to him. The *fantôme* drank it.

When everyone was awake, Miles said maybe they should go the fifteen kilometers to Hombori. This was for Deon's sake.

Rodney looked at Karl. They wouldn't be going to town. Miles didn't think he was testing Wolfy, but perhaps he was.

"But we're going to finish that route," Wolfy said. She looked at Deon and then back to Miles.

"I'd like to see a little of town," Miles said. Wolfy said she would go with Miles. After Rodney had checked with the Spaniard to make sure the east face line was new, he and Karl returned to Wamderdou, carrying their fixed lines. Like part of the group, the *fantôme* followed Deon, squeezed into the Spaniard's car next to Miles and Wolfy and closed the door. He unrolled the window. He'd been in a car before.

The townspeople gathered around them, as interested in the *fantôme* as in the foreigners. They walked through the marketplace, divided between men roasting meats and smoking cigarettes on one side and women selling goods laid out on cloth on the other. Wolfy declined meat offered to her on a stick, but Miles ate some. He allowed himself to eat meat if he deemed it culturally appropriate. He passed on roasted bat, but later he had a plate of fish. When he threw the scraps on the ground as he'd seen others do, children ran up to eat from the bones. They knew that as a tourist, Miles would not have stripped the fish of all its meat.

The sun grew hot. A small boy told them the Chief wanted to see them. They met the Chief in his compound; he wanted to examine the *fantôme*. The boy stood still as the Chief lifted his arm, stroked fingers through his underarm hair. The Chief examined the boy's head and around his ears, opened his mouth and looked at his teeth. The Chief asked Deon and Wolfy to leave. Then he had the boy drop his pants. Afterward, outside in the Chief's courtyard, the Chief repeated his name and office, extending his hands to the boy. The Chief repeated this many times, and after much coaxing, the boy spoke what they believed to be his name.

Miles could read French better than he understood it spoken, so he asked the Chief to write down his observations. Then Miles read the Chief's remarks for Wolfy and Deon, told them that the Chief believed that the boy was a foreigner from a place far away. But the Chief also believed he might have come from the ancestors, before the French, the Moors or the Dogons. The Chief did not discount the possibility. Maybe the boy's people were formerly here. Maybe they took the camel trains away.

After tea, the Chief arranged for a Land Rover, and, with a nephew driving, he took them through the town. They passed the shanties built of garbage on the outskirts, the sick and starving, and drove into the desert to Hombori Tondo. They drove through a boulder field toward a pink sandstone village carved high up in the cliffs. Miles's ability to understand the Chief's French improved as they drove, and he told Wolfy and Deon what the Chief said, more or less. The *fantôme* crawled over the back seat and sat in the back of the Land Rover with his knees against his chest.

They climbed ladders and fixed ropes up into the village of conical mud structures, ancient mosques and the carved caves of the Dogons and Tellem. They passed through narrows and up over boulders, stepping on depressions in the rock worn by former hands and feet. The Chief and the nephew helped Deon. At the end of one of the narrows, at the cliff wall itself, the nephew removed a weathered strip of plywood from a fissure and gave the Chief a plastic flashlight from the cloth bag he had slung over his shoulder. The fissure in the rock split down into the cliff, and Miles, Wolfy and Deon had to step over the fissure and into the cave. The Chief held Miles's arm. Wolfy didn't need any help. Then Miles encouraged Deon, who finally leaped across and into his arms. Miles was momentarily aroused and just as quickly worried about Wolfy's jealousy. Only when they were safe inside did the *fantôme* follow.

The cave was cool, almost cold after the heat of the sun. Light filtered in from the split in the rock above them. Through the slit in the rock, Miles saw sky and knew that at night the stars would be visible. They stepped on what Miles soon realized were human bones. The Chief walked with little concern, and the bones clacked under his feet. The others did the same, all but the *fantôme*, who walked gingerly and didn't make a sound. The air was rich with the smell of guano, and Miles also smelled cool water. The fecund odor and the small sleeping breaths of the bats mixed with the presence of the dead. The Chief beamed his flashlight on figures painted on the walls of the cave in a brown the color of dried blood. He shone his light on several symbols, their outlines etched by sharp rocks. He brought the *fantôme* closer and had him look at the markings. Wolfy slid in close to Miles. Deon peered over their shoulders, her hand on Miles's waist. Miles felt as though he were at the origin of time.

Even though the *fantôme* did not seem to recognize the symbols on the cave wall, the Chief held a celebration in his honor that evening. After the evening prayer, the Chief sent his nephew in the Land Rover to inform the Spaniard and his Peul wife and collect Karl and Rodney. The street was alive with music and dancing. *Griots*, the storytellers, played large beaded gourds; others played guitars and drums. The air and ground vibrated with the stamping of girls in yellow skirts, their feet marked with intricate designs in henna, some—the very young—with tightly woven braids, smooth brown skin, oval faces and eyes. The Chief's wife wore a rich blue robe and headscarf, huge earrings of red and gold and a golden nose ring.

Wolfy wouldn't eat the food, and neither would Rodney, who feared getting sick, or Karl, who had an intestinal condition and restricted his own diet. They had boundaries. There were always boundaries. The skin was a boundary. The lens of the eye. Miles hated that, the separateness, and even though it made Wolfy distant, he ate.

Deon picked at a few things, and the *fantôme* ate slowly and seemed to wonder what it was all about. The *fantôme* knew he wasn't a god or an ancestor. But he seemed to know he was being honored. Miles watched an adolescent girl with pleated hair twirl in front of his eyes, and the old women held hands in front of their mouths and trilled, the gourd rasping, all of it an intoxication, the thrill of sound, the whirling of yellow hems and feet. In the midst of the dancing, Miles thought of the cave full of bones and the polished fissure worn smooth by generations of bodies passing through, returning the dead.

Wolfy said to Miles, "You're giving her a lot of attention."

"Who is that?" he asked. He didn't know whom she meant, but thought she must mean Deon. He'd talked to her about the food, but that was it. Maybe earlier? The girl dancing? He took Wolfy's hand, and she let him hold it, loose and uncommitted.

Miles's mood turned, and he saw that the dancing girl's legs were thin as sticks; he remembered the shanties they'd passed outside town and the children eating his discarded fish bones. After a while, when Wolfy still wouldn't speak to him, he said, "I think you're jealous of him." He nodded toward the *fantôme*. "Isn't that what this is about?"

Later the Chief made a place for the *fantôme* to stay, left with him and then came back to tell them that the *fantôme* had returned to the mountains.

In the morning Miles was sick, and from his tent he heard Rodney insisting that Wolfy come back to the great roof. Wolfy poked her head into their tent and told Miles she was going.

"Go," he said.

"I guess it's convenient that you and Deon are sick together."

He shook his head. Nausea overwhelmed him for a moment. "Please get out of here."

When the heat was too much, he got out of the tent. Deon emerged from the hut. They wondered together where the *fantôme* was, whether he'd gone with the others. Miles rubbed sunscreen over his face, though not on his forehead, where it would seep down to sting his eyes. He put his hat back on.

Deon said, "I think I'm going to throw up."

Later, sitting on the edge of the tent platform sipping tea, Miles told Deon he'd go look for the others. "I can't spend too much time with you because Wolfy gets jealous."

"I know," Deon said.

"I don't know what to do about it."

"She and I have been friends for a long time, and just because I'm a total narcissist doesn't mean I don't understand her—a little," Deon said. "She tries to keep everything in its place, but it makes her crazy. Ordering brings chaos. It doesn't take it away. What she's got to do is move in the other direction." She put her hand on his for a moment. Her palm was cool on his knuckles. They swung their legs and looked off toward Le Main de Fatma.

"Unfortunately, I love all of her, not just the parts I like," Miles said.

Deon lifted her hand, said, "Well, go get her, you fucking sap."

Walking, with only the daypack, was the best thing for him. He took off his hat, and the sun warmed his forehead. He breathed in the dry air. In the distance, a haze obscured the horizon line. He rounded Le Main de Fatma. In many ways it didn't look much like a hand, but as he walked, his perspective changed, and he saw the wrist turn and gesture toward the sky. He thought again of "Ozymandias." These fingers twelve hundred and two thousand feet high were all that were left, and someday they would be gone too.

When he found the climbers, he saw all the work Rodney and Karl had done the previous day. They had fixed ropes up the first two pitches of the climb, and high above he saw Wolfy below the roof. Immediately his gut wrenched. He scanned the rock with Rodney's binoculars and saw Karl dangling from a fixed line anchored to the summit with a video camera on a sling. Miles swung the binoculars to the right, found Rodney on the ledge, anchored and belaying Wolfy. Wolfy was twenty feet higher and hung from protection, two equalized pieces, wedged into the dihedral below the roof. Miles arranged some rocks so that he could lie down on his back and view the action. For the rest of the afternoon, Wolfy hung and then attempted the roof, and each time she fell, swinging from the rock. Miles saw that the problem was not physical.

They came down early, having failed to pass over the roof. When Wolfy descended the last fixed line, Miles got up and found himself, without his knowing it had happened, covered with a layer of desert dust. He greeted her at the base of the rock. She asked, "Where's Deon?"

Miles knew that through a complex logic, from meat to Deon to Rodney's belay to Miles, Wolfy held him responsible for her failure. Maybe he was responsible.

They began in the tent. Wolfy did not broach the subject, but Miles knew what she was thinking. Though their sleeping bags were opened toward each other, their bodies did not touch. She read a book with her headlamp on.

They ended out in the desert, under the stars, meteors falling, streaking and burning up in the atmosphere. Miles knew what Wolfy wanted. She wanted him to convince her that he was not attracted to Deon. There was nothing rational about it. Wolfy wasn't jealous of the real Deon. But Wolfy believed that the only thing that would make her feel okay was to have this specter of Deon cast down. And she resented like hell that Miles wouldn't do it for her by answering her questions in the ways she wanted. Miles wouldn't. Not only would Wolfy never believe him, but Miles believed it was wrong to do that to Deon, or to anyone.

He gestured. "Look where we are. It's unbelievable."

The desert winds were up, and he could hear the wind roaring as it funneled through the spires of Fatma. The wind sucked their voices away into the low pressure, the thermal differential, to fly over the sand, the huts, the villages and into the desert. Miles said, "We're here, but we're living in your head."

Though the *fantôme* had not come to the camp the day after the party, he was back the following morning, sitting on the wall and waiting for the group to rise. Why he chose not to come and then to return, no one could answer. Maybe he'd also been sick from the village food. Maybe something else. But Rodney had other concerns. He had the idea that Wolfy should try the roof again fresh, but that Deon should come to the cliff too. If all else failed, his idea was to have the *fantôme* climb the roof.

"He's not interested in your white route," Deon said. "A straight line up a rock, like there's a straight fucking line anywhere around here."

"Isn't that up to him?"

"It's too dangerous," Wolfy said.

"Anyway, I was planning on doing something else," Deon said and cocked a hip.

"Please," Rodney said, indulging her.

Karl said, "He'll wear a rope, of course."

They rigged in the morning. When it came time to make the attempt, Wolfy said she needed Miles to belay. This was an apology but also, Miles knew, a necessity. They all jugged up the fixed lines to the crux. Karl hung from the summit with his video camera, Miles belayed and Wolfy climbed from the crack and over the first crux she'd done two days earlier. She had those moves wired now, and they were no problem for her. Miles looked down and saw the tiny figures of Deon and the *fantôme* at the base of the cliff, the red glint of the binoculars in Deon's hands. Then she handed the binoculars to the *fantôme*.

Wolfy reached the crux and pinned her right foot out on the dihedral below the roof. She set her hands and began to move upside down in the crack. Miles leaned out from the rock, pulling the sling taut that held him to his anchor and looked up at her. Just at the edge of the roof, she reached out, swung her right foot to the right and held a thin edge with the tips of her fingers, grasping with her right hand above for something, anything. Problems were usually footwork or mental, in that order.

But the move could be too hard. Those were ideas to keep away from. Her right foot agitated for more purchase. "Watch me," she yelled. Then she fell.

There was a certain terror to watching her fall, knowing the rope would pull at the 'biner attached to the protection in the rock, fearing that the cam could pull free, snap Wolfy down to be caught on Miles's anchor. He had three pieces in the rock, but after that, there was nothing. In the end, they depended on these pieces of metal and the rock and the rope. If any of them failed, they'd be dead—nothing on earth could stop them from dying. But gear seldom failed. If accidents happened climbing, it was ninety-nine times out of a hundred climber error.

Wolfy jerked at the end of her rope. Carabiners and slings clinked, pulled taut from the rock face. At the other end, the rope yanked Miles's belay device, belay loop, harness and waist. Threaded in the cracks, the cramming devices and nuts bit into the rock. Everything held.

Before lunch they descended again. In the heat of midday, Rodney pantomimed what he wanted the *fantôme* to do. As he tried to get his points across, sweat rose on Rodney's forehead. The boy, however, remained chalky and dry. Miles helped the boy put on a harness. On the ground, using a crack at eye level, Rodney and Karl showed the boy how to clip into the protection that Karl had placed above the roof, once the *fantôme* got over the roof—if he did. They demonstrated to him that he'd be safe tying his harness to a cam wedged in the rock. They had the *fant*ôme climb up and drop onto the gear. At first the boy didn't want to do it. He had to be eased from the rock by Karl and Rodney, to show him it was safe. To Miles, the whole thing seemed like a bad idea.

They ate Tasty-Bites from the pouches. Miles gave the boy an extra pair of his climbing shoes to wear. The boy put them on and smiled, looked at his feet. This was the first unreservedly positive expression Miles had seen from him. Then Rodney and Karl and Miles ascended up their fixed lines back to their anchors on the third pitch. The *fantôme* followed without tying in, free soloing up the first two pitches. The harness was cumbersome for him and seemed to make the boy self-conscious.

At the anchor, Miles clipped in, seven hundred feet above the desert floor, while Wolfy and Deon watched from below. He tied the *fantôme* into the end of the rope and showed the boy how the belay would catch the rope, should he fall. Miles wasn't sure what the boy understood. The wind rose. Miles felt his sunscreened skin covered in grit.

The roof loomed above them, casting dark red rock against the sky. The boy began his climb out from the crack. The moves here were likely more difficult than anything the boy had ever done before. He had never needed to climb anything like this. Deon had said the boy was loose, and Miles thought he was like water. He'd spent years flowing up and over the cracks and crags of Fatma, against gravity. Like water, he went where he could, finding routes by merging body and rock, animate and inanimate. The boy would never conceive of doing a climb like the one Rodney had devised. There was no need to go *straight* up Wamderdou.

The boy moved away from the anchor, spent some few seconds clipping into the bombproof piece above the anchor and to the right of Miles. He had understood that much, thank God. Then he proceeded to the first crux that Wolfy had negotiated the other day. The boy had watched her do it, and he imitated her, grasping the small edge and pushing off to stretch his arms up toward a sloping handhold. The rope seemed to bother him, and then his leg started to shake.

They hadn't seen the boy afraid before. His arms were longer than Wolfy's and he grasped the sloping rock and pulled himself up. Sweat popped on his forehead and stained his shirt between his shoulder blades. His knees still shook as he worked his way up under the roof. The boy didn't stop and consider. Miles knew what was driving him. He couldn't retreat. He had to go forward. He moved into the layback off the crack and spread his arms, one hand upward into the crack; then his feet cut loose and swung.

He would never make it. The boy hung on with one hand, stuck a toe on the rock below the roof and then reached across his chest with his other free hand. He was perpendicular to the ground now. His right hand reached up and over and out of Miles's sight. Then he swung his midsection, got a foot up on a bulge and slid up and out of Miles's view. He'd done it. Miles felt the rope pull, and he fed slack along with the even tug. He paid out, and then more. From his fingers on the rope, Miles knew the boy was pulling rope to clip it into the protection above the roof. Miles's heart was slowing. He was filled with elation for the boy. Rodney was talking in his ear—they'd done it. Miles was listening, not paying attention to the belay.

The boy was well over his last piece of protection. He'd gathered rope to clip the carabineer over the roof but hadn't clipped it. He fell for no good reason. He fell because he'd already done the hardest part. Listing for a moment at the lip of the roof, he toppled backward, gaining speed. In seconds, the rope snapped through the carabineers and pulled the cams and nuts taut in the cracks and yanked Miles from his anchor. The slings pulled. The cams bit into rock. Then the rope took the boy's weight and elongated, sapping his momentum.

Miles's heart beat hard, but he had the boy locked off and safe. Moments passed as the boy dangled at the end of the rope, hanging in space, motionless. He rotated. He seemed asleep. His arm moved as if pushed by a breeze. One leg twitched. Miles didn't know what to think; he didn't think anything. After moments, the boy crunched up. He opened his eyes and gazed at the rock in front of him. He reached a hand out toward it.

Miles, Rodney and Karl helped the boy down the face of Wamderdou. When he'd reached the bottom, Deon and Wolfy hugged him, pulled his small body into theirs. With flaccid muscles, he looked like skin over bones as they compressed him.

Wolfy came to Miles. She trembled for a moment, squeezing him. "That scared me."

Miles stayed at the base, appreciating Wolfy's power as she jugged up the fixed lines, her resolve now set like the tectonic pressures that produce rock. She took a belay from Rodney and strung out the lead, wedging into the roof dihedral, jamming one hand deep in the crack, bats be damned. She'd seen the boy do it, and she knew she could do it too. She swung her feet out, cut loose and pinned a heel on the edge of the great roof. For a moment, with her heel and one hand on the ledge of the roof, she let her arm swing down and shook it out. She had it. The sun was lowering, and above her a few bats circled erratically. She pulled herself over, clipped in and climbed to the next belay ledge, set an anchor. The wind rose, howling through the spires. The boy sat at the base of Wamderdou. At some point he got up and wandered away.

The next day, they were clear that the boy would not be returning. Karl, in ominous baritone, said, "He'd never died before. That's why."

Rodney and Wolfy linked the climb. They would always have that together, for their lives, into the future. Karl and Miles weren't able to pass the crux and took the escape route to the top. On the summit of Wamderdou, they stood together. Miles looked at Wolfy: harness, black climbing pants, green windbreaker, her yellow pigtails pleated on her shoulders. The haze of the *harmattan* was visible everywhere on the horizon. Ozymandias, time. Glory was fleeting, but it was still glory, and Wolfy's was real. She claimed Wamderdou.

When they reached the base, Miles drew Wolfy away. They took a wide path, circumnavigating the spires. He turned her to face the fingers of Fatma reaching for the sky. He wanted to show her what he'd seen the day he'd been sick and walked alone; he wanted to share that with her, but their perspective was not yet right.

They walked in loose sand, rounding the far side of Kaga Tondo. "Just a little farther," he said. Miles stayed trained on the fingers of Fatma, watching. Then, as they walked, the wrist turned; the fingers spun, melded and spread just so, transforming the spires of rock into a gesture rising from the orange desert. Miles knew it was not a hand but only resembled a hand, and that was enough, a metaphor that any person could see and feel, in this spot—a connection of people and earth, an awakening that could be shared by every living human being on earth, invoking in each awe, supplication and adoration, those divine impulses that drew to this sacred place nomads, travelers, people of every disposition—the Tellem, Dogons, Muslims and French, those many people of Mali and all wandering pilgrims—to see God in self but also in a gesture of rock against sky.

"Do you see that? Amazing, isn't it?"

Her pale-blue eyes, the sun golden on her skin, the last flits of light in her yellow hair, faded. "I guess slave traders pass through here," Wolfy said. "That boy's sister was traded."

"I know," Miles said.

They walked around Kaga Pamari and over to their left saw Wangel Debridu. Nearing camp, Miles realized that Wolfy was crying. He pulled her close.

She wiped her eyes, but the tears kept coming. "If you died, I wouldn't want to go on."

"Sure you would," he said. "You will go on."

Her tears really started now. He said again, "You will," and wrapped her in his arms. She sobbed, and he felt the power of her, her force and intensity now serving this purpose, weeping for his death, her shoulders pulled up and wracked down, the wetness of tears, the remarkable being of her, from her toes to her fingertips.

Back in San Francisco, Wolfy would occasionally see Deon, who would curse her latest fling, sometimes a boy, sometimes a girl. Miles, getting the news secondhand, knew it would be the rare person of any gender who could keep up with Deon. Then both Miles and Wolfy went to Sausalito for Deon's student sermon. She stood at a lectern, her fingers curled over the edge. Her voice rang out as she defined chaos as a place without distinction, a place of tranquility. Her words took force as her shoulders drew up with breath; she spoke over the crowd of parents and well-wishers, above the confusion of her own life. When she was done and they found each other in the crowd, Deon took their hands and said, "Well, how the fuck was that?" They admitted it was really *fucking* good.

The last Miles heard, Rodney was off to China. He called to ask if Miles had seen his binoculars. Miles didn't have them. Miles remembered the boy holding them, scanning the crags. If the boy had stolen them, Miles was glad of it.

More time passed, and Miles forgot about the *fantôme* and Le Main de Fatma. Then one day, years later, Miles and Wolfy's baby girl toppled backward off the sofa. With the instinct a parent has, Miles caught her, and as he held her in his hand, he remembered the boy falling after the roof of Wamderdou—because he'd already accomplished the impossible, on a climb Rodney forever named Wamderlust. The boy had dangled there, inert, and then reached a hand out toward the rock. And Miles remembered Karl, dressed in black stovepipe jeans, intoning in his baritone, "He'd never died before."

He remembered their last day: Karl asked Deon if she would like to see the Bandiagard escarpment where many ancient villages were located; Rodney went to town to arrange for a vehicle to take them back to Bamako; and Miles and Wolfy rented a moped and drove to the village they'd visited with the Chief. They arrived with only a daypack. They'd never climbed without ropes, but this last day they did, for fun, forgoing ladders and rope and instead scaling the rock like the ancient people who had made this their home. From the base of Hombori Tondo, they free soloed to the cave of bones.

Miles swiveled his daughter down and placed her feet on the floor. She crumpled to her knees and crawled to her striped tiger with yellow plastic eyes. Lives were trajectories and also endlessly conical. Spiraling up or down, Miles didn't know. And it didn't matter. They touched each other. His daughter would climb soon, and he would want to tell her the story of the *fantôme* of Fatma, the story of a boy and sister abducted by traders and transported over foreign landscapes, a boy who escaped, a boy who'd been in war, a boy drawn up into the hand of fate.

Perhaps the boy had always intended to leave the spires before the *harmattan* came. Perhaps he had needed that time to gather strength for the journey ahead, for his assault on the fortress that held his sister. Perhaps he had needed binoculars. Or perhaps his story did not yet take that route.

Miles watched his daughter tug at the stuffed tiger. He thought of a boy in the Sahel. One day the boy counseled a girl with small stones not to pass where the mamba snake had its lair. He climbed and fell. He died and found himself on the end of a rope—a boy who had forgotten and then remembered.

The Wall

Emma Törzs

After my brother Jonah's funeral, I didn't fly home with my parents. Instead I stayed behind with Eva in her shoebox apartment in Tel Aviv and spent a couple nights learning to go down on her, an act that felt surprisingly natural once I got used to the right-up-close-ness of it. I'd never been with another woman before, but we didn't talk about that. Mostly we were quiet or talked about Jonah. Though Eva and I had met for the first time at his funeral, she'd been serving with him for over a year, and he'd shown me many pictures of the two of them in their sand-green IDF uniforms, their arms slung around one another's shoulders in the casual way of soldiers everywhere. In e-mails he'd referred to her breezily as "my best bud," but when he'd come home on leave the last time, he'd gotten uncharacteristically wasted on a twelve-pack of High Life and said to me, "I can't stand it, Miri. I want her so badly I can't pray, I can't sleep. I'm on my knees asking God to either turn her straight or gun her down so I don't have to look at her anymore, and then I spend all night begging forgiveness for thinking such fucked-up shit."

Before Eva, I had never seen my twenty-three-year-old brother in love or even in lust, which I'd pop-psychologized as a reaction to the trauma of his puberty; he'd dreaded its coming for years even before the physical changes began. He was terrified of losing his voice. And I was frightened too: just a year and a half older than he, I'd grown up to the sound of his blue-sky treble floating around our house, the foresty trill of arpeggios from behind his bedroom door, and I was used to a life organized by his choir practice and performances. He'd been singing since he was four years old and had been gifted in the oldest sense of the word, as if a hand had reached down and pressed light into his throat. We'd both been raised by secular Jews, but Jonah was raised by his choir as well and was a believer. He'd been raised on music steeped in God.

"The Christian God," I'd argued once, home freshman year of college for winter break. I was sitting at our kitchen table watching him blend peanut butter and bananas into ice cream, as always working tirelessly against his twiggy teenaged metabolism. "All those old songs are about Jesus."

"It's got nothing to do with words," Jonah said over the screech of the blender. "I didn't listen to the words. I listened to the *feeling*."

He was seventeen then and had known for several years that his voice was never coming back. He could still sing better than most, but his tone was uneven, his range stilted, all the buttercup richness graveled down. His coach had told our parents there were some boys who never came to terms with the change, never figured out how to handle their new instrument, and gently recommended that Jonah begin to see a therapist instead, "to address the mind behind the larynx." But by that time he was beginning to lift weights and had subbed out choir practice for the temple and the gym, and my parents figured he was moving on.

"All praise music, all worship music, it's the *music* that tells you what the song's about," said Jonah, pouring his viscous beige shake into a glass. "The lyrics are just a key, like on a map. A compass rose. But you don't need the idea of north if you know which way is up."

He took a sip of his drink, his corded neck contracting and releasing. This new body of his called attention to itself in a way that frightened me: the popping veins, the hammy arms swinging from bricked shoulders, the pulse beating beneath the stretched-tight skin of his temple, all of it a constant unwelcome reminder of human meatiness. Only his face was the same as it'd always been. Narrow, alert, a delicacy about his mouth like he was holding a diamond on the tip of his tongue. He'd begun wearing a knitted black kippah, and the whole effect—the jacked-up body, the little Jewish head—was disconcerting.

"You weren't this religious when you were actually singing, though," I said. "Why now?"

He sat down across from me. "God gave me my voice," he said. "And then He took it away. Think about it, Miri. Why would He do that?"

"Punishment?" I said.

"No," said Jonah, and he'd made a swishing, side-to-side motion with his hand, almost like the Queen's wave. "Redirection. I have a new compass now."

I didn't know it at the time, but his compass was already set east, toward the Israeli army, and that very spring he made aliyah to Israel and became a *chayal boded*: a "lone soldier." At his funeral four years later, I saw the phrase written down in English characters for the first time and realized it wasn't "loan," as I'd always thought of it—like we were loaning Jonah out and would get him back eventually—but "lone" like only, like alone.

The night after Jonah's funeral, Eva came to my hotel room while my parents were out. It was the first time I'd seen her out of uniform. She was Israeli but of Russian-American descent and was as blonde and pale-eyed as an Iowa farm girl, though slight rather than sturdy. Her short curls were wild outside the confines of her green cap, and as a civilian she was wearing Chuck Taylors and boys' skinny jeans like a beautiful, clear-skinned version of the skaters I'd had crushes on in junior high. We sat pressed close together on my parents' enormous hotel bed and watched the videos of Jonah that Eva had shot with her phone. She said, "I know some people won't want to look so soon, but I brought them just in case," and I said, "I want to see anything you have."

The videos were small on the phone's screen, but the sound was clear and very loud, and the first voice from the speakers was Jonah's. He was speaking Hebrew, a language I'd only heard him use during prayer, never like this, in everyday life, sitting on a stone wall in his uniform and chatting to someone just beyond the screen.

Eva tried to translate—"He says, 'Does anyone have a pen?'"—but I shushed her. I wanted to hear only Jonah. Better, maybe, that I couldn't understand him: the sound of his voice alone had lined my eyes with tears. He was laughing, tan, dusty. Coke-commercial happy, the way you want your loved ones to look in memory. A black-nosed machine gun was hanging at his side, loose and casual like I'd carry a purse, and behind him I could see the turrets of Old Jerusalem and the golden gleam of the Dome of the Rock.

Another soldier had come into the picture to hand him a pen and a small pink notepad. She was narrow as a dart and moved in flutters. I vaguely recognized her from the funeral, remembered her dark hair sticking to her tear-wet face like a net.

"That's Noa," Eva whispered, her lips nearly touching my ear. "She likes your brother. Look! It's so obvious."

Noa was flickering her fingers through the ends of her ponytail, and I saw that she couldn't meet Jonah's eyes when he spoke to her, though she was smiling, close-mouthed and nervous. For a moment I let myself spin my brother's life out past the frame of the camera: Noa in white, shards of wedding glass beneath their feet, a faux-Bauhaus apartment in Tel Aviv and a yarmulked toddler with a serious brown face and Jonah's lost little eyes. But even had he lived, that life was only fiction. He was looking uncaringly beyond Noa, at the camera, at Eva.

I was crying, and Eva took my hand to squeeze it tightly. I felt so heavy—drowning in silty water—yet at her touch I felt, too, the lifting of my lungs, a surface-focused surge between my legs: the lightness that comes from desire, from wanting something. I thought, simultaneously, *This feeling means I'll be okay* and *This feeling means I'm lost forever*. The contradiction made me dizzy.

"What is he writing?" I said, in part to distract myself. "On that little pink paper?"

"A prayer," Eva said. "For the Wall."

"What do you mean? What wall?"

"The Western Wall," Eva said. "Come on. You know this wall. In Jerusalem?"

"What kind of prayer?"

"It's custom," she said, "to write a prayer and put it in the wall. In between the stones. If you go and you look, you can see all the cracks are filled with paper."

"What did Jonah pray for?"

Eva lifted one shoulder and looked down at our hands, still intertwined. "He didn't say. You know, it's private."

"When was this?"

"A week or so ago. A few days before the accident."

We were talking over the recording of Jonah, and I felt a pang of guilt for muffling his voice. When he'd been sad he'd always wanted silence, but I was unlike him in that regard. What I wanted was to hear everything, to know what was running through Jonah's inscrutable head in his last days, whether he knew they were his last days, whether he was happy, miserable, yearning; I wanted to know what he had prayed for at the end. I wanted a window beyond the screen—I wanted that piece of paper.

Eva leaned into me, her shoulder warm and strong, while offscreen she laughed, the camera shaking up and down. I leaned back into her and stared at my brother's pixelated hands, now folding up that slip of pink, his words disappearing within the pleats. When Eva kissed me a while later, I couldn't tell if I was stealing Jonah's dearest wish or granting it.

The next morning my parents flew home and I stayed. After I dropped them off at the airport, I went walking in Jaffa alone, my eyes swollen nearly shut from crying, the sun hovering dry and hangover-bright. The interior of the neighborhood was packed with market stalls, densely colored and clattering with jewelry and knock-off sunglasses, but I was too dazed to shop and too superstitious to indulge in shallow pursuits so soon after Jonah's death. Instead I aimed for the narrow outlying roads and the shade of buildings constructed like tight-fitting castles, made to withstand heat, salt. The crackling blue of the Mediterranean winked from the gaps between their roofs. There was a promenade that drew a line between the city and the sea and looked out over the ancient port, but I wasn't ready yet for tourism, or beauty. I wanted hush. I wanted to be alone with four thousand years' worth of ghosts who'd walked these streets, among them Jonah. His was the direct gaze turned at me from a blind and phantom crowd.

"Think of all the grieving sisters who've come before you," our rabbi had said to me at the memorial service back home. "You're in eternal, sympathetic company. Take strength from them."

But this was like being told to choke down an unwanted meal because somewhere starving children were sucking on rocks: the knowledge of their pain only served to magnify my own. I'd feed those children if I could! And were it up to me, we all would have our brothers back.

A surge of American teenagers spilled out from a nearby alley, bleary-eyed and sweaty and sucking on Nalgenes. Birthright: you could spot them a mile away. I hadn't gone on the trip, though it was free, but I'd applied as a freshman, while Jonah was skipping his eleventh grade classes to go to synagogue and before he'd mentioned anything about the army. I was attending a private liberal arts school in the West, and my friends had shamed me into declining the offered acceptance. "It's brainwashing," they'd said. "It's propaganda to support an apartheid state." Almost nobody at home knew my brother was a soldier. If asked about him, I usually said he was in security.

When I got back to Eva's apartment I told her about leaving my parents at the airport, about how at the last minute I hadn't been able to stop reaching for my mother. We would back away from our embrace as if to end it, and then suddenly we'd stumble forward again, magnetized by grief.

"Well, of course," said Eva. "Now you know what it really means to say goodbye."

For Eva, everything was "Well, of course." It was one of the things I liked best about her, her ability to accept, to explicate. Her shelves were full of Buddhist koans and illustrated nature guides, and she watched TED talks on the power of positive thinking. She never seemed to question her own emotions, and, more importantly, she never questioned mine. Probably this was also what Jonah had liked about her.

That night, wrapped in Eva's yellow sheets, I said, "You and me, us sleeping together—do you think it's just, I don't know, a product? A reaction to the situation?"

"Definitely," she said, and I surfaced from my bog of sadness for long enough to feel indignant. I guess I'd wanted her to say something like, *You're beautiful, you're intelligent, who wouldn't want to sleep with you?* "We were already connected," she continued. "We shared somebody between us. So I think it's natural to want to extend our connection because in this way we extend our connection to Jonah, too."

I brushed my knuckles across her bare breast and watched the pink skin around her nipple tighten and wrinkle. How many times had Jonah imagined touching Eva like this? Was he all-knowing now, could he see me? I wished I could open up my body to his spirit and let him have this in my place. "Did you love my brother?" I asked.

"He was my favorite person," she said. The whites of her eyes began to redden, and I watched tears rise up. "I loved him a lot."

I wanted to ask, of course, if she'd known how he felt about her, but it wasn't my secret to give away, and I didn't want to complicate her memories or sully them. So I said, "I guess you know a lot of people who have died."

"No," she said, and her hand, which had been resting on my waist, slipped away.

"But you're all soldiers," I said.

"We're not all of us in the army very long," she said. "And some of us have more dangerous jobs than others."

I didn't really know what kinds of jobs Jonah and Eva had; all I knew was they weren't high-risk. Jonah had wanted combat, had wanted "to protect," which I'd always heard as "to kill," though perhaps that wasn't fair to my righteous little brother—but after training and testing he'd been assigned a different position, instead, one that he'd described in an e-mail as "essentially fucking useless, pardon my Hebrew. Everyone keeps saying every position is important but you know they don't have to say that to some of the other guys. Those guys know without being told."

He had claimed he was in no immediate danger, yet he'd died. He had fallen from a rooftop, off duty, late at night. So the story went.

"You don't think Jonah jumped," I said to Eva, trying hard to leave the question mark out of it.

"An accident," she said.

"He couldn't have been buried on Mount Herzl otherwise, could he?" I said. "Aren't those the rules?"

"Rules, rules," she said, guttural and gentle. "What does an American know about rules?"

I swallowed down a lozenge-lump of tears. I knew that Jonah had wanted them, rules and structure, but he'd signed his life over to chaos instead. The army was all directive, yes, but war was the opposite; war had no boundaries. It was insubordinate. Yet I couldn't help but wish that Jonah had gone in an explosion or a hail of gunfire, something heroic, something conclusive, something I could mourn as tragedy alone without the complications of *if* and *why*. I'd never before wished such brutality on another person. I thought of Jonah wishing Eva dead out of his thwarted love for her, and wondered if our violence stemmed from the same dark place in our hearts.

I reached out and placed my hands around Eva's slender throat. I felt it move as she swallowed, but she didn't pull away. I ran my thumbs across the soft underside of her chin. "I want to go to Jerusalem," I said. "I want to go to the Western Wall and find out what Jonah wrote on that piece of paper."

"You can't," she said. "There are thousands of prayers in that wall."

"I'll find it."

"Miri, Jonah was on the men's side. The Wall is divided between men and women, and it's illegal for you to cross over."

"That's bullshit!"

"It's a place of worship," she said. "Let go of my neck."

I was crying. I kissed her throat where my fingers had been squeezing. "Please," I said. "Please help me. Please at least help me look."

Finally she said, "Maybe it could be good."

So two nights later, in our bedroom at the hostel in Jerusalem, Eva helped me bind my breasts with an Ace bandage and blue duct tape, straining and tugging like a maid squeezing a lady into a corset, while I tried not to inhale.

"Your left one is bigger," said Eva, reaching around to smush it down with her palm.

"Someone once told me everybody's is," I said. "To protect your heart."

"The men's side is on the left," said Eva. "It's bigger, too."

It took me a moment to realize she was speaking not of breasts anymore but of the men's side of the Wall, and a needle of nerves pierced my foggy resolve. I hadn't asked the consequences—hadn't wanted to know—but it was religious and therefore military law I was defying, so were I caught I'd be—arrested? Deported? Stoned to death by a hollering crowd? This was the Middle East, after all . . . but was it *that* Middle East?

I imagined my brother turning over in his fresh grave, despairing of my ignorance.

Eva handed me a gray button-up shirt, a boy's size large: hers. The baggy men's khakis were hers too, as were the high-top sneakers. My short hair was slicked up beneath a kippah, and with eyeshadow I'd darkened my brows, added tentative sideburns and shaded the hint of a mustache on my upper lip. The whole dress-up procedure had felt goofy, almost Chaplin-esque, but then I straightened the shirt and turned to the mirror on the back of our door and found a boy staring back at me.

Over my reflected shoulder I saw that Eva's face had gone very still, her eyes locked on mine in the glass, and I knew that she saw him, too: my brother. I looked just like Jonah.

Or—though Eva couldn't know this—I looked like Jonah at fourteen, the year he'd received a razor and a can of shaving cream for Hanukkah. "Time to get that awful fuzz off your face!" my mother had said, trading a grin with my father, and only I had seen the panic quiver briefly in my brother's mouth, the way his hand had gone slack around the gifts. Already his voice had begun to crack. My face, now, was a parody of Jonah's prepubescent face, before the final breaking of his voice. Before the protein shakes, the push-ups, the long hours at the synagogue and then the gun range. I felt a telltale tremor in my eyes.

Before I could give in to grief, Eva grabbed my arm and spun me away from the mirror.

"Kiss me," she said. "I've never kissed a boy before."

I took a breath and imagined myself three inches taller, imagined my shoulders were broader and my arms stronger. I pulled her close and kissed her with Jonah's lips. When we pulled away, her brow was furrowed and she shook her head. "This is a terrible idea," she said.

"Too late," I said.

It was a half-hour walk from our hostel to the Old City of Jerusalem. The evening was warm, filmy. I felt conspicuous in a way I'd never before experienced, fearful of being looked at and discovered, and I was terribly aware of the eyeshadowed stubble on my upper lip and the sweat that was beading there. I kept turning to Eva for her to check. "It's not running? It's not smudged?"

"It's fine," she said. Her mood had darkened in a way I couldn't define. She kept looking at me, then looking away, shaking her head a little, mouth set.

"Are you scared?" I said.

"Of course not," she said.

"You're acting strange."

She was quiet, but she looped her arm briefly in mine, pressed her cheek against my shoulder and then released me.

The modern Jerusalem was both familiar and foreign, a Western-style city that wouldn't quite let you forget the history it had paved over, but as we neared the great stone walls of the Old City things took on a story book sheen. There were rustling palm trees, cypress, streets of ecru cobblestones and, in the distance, the calm green rise of the Mount of Olives. Hawkers and tourists of every ilk milled about, snapping pictures and reading aloud from tour books in the fading light, and when the Muslim call to prayer sounded from a loudspeaker within the walls, I saw a group of gold-decked, lipsticked women make the sign of the cross and bow their heads in synchrony. Was it a show of solidarity or a ward against difference? Either way, the sight chilled me.

We followed a group of forelocked, hatted Hasidim through the tall arch of a dark-hollowed doorway in the side of the wall, and I reached for Eva's hand, but she pulled away, neatly, instantly. Up till then, she'd always been under my reaching fingers when I needed her. "Do you want a tour?" she said. "Or straight to the Wall?"

"Straight there," I said, and added, "Maybe next time," feeling the dishonesty even as I spoke. Already I knew I didn't ever want to come back. It should have been Jonah at my side, showing me around with a proprietary grin and narrating the history of every rock with his blend of solemnity and irreverence. *This is where Solomon built the first temple, this is where Muhammad prayed, this is where Jesus stopped to take a piss*. Even as devout as he became, Jonah could always take a joke. I felt a flash of pure resentment toward Eva: for not taking my hand, for not being Jonah. Then wondered if she felt the same toward me.

"This way," said Eva and gestured toward a crowded, fast-moving line. "Security."

"How do I look?" I said.

"No one will say anything."

Again I tried to take her hand, and again she evaded me, flushing this time. "Eva," I said, very quietly, "as far as anyone knows, I'm a guy. You can hold my hand."

"It's not that," she said. "I just don't feel like touching right now."

When she said that, suddenly it was all I wanted, to be close to her, to hold her hand in mine and get my body up against hers. I moved so I was flush against her back, and she stepped forward so quickly she nearly collided with a small child in front of her. "You don't have to *act* like a boy," she snapped.

"I'm nervous," I said.

"Deal," she said, terse like a soldier. She *was* a soldier. For a second this fact calmed me, as if she were an authority, a protective force, but then I remembered that everyone in this country was a soldier. I was surrounded by them. My pulse banged up again.

Yet despite my frantic heart, we made it past security without a hassle. There were two gun-strapped young men operating the x-ray machine through which I fed my backpack, and they seemed both more and less alert than I was used to: more alert to the prospect of violence but less interested in me as a body, their eyes flicking over me incuriously in a steady nongaze. Behind me, Eva said something in Hebrew, and all three of them laughed.

"You see?" said Eva, herding me toward the mouth of a small tunnel. "They're looking for weapons, metal. Not for cross-dressing American girls."

By this time the sun had set completely, and we came out onto a crowded stone plaza that glowed under yellow floodlights, thick with tourists and armed soldiers and headscarved groups of teenaged girls. Everyone moved as if in schools on the same tide, drifting closer to the lit-up stone facade of the Wall. Though it was straighter and more focal than the other walls of Old Jerusalem, at first it seemed smaller than I'd imagined—I could see the dark points of trees growing on a slope behind it. But then we drew closer, and it began to tower over us. It was very old, and you could feel its age. Here and there some greenery had sprouted from the pale limestone bricks and clung like floating bushes, with white birds darting between.

We walked to the metal-and-mesh partition that portioned out the space before the Wall like a stage. People filed in through the wide paths on either side. "There's the entrance for the women," said Eva. "And here is the men's."

The women's side, the right side, was smaller by more than a third. While the men were shouting and singing and dancing, sending up a great noise, the women made barely a sound.

"We're not permitted to pray out loud," said Eva. "You shouldn't either, they'll hear your voice and know. So look—your brother was there, toward the end, and he put his paper into the rock about here." She tapped her shoulder, chest-height for me, and it occurred to me to wonder how she knew this; she must have been watching him. Wishing she could join him? Wondering, as I did, what he'd prayed for?

"I'll wait for you here," said Eva.

"You're not going in on the women's side?"

Her arms were crossed, her gaze distant. "Been there, done that," she said.

Nobody paid me any attention as I made my way to the men's side, pulse racing. I tried to walk with utter certainty and confidence, as if I belonged, when in fact I was out of place from my body right down to the level of the soul. The faces of the men surrounding me were physically distinct from one another—darkly bearded Orthodox, gold-necklaced tough guys, gawky pocked and furtive teenagers—but they were united in their expression: awe. Reverence. As I entered the courtyard of the Wall, prayer rose up all around me, chanted, sung, murmured. Men spoke from memory or read from printed pages, their words one lost note in a full orchestra and becoming distinct only as I passed, like snatches from a car radio. The lights turned everything a variegated sepia. Of all the words I heard, I understood nothing save for *Adonai*. Some men had their eyes raised to heaven; some were staring at the ground. Many were shouting their prayers, hollering in big groups with arms linked like a sports mob. Many were weeping. Several had uniforms and guns.

Never in my life had I been exposed to so much male emotion, and never in my life had I felt so scared and faithless. The energy was palpable, and for me it was not the energy of God but of men. It pushed at me from all directions, and if a hot-blooded wind were to rise and billow, I knew I could be stampeded by it. I felt the press of tape and bandaging, as if my breasts were straining to break out and expose me, but really it was that my breath had quickened, so I was nearly hyperventilating, my lungs inflating too much and then failing to contract. I'd thought at least I might feel one wet wavelap of the oceanic love that Jonah had always professed to experience, but I felt only a titanic, formless terror. Would it be different on the women's side, in silence? Would I feel different if I were here undisguised?

I had just two options: backward, or forward. I sucked in a deep breath and tried to imagine how my brother would feel in this same situation. He no doubt would feel—had felt—elated. Full of God's grace. Like he was part of something larger than himself, like he had a calling, like he was joined with these other men in an unearthly brotherhood that would protect and nurture him all through his life, and beyond. While he was alive I had been wary of these ideas, but now that he was dead, they felt sacred to me on his behalf. I would never be religious—but wasn't I now feeling the foundation of all faith? Fear. And grief, which has its roots in fear and in love. Love and fear.

Fear, I had covered. Now to concentrate on the other. I had loved Jonah and would always love Jonah, but my love for him had nowhere to go anymore, except deeper. So I went deeper; I moved onward. And once I was close, I felt my panic subside. The Wall was cool to the touch, and the placid stone face of it soothed me. The men here toward the front were quieter than the men in back, many of them sitting on white plastic lawn chairs, books in laps, shawls on shoulders, foreheads touching or nearly touching the rock. Every available crack was stuffed with paper like multi-colored grout, and men were stepping forward to add their prayers. I laid my palm flat against the Wall as I could see others doing and then began to move slowly sideways, fingers trailing as I searched the cracks. Yellow, white, blue and, yes, pink, there and there and there and—

Everywhere, it was everywhere, pink paper folded up and crammed into the wall like gum in a shoe. From where I was standing—five meters in, chest height—I could count at least ten within arm's length. I glanced up, around. The men on either side of me were both older, one bald and wearing the kind of comfortably hideous leather shoes I associated with German tourists and one dark-skinned and mustached in a navy suit. Behind me, of course, was the crowd, but why would they pay attention to me, one figure of many, my fingers hidden by my body as I picked loose a slip of pink paper? I closed it in my fist, shoved it in my pocket, moved down a step, removed another, then another, another. I lined my pockets.

Somebody spoke loudly in my ear, so close I could feel his breath, and I jolted, whirled around. The bald man was staring at me, his pale eyes wide under white eyebrows, his mouth moving in a language I didn't know. Beneath the floodlights his face was shaded and bloodless.

"Sorry," I said, in as deep a voice as possible. I was facing the surge again, and again felt the tide of panic begin to swell. My back was to the Wall now. I could be crushed against it.

"English?" the man said. I tried to edge away but was blocked in by plastic chairs and male bodies. I nodded, unable to unhitch my vocal chords.

"I said to you, what are you doing? Why you are removing these? Some kind of joke, hmm? I put mine just one minute ago and now. . . ."

"Did I take yours?" I squeaked.

"Yes!" he said. "You take mine, you take others, I see you!"

Other people were beginning to glance at us now, and I said, trying to stay quiet, trying to keep my voice boyish, "I'm looking for my own, I put it here yesterday but I—I changed my mind about . . ."

"You cannot *take back* prayer," the man said, but he was lowering his voice to match my volume, and he nodded and smiled benignly at a Hasid who'd begun to glare at us. "They are in your pockets?"

I put a hand into the pocket of my pants and withdrew three of the four prayers I'd squirreled away, and held them out to him on a trembling palm. He snatched them up and quickly unfolded each one in turn, nodded in satisfaction when he found his own and then re-inserted all three into the Wall, muttering a prayer for each. I willed myself to leave, to walk away, but was frozen with fear and regret, and he turned back to me and grabbed my arm. He brought his face very close to mine, his nostrils flaring, eyes widening in recognition. My heart stopped.

"Who do you think you are?" he said.

I couldn't speak.

"This is a sin against God," he said, and his grip around my arm grew painful. His face burned dark with fury. "Should I shout and bring the soldiers?" He shook me hard, making my head wobble on my neck. Again people had begun to watch us, and his neck corded tight as I sweated and shuddered. "No," he said. "I will not bring God's eyes away from all these men and onto you. You don't deserve the light of His attention." He let me go and wiped his palms on his pants with pure, unfeigned disgust. "God turns his back on you," he said. "He will never look for you."

He put his own back to me, and for a moment I was still so petrified I couldn't get my legs to move. Then my blood surged and I aimed my body toward the exit like a bullet. There was one remaining stolen piece of paper in my pocket, and it seemed like a sign, like a gift, like it *had* to be Jonah's if there was any mercy to be found here. I pushed back through the crowd with my face hot and my heart banging, my mouth dry, my skin prickling each time somebody brushed against me. All the blood seemed to have left my extremities, and my fingers were cold even in the murky heat of the evening. When I stumbled out onto the plaza and saw Eva still standing cross-armed and patient, I felt relief pour over me like fresh water.

"You have it?" she said, straightening at my approach.

"I got only one," I said. "I haven't looked at it yet. I'm panicking."

"Let's go," she said, and I let her lead me back through the dark tunnel and the lines of people waiting to be patted down, past the information booths and back through the arched gate, out of the Old City and into the new. We walked a block without speaking and then sat on a bench beside an Arab gift kiosk, beneath a streetlamp. She didn't touch me, but I leaned into her, wishing she were larger, wishing I could put my head on her shoulder and dissolve. The man at the kiosk glanced at us and then went back to fiddling with a staticky boom box.

"Someone saw what I was doing and knew," I said. "He looked at me and knew."

Eva tensed all over and glanced behind us, as if expecting to see soldiers come lumbering out of the shadows with their weapons raised. I said, "He let me go, but I think he put a curse on me." I thought of original sin, of the original curse. "Am I the first woman to ever cross the line?"

Eva said, "Of course not. What did you find?"

I took the pink paper from my pocket with unsteady fingers and started to unfold it, then stopped and handed it to her. "I can't," I said. "Will you?"

She hesitated. "You know the chances are very small it's Jonah's."

"Read it out loud."

Eva held the paper with her thumb and forefinger, staring. Then she took a deep breath and unfolded it. There was an agonizing silence.

"It's in Spanish," she said.

I tried to latch onto that, my mind racing through all the possibilities—Jonah had taken Spanish in high school, he'd liked Bolaño, so maybe, maybe—

"Let me see," I said, and snatched the paper. The handwriting, slanted and all caps, was nothing like Jonah's neat, almost typeset hand. It was the same phrase repeated three times like in a fairy tale, more spell than prayer. *Que Sebas me ame. Que Sebas me ame. Que Sebas me ame.*

"What does it say?" I asked Eva. "Can you read it?"

"I don't speak Spanish," she said.

"Shit," I said and crumpled the paper in my fist. "Shit."

"Miri," she said, "Jonah probably wrote something stupid. Please, God, no more hummus for breakfast, or please, God, give us good wi-fi tonight. He always saved his real prayers for his own head."

I wiped my eyes and didn't speak. Even to myself I couldn't quite articulate why the idea of finding Jonah's prayer had meant so much to me, why I'd so badly needed to touch it and feel it manifest in my fingers. The radio at the kiosk behind us crackled through stations, searching, searching, and Eva plucked the pink paper from my grip. She smoothed it out against her knee. "Everybody wants the same thing, anyway," she said.

"Do they?" I said and put my hand on her thigh.

"Stop," she said, moving her leg. "Stop touching me with that stuff on your face. Wipe it away first."

"Why does it matter?"

"It scares me," she said. "You look too much like Jonah."

"Why does that scare you? You say you loved him."

"Yes. *Because* I loved him."

"How much, though?" I said. My hand had returned to her thigh, and my fingers dug hard into her jeans. "How much did you love him?"

"Quit it, Miri."

"Did you love him enough?"

Eva shoved my hand away and slid down the bench from me, her mouth trembling, her eyes full, breath coming hard. She sniffed wetly, and as I watched, a fleck of mucus flew from her nose and landed on her clenched fists. Suddenly I saw her clearly: a young girl crying on a bench, her skinny limbs shaking, her body blurred around the edges in the fading light, and me with my eyes flashing at her like bared teeth. I dropped my gaze. I had wanted to think of Eva as a simple gift, lovely and unyielding, a woman sent to comfort me and lead my body through the desert of my grief. I'd wanted to think of her as mine and Jonah's. Ours. But I knew then she was nobody's.

Jonah would disagree with me. He would say she was God's. He would say it with desire for both Eva and for God, a longing so deep it had its roots in anger.

"Are people at peace when they pray?" I said. "Is that what God is for?"

Eva let out a shuddering breath. "Pray, and let me know."

I tried one more hopeless time to kiss her, but she turned away, and my lips landed on her cheek, sisterly. Behind us, the man at the kiosk had finally found a song he liked, and he raised the volume till a single soaring melismatic voice was blasting through the cheap radio speakers, singing low, then up, and up.

Contributors' Notes

Jennifer duBois's debut novel, *A Partial History of Lost Causes*, was the winner of the California Book Award for First Fiction, the Northern California Book Award for Fiction, and was a finalist for the PEN/Hemingway Award for Debut Fiction. Her second novel, *Cartwheel*, was the winner of the Housatonic Book Award fiction and was a finalist for the New York Public Library's Young Lions Award. The recipient of a Whiting Writer's Award, a National Book Foundation 5 Under 35 Award, and a National Endowment for the Arts Creative Writing Fellowship, duBois teaches in the MFA program at Texas State University.

Jason Brown was a Stegner Fellow and Truman Capote Fellow at Stanford University, where he taught as a Jones Lecturer. He now teaches in the MFA program at the University of Oregon. He has published two books of short stories, *Driving the Heart and Other Stories* (Norton) and *Why the Devil Chose New England for His Work* (Open City/Grove Atlantic). His stories have appeared in *Best American Short Stories, The Atlantic, Harper's, TriQuarterly*, and other magazines and anthologies. Several of his stories have been performed as part of NPR's Selected Shorts.

Otis Haschemeyer has an MFA from the University of Arkansas, attended Stanford University as a Stegner Fellow, and spent a year at the *Cité Internationale des Arts* in Paris, France. His creative nonfiction, stories, and poems have been published in *The Sun Magazine, The Alaska Quarterly Review, Barrow Street, Southern Indiana Review* and others. He teaches creative writing at the University of Oregon.

Roy Kesey is the author of two novels, two short story collections, and a historical guidebook. He is also the translator of Pola Oloixarac's debut novel *Savage Theories* (Entropía/Soho Press) and her forthcoming novel *Dark Constellations* (Literatura Random House/Soho Press). He has won an NEA grant for fiction and a PEN/Heim grant for translation. His work has appeared in over a hundred magazines and anthologies, including *Best American Short Stories* and the Norton anthologies *New Sudden Fiction* and *New Micro.*

Alice Fulton's latest volumes are *Barely Composed*, a poetry book published by W.W. Norton, and *The Nightingales of Troy*, a collection of linked stories, also from Norton. Her honors include an American Academy of Arts and Letters Award in Literature, the Bobbitt National Prize for Poetry from the Library of Congress, and fellowships from the NEA and the MacArthur Foundation. She is currently the Ann S. Bowers Professor of English at Cornell University.

Fiona McFarlane is the author of *The Night Guest* and *The High Places*, which won the 2017 International Dylan Thomas Prize. She lives in Sydney

Austin Ratner is author of four books, including the novels *The Jump Artist*, winner of the 2011 Rohr Prize for Jewish Literature, and *In the Land of the Living*. He studied at the Johns Hopkins School of Medicine and the Iowa Writers' Workshop and has written nonfiction for *The New York Times Magazine*, *The Wall Street Journal*, *The Jewish Daily Forward*, and *The Psychoanalytic Review*, among other publications. He lives in Brooklyn, NY with his wife and two sons and teaches at the Sackett Street Writers' Workshop.

Yuko Sakata has an MFA in fiction from the University of Wisconsin—Madison. She is a recipient of the August Derleth Prize and a fellowship from the MacDowell Colony. She has worked as a production editor for Devil's Lake. She is also a dancer and a translator.

Tamara Titus's short fiction has appeared in *Glimmer Train*, *Sou'wester*, *Emrys Journal*, and other publications. She is the recipient of a Regional Artist Project Grant from the Arts & Science Council of Charlotte–Mecklenburg, as well as a North Carolina Arts Council fellowship in fiction. She co-edited *This is the Way We Say Goodbye* (the Feminist Press, 2011), an anthology of women's essays on caregiving, and in 2013 she received an Honorable Mention from the James Jones Fellowship Contest for her novel-in-progress, *Lovely in the Eye*. Currently, Tamara spends her time writing and editing, caregiving, and serving on the Charlotte Historic District Commission.

Emma Törzs is a writer, teacher, and inveterate waitress based in Minneapolis. Her short fiction has been published in journals such as *Lightspeed*, *Ploughshares*, and *The Threepenny Review*, and honored with a 2015 O. Henry Prize. She's the recipient of grants from the Loft Literary Center, the Jerome Foundation, the McKnight Foundation, the MRAC, the MSAB, and Norwescon, and is an enthusiastic graduate of Clarion West '17.

Melissa Yancy's short fiction has appeared in *One Story*, *Glimmer Train*, *Zyzzyva*, and many other publications. Her story collection *Dog Years* was selected by Richard Russo for the 2016 Drue Heinz Literature Prize, and received a California Book

Award for first fiction, a PEN/Hemingway Award Honorable Mention, and was longlisted for The Story Prize. She is the recipient of a 2016 NEA Literature Fellowship. She lives in Los Angeles where she works as a fundraiser for healthcare causes. She can be found online at melissayancy.com.

Rachel Yoder is a founding editor of *draft: the journal of process,* which publishes first and final drafts of stories, essays, and poems along with author interviews about the creative process. She is also the host and creator of The Fail Safe, an interview podcast about writing and failure. Her writing has appeared in *The New York Times, The Chicago Review, The Paris Review Daily*, and *The Sun Magazine*, as well as many other online and print journals. She was awarded a 2017 Iowa Artist Fellowship from the state of Iowa. She lives in Iowa City with her family and directs literary programming for the Mission Creek Festival. She can be found online at racheljyoder.com.